The
Quilter's
Apprentice

*Also by Jennifer Chiaverini
in Large Print:*

The Cross Country Quilters
The Runaway Quilt
The Quilter's Legacy

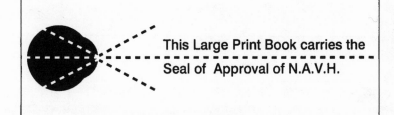

This Large Print Book carries the
Seal of Approval of N.A.V.H.

An Elm Creek Quilts Novel

The **Q**uilter's Apprentice

Jennifer Chiaverini

Thorndike Press • Waterville, Maine

Published in 2003 by arrangement with Simon & Schuster, Inc.

Thorndike Press® Large Print Women's Fiction.

The tree indicium is a trademark of Thorndike Press.

The text of this Large Print edition is unabridged.
Other aspects of the book may vary from the original edition.

Set in 16 pt. Plantin by Elena Picard.

Printed in the United States on permanent paper.

Library of Congress Cataloging-in-Publication Data

Chiaverini, Jennifer.
   The quilter's apprentice : a novel / Jennifer Chiaverini.
      p. cm.
   "An Elm Creek Quilts novel" — T.p. verso.
   ISBN 0-7862-5740-7 (lg. print : hc : alk. paper)
   1. Compson, Sylvia (Fictitious character) — Fiction.
2. Female friendship — Fiction. 3. Pennsylvania —
Fiction. 4. Quiltmakers — Fiction. 5. Aged women —
Fiction. 6. Quilting — Fiction. 7. Large type books.
I. Title.
PS3553.H473Q55 2003
   813′.54—dc21   2003054112

For Geraldine Neidenbach
and Martin Chiaverini
with all my love

As the Founder/CEO of NAVH, the only national health agency solely devoted to those who, although not totally blind, have an eye disease which could lead to serious visual impairment, I am pleased to recognize Thorndike Press* as one of the leading publishers in the large print field.

Founded in 1954 in San Francisco to prepare large print textbooks for partially seeing children, NAVH became the pioneer and standard setting agency in the preparation of large type.

Today, those publishers who meet our standards carry the prestigious "Seal of Approval" indicating high quality large print. We are delighted that Thorndike Press is one of the publishers whose titles meet these standards. We are also pleased to recognize the significant contribution Thorndike Press is making in this important and growing field.

Lorraine H. Marchi, L.H.D.
Founder/CEO
NAVH

* Thorndike Press encompasses the following imprints: Thorndike, Wheeler, Walker and Large Print Press.

Acknowledgments

I am deeply grateful to the many people who have made this book possible:

My editor, Laurie Chittenden, for opening her heart to this story and helping to make it even better; and my agent, Maria Massie, for her help and advice.

The members of QuiltNet, for their friendship and generosity.

My teachers, especially Percival Everett and James Walton, who told me I could do this.

The members of the Internet Writing Workshop, especially Lani Kraus, list owner, who supervises a wonderful forum for aspiring writers; Dave Swinford, administrator of the novels list and one of the nicest people on the net; Jody Ewing, for her kindness; and Candace Byers, Warren Richardson, and Lesli Richardson for their critiques.

My friend Christine Johnson, who read

every chapter and never failed to encourage me when I needed it most.

Geraldine, Nic, and Heather Neidenbach; Virginia and Edward Riechman; and Leonard and Marlene Chiaverini, for their love and support.

And most of all, to my husband, Marty, for everything.

Chapter 1

Sarah leaned against the brick wall and tried to look comfortable, hoping no one walking by would notice her or wonder why she was standing around in a suit on such a hot day. She shaded her eyes with her hand and scanned the street for Matt's truck — their truck — but she didn't expect to see it. He wasn't late; she was early. This interview had been her shortest one yet.

A drop of perspiration trickled down between her shoulder blades to the small of her back where her silk blouse was tucked into her navy skirt. She removed her suit jacket and folded it over her arm, but she knew she wouldn't feel comfortable until she was back in her customary T-shirt and shorts. A barrette held her hair away from her face, and the back of her neck sweltered beneath the thick, brown waves. The people who slowly passed on their way to jobs, shopping, or summer classes at nearby Waterford College looked as uncomfortable and as drained by the humidity as Sarah felt. In a few months, she knew, she'd be griping about the snow like everyone else in central Pennsylvania, but today she longed for autumn.

The handle of her briefcase began to dig into her palm. As she shifted it to her other hand, she glanced at the revolving door half a block away. With her luck, some of the interviewers would leave early for lunch and spot her lingering there. They'd probably urge her to wait inside in the air-conditioning, and then she'd have to figure out some polite way to refuse. That, or slink back inside like a reprimanded child. The thought of it made her shrink back against the wall.

Two staccato beeps of the horn sounded before Sarah saw the red truck pull up and park along the opposite curb. She pushed herself away from the wall and hurried across the street.

"How'd it go?" Matt asked as she slid into the passenger's seat.

"Don't ask."

Though she had tried to keep her voice light, Matt's face fell. He started the truck, then reached over and patted her knee. "I

10

guess you already know how sorry I am about all this."

"Sorry about what? You're early."

"You know what. Don't pretend you didn't understand. If not for me and my job, we never would've moved here."

"It's not like you dragged me here by my hair." Sarah closed her eyes and sank back into her seat. "It's not your fault I don't have a clue how to make it through a job interview without sounding like an idiot."

"You're not an idiot."

"And you're not responsible for my unemployment."

"Well, I feel bad anyway," he responded as he pulled into traffic. "I mean it, Sarah. I'm really sorry."

Of course he felt sorry. So did she, but feeling sorry didn't make her any less unemployed. Apparently, neither did working her tail off to graduate with a great GPA and sacrificing every other available moment to part-time jobs and internships to gain work experience. Even the years she had invested in her last job apparently did her more harm than good. Potential employers took one look at her résumé, noted all the accounting experience, and refused to consider her for any other kind of work.

Sometimes Sarah thought back to those

first years after college and wondered how she and Matt ever could have been so hopeful, so optimistic. Of course, their prospects had seemed brighter then, colored by newlywed joy and professional naïveté. Then the newness faded from her job as a cost accountant for a local convenience store chain, and the days began to follow each other in an unrelenting cycle of tedium. Matt enjoyed his job working on the Penn State campus, but just after he had been promoted to shift supervisor, the state legislature slashed the university's budget. College officials decided that they could do without new landscaping more easily than library books and faculty salaries, so Matt and many of his coworkers found themselves out of work.

They soon learned that open positions were hard to come by in a medium-sized college town in the middle of Pennsylvania. Matt couldn't find anything permanent, only occasional landscaping jobs for some of his former agricultural science professors. One by one, his former coworkers found jobs in other towns, sometimes in other states. But Matt was determined to find something in State College, the town where he and Sarah had met, where they had married, and where one day, they hoped to raise children.

Eventually even Matt's natural optimism waned, and he grew more discouraged every month. Soon Sarah found herself slinking off to work every morning, wondering if she should be doing something more to help him find a job and fearing that if she did get more involved he'd think she doubted his ability to find a job on his own.

As time passed, the sharpness of her worries dulled, but they never completely faded. Matt made the best of the part-time work he managed to find, and Sarah was proud of him for it. She watched him persevere and tried not to complain too much about the drudgery of her own job. Instead, year after year, she put in her hours and collected her paychecks, and thanked her boss for her annual bonuses. She knew she should be grateful, but in her heart she felt something was missing.

One December, as she and Matt decorated their Christmas tree, Sarah counted the number of Christmases they had spent in that apartment.

"Has it been that many?" Matt asked. His eyes grew sad. "I thought we'd have a house of our own by now."

Sarah placed another ornament on a

high branch and thought quickly. "Lots of people wait much longer than this before they buy a house. Besides, I like it here."

"So many years in this apartment, and too much of that time without steady work."

"So many years of bean counting. It's amazing my brain hasn't melted into mush."

Matt tried to grin. "Maybe we're just having a midlife crisis."

"Speak for yourself. I don't think I've hit midlife just yet."

"You know what I mean. Wouldn't it be nice to get a fresh start, knowing now what we didn't know then?"

She reached out for his hand and squeezed it to show him she understood.

A few weeks later, a group of their friends gathered at their tiny apartment on College Avenue to welcome the New Year. They spent the day watching bowl games and proclaiming the superiority of the Nittany Lions, and in the last half hour before midnight they watched the ball drop in Times Square on television and took turns announcing their New Year's resolutions. Everyone burst out laughing when Sarah resolved to take the CPA exam so she could go into business for herself.

They quite rightly noted that a CPA's life wasn't much of a departure from the work she already knew and despised. She saw their point, but any change, however slight, would be a relief.

Then Matt stood up and announced his resolution: to find a permanent job even if it meant leaving State College.

Sarah raised her eyebrows at him, a silent message he immediately understood. He quickly added, "As long as that's okay with you, honey. As long as you don't mind moving."

"I'd rather not, if you want to know the truth."

"But we both want a fresh start. You've said so."

"I think it's time to cut you off." She smiled to soften her words as she took the beer can from his hand. It wasn't his resolution that troubled her so much as the way he had presented it, springing something that big on her so unexpectedly — and in front of an audience. Matt was methodical and patient, never one for surprises. It wasn't like him to make decisions that affected them both without talking to her first.

She waited until the guests had left and the mess from the party had been cleared away. Then she cornered him in the bathroom as he brushed his teeth. "Do you think you could warn me next time before you make major life decisions for us, especially if you're going to do it in front of all our friends?"

Matt spat out his toothpaste. "I'm sorry, Sarah. I spoke without thinking." He rinsed his mouth and spat again. "Actually, that's not entirely true. I've been thinking about this a lot."

"About moving?"

"About getting a fresh start somewhere else. Come on, Sarah. You hate your job; I can't find one. It couldn't be any worse in a new place, and I'm willing to risk that it would be even better." He studied her for a moment. "Are you willing to risk that?"

Sarah watched him, and thought about how long he had been looking for permanent employment, how he sometimes scraped together a full day's work out of a few odd jobs, and how her own career bored her so senseless that she hated to get up in the morning.

"I'll sleep on it," she said.

In the morning she told him she was ready to risk it, too.

A few weeks later, Matt finally landed a job — a job in a town more than two hours' drive away. Sarah celebrated with him and tried not to be too dismayed when he described Waterford, an even smaller college town in an even more remote location in Pennsylvania with an even tighter job market than State College. But how could she refuse when Matt was so elated at the chance to work again? And how could she not side with Matt after her mother had shrieked into the phone, "You mean you're giving up your professional job to go with that — that — that gardener?"

Sarah had curtly reminded her mother that "that gardener" was her husband and that he had a bachelor of science degree in landscape architecture, and added that if her mother didn't approve Sarah wouldn't bother to leave a forwarding address. Her mother had never understood about Matt, had never tried to understand. She just set her mouth in a prim line and refused to see what Sarah saw, that Matt was an intelligent, thoughtful, caring man with a good heart and a love for earth and rain and all growing things. If Sarah's mother wailed and moaned to think that her daughter was yoking herself to a country bumpkin, she had it all wrong.

Sarah reached over and stroked Matt's curly hair. From April through October he

17

had sun-streaked blond hair and a perpetually sunburned nose. "It's only been eight weeks. I didn't expect to find something as soon as we rode into town. That's not realistic."

Matt glanced at her before returning his gaze to the road. "I know you said not to ask, but how did it go?"

"Same old thing," Sarah grumbled. "The more I talked, the more his eyes glazed over. And then he said, 'Frankly, we're looking for someone who conforms better to our company persona.' And then a smile and a handshake and he was showing me the door."

"What's a 'company persona'?"

"I think he meant I wouldn't fit in."

"They usually at least think about it for a day or two before rejecting someone."

"Thanks, sweetheart. Now, which part of that remark was supposed to make me feel better?"

"You know what I mean." Matt gave her an apologetic look. "Did you tell them that you don't want to work in accounting anymore?"

"Yeah, but that didn't help. I feel like I've been typecast."

"Well, don't give up, honey. Something will come along."

"Yeah." Sarah didn't allow herself to say anything more because she wasn't sure she'd be able to keep the sarcasm out of her voice. Something will come along. That's what she had told Matt at least once a week while he was unemployed, and he'd never believed it. But now that he was the one repeating the refrain, it took on the status of gospel. She loved Matt, but sometimes he drove her nuts.

Matt signaled for a left turn and pulled off the main street onto a gravel road. "I hope you don't mind a detour."

"Where are we going?" Sarah asked as the truck jolted unsteadily down the narrow road, leaving a cloud of dust behind it.

"A new client stopped by the office yesterday to set up a contract. She brought a few photos of her house, but I need to take a look at the grounds myself before Tony can finalize the agreement. It's just a little place, just some lady's little cottage. I thought maybe you could help me find it."

"Fine by me. I'm not in any hurry." It wasn't as if she had anywhere to go. She looked around but saw no houses, only farmers' fields already knee-high with pale green cornstalks, and beyond them the darker green of rolling hills covered with trees.

The road forked ahead, and Matt turned the truck onto an even narrower road that arced sharply to the left into a thick forest. "See that road?" Matt asked, jerking a thumb over his shoulder at the fork they had not taken. "That leads right up to the front of the house, or it would if the bridge over Elm Creek wasn't out. The lady who owns the place warned us to use the back way. She said she's tired of having people complain about having to hike into town to call a tow truck."

Sarah smiled weakly and clutched at her seat as the truck bounded jerkily up a gradual incline. Pennsylvania roads were infamous for their potholes, but this drive seemed worse than most. As the grade became steeper, Sarah hoped that no one was approaching them from the opposite direction. She doubted that both cars could stay on the road without one of them scraping a side on a tree. Or worse.

Suddenly the forest gave way to a clearing. Before them stood a two-story red barn built into the side of a hill. The road, now little more than two dirt trails an axle's width apart surrounded by overgrown grass, climbed away from them up the hill and disappeared behind the barn. Matt shifted gears and followed.

Just beyond the barn, the path crossed a low bridge and then widened into a tree-lined gravel road. "Elms," Matt noted. "They look healthy, but I'll have to check. The house should be around here somewhere."

Sarah glimpsed something through the trees. "There. I see it." And then, as they approached and she was able to see more, her eyes widened. Matt's description hadn't prepared her for anything this grand. The gray stone mansion was three stories tall and L-shaped, with Tudor woodwork along the eaves and black shutters bordering each of the many windows. The shorter branch of the L pointed west, toward them, and the other wing stretched to the south. Where the two wings met there were four stone stairs leading to a door.

"You call this 'some lady's little cottage,' Matt?"

The truck slowed as they pulled into a gravel driveway encircling two enormous elm trees. Matt stopped the truck and grinned at Sarah as he put on the parking brake. "What do you think? Pretty impressive, huh?"

"That's an understatement." Sarah left the car and shut the door behind her without taking her eyes from the mansion. A twinge of envy pricked her conscience, and she hastily buried it.

"I thought you'd like it." He came around the truck to join her. "Tony was lucky to get her as a client. I can't wait to get a look at the rest of the grounds."

They climbed the steps and knocked on the door. Sarah closed her eyes and savored the breeze while they waited. Despite the bright afternoon sun, it felt at least ten degrees cooler there than in town.

After a few moments Matt knocked again. "Maybe nobody's home."

"Did they know you were coming?"

"Tony told me he made an appointment for today. I usually call to confirm, but they don't have a phone here." He raised his hand to knock a third time.

Suddenly the door swung open. Hastily, Matt dropped his hand to his side as a woman who looked to be in her mid-seventies wearing a light blue dress appeared in the doorway. She was taller than Sarah, and more slender, with silver-gray hair parted on the right and blunt cut a few inches below her chin. The only softness to her face was in the gentle sagging of skin along her jaw and in the feathery lines etched around her eyes and mouth. Something in her bearing suggested that she was used to being obeyed, and for a moment Sarah wondered if she ought to curtsy. Whoever the old woman was, she fit the proud old manor as surely as Matt fit his sturdy, reliable pickup, as surely as Sarah herself fit — what? She couldn't think of any way to finish the thought, and she wished she could.

The woman put on a pair of glasses that hung around her neck on a fine silver chain. "Yes?" she asked, frowning as if she wasn't sure she liked what she saw.

"How do you do, ma'am. I'm Matt McClure from Exterior Architects. I have an appointment to photograph the grounds for the restoration you requested."

"Hmph." The suspicious gaze shifted to Sarah. "And who are you?"

"Oh, I'm — uh, Sarah. I'm Matt's wife. I'm just here with Matt." She gave the woman a quick smile and extended her hand.

The woman paused a moment, then shook her hand. "Well, you probably know that I'm Sylvia Compson. You may call me Mrs. Compson." She looked Matt up and down and frowned. "I expected you earlier." She turned and walked into the foyer. "Well, come on, Matt and 'Uh, Sarah.'

Come on inside. Shut the door behind you."

Sarah and Matt exchanged a quick look, then followed Mrs. Compson inside. She entered a doorway on the left and led them into a spacious kitchen. The left wall was lined with cupboards and appliances, and there was a window over the sink. A microwave oven rested incongruously on a counter next to a rickety old stove directly across from them. There was an open doorway on the other side of the stove, and a closed door on the adjacent wall. A long wooden table took up the center of the room. Mrs. Compson eased herself onto a low bench next to the table and regarded them for a moment. "Would you like a glass of lemonade, or perhaps some iced tea?" she finally asked, directing the question to Matt.

"No thank you, ma'am. I just need you to show me the grounds so I can take a few pictures, and then we'll be on our way."

Her eyes still on Matt, Mrs. Compson jerked her head in Sarah's direction. "What about her? Maybe she wants something."

"A glass of lemonade would be wonderful," Sarah said. "Thank you. I've been standing outside downtown and —"

"There are glasses in the cupboard and a pitcher of lemonade in the icebox. Don't expect me to wait on you."

Sarah blinked. "Thanks. I'll just help myself." She gave the woman a tight smile and walked around the table toward the cupboard.

"And now I suppose we'll all have to wait around while you sip your beverage, even though you've come here later than your appointment and you've already kept me from my work long enough."

Sarah stiffened. "If it's that much trouble —"

"Mrs. Compson," Matt broke in, shooting Sarah a helpless look over the old woman's shoulder. "Tony made the appointment for two. We're five minutes early."

"Hmph. Ten minutes early is 'on time' and fifteen minutes is 'early,' if one cares about one's first impression. Now, is she going to get on with that drink or will she stand there gaping at me until she puts down roots?"

"Mrs. Compson —"

"Don't worry about it, Matt," Sarah interrupted, hoping she was meeting Mrs. Compson's stern gaze with one equally strong. "I'll wait for you here." A beautiful estate to explore, and to keep Matt's client happy Sarah would see no more of it than this one room. Still, she'd rather have a glass of lemonade than another moment of Mrs. Compson's company.

Mrs. Compson nodded, satisfied. "Come on," she said to Matt, rising stiffly from the bench. "I'll show you the front grounds." She left the kitchen without a backward glance.

Astonished, Sarah caught Matt's sleeve as he turned to go. "What did I do?" she asked, whispering so that the old woman wouldn't overhear.

"You didn't do anything wrong. I don't know what her problem is." He glanced at the doorway and shook his head in exasperation. "Look, why don't I take you home? I can come back for the pictures another time."

"No, that's okay. That would just make things worse. I don't want you to get in trouble."

"I won't get in trouble."

"It's all right. I don't mind waiting here. Really."

"Well, if you're sure . . ." Matt still looked doubtful, but he nodded. "Okay. But I'll be as quick as I can so we can get out of here." He gave her a quick kiss and a reassuring smile before hurrying out of the kitchen after Mrs. Compson.

Sarah watched him go, then sighed and opened the cupboard doors in search of the glasses. She wondered why the woman had even offered the drink in the first place, if it were so much trouble. She found a glass, and as she shut the cupboard, she glanced out the window and spotted the truck. She considered waiting there until Matt finished, but then the old woman might think she'd scared her off, and Sarah wasn't about to give her the satisfaction.

The refrigerator stood next to the closed door. After pouring herself some lemonade and returning the pitcher, Sarah sat down on the bench and rested her elbows on the table. She sipped the cool, sweet liquid and looked around the room. Matt might not finish for an hour, maybe more. Her gaze rested on the closed door next to the refrigerator.

Curious, Sarah rose and shifted the glass to her left hand. She wiped the condensation off her right hand and tested the doorknob. Finding it unlocked, she opened the door and peered inside to find a tiny room. It was a pantry, apparently, judging by the shelves filled with canned fruits and vegetables and cloth sacks whose contents she could not determine. She closed the door and, after a quick glance in the direction the old woman had taken, stepped through the open doorway to the left.

She found herself in a sunny, pleasant sitting room, larger and wider than the kitchen, with overstuffed furniture arranged by the windows and the fireplace. Cheerful watercolors hung on the walls, and a small sewing machine sat on a nearby table. A chair stood nearby as if someone had been sitting there recently. Two pillows and a small stack of neatly folded sheets rested on the largest sofa, right next to —

Sarah caught her breath and walked over for a better look. She unfolded the blanket with one hand and draped it over the sofa. *Not a blanket, a quilt,* she corrected herself, stroking the fabric. Small diamonds of all shades of blue, purple, and green formed eight-pointed stars on a soft ivory background. Tiny stitches formed smaller diamonds within each colorful piece, and the lighter fabric was covered with a flowing, feathery pattern, all made from unbelievably small, even stitches. A narrow vine of deep emerald-green meandered around the edges. "How lovely," Sarah whispered, lifting an edge up to the light to better examine it.

"If you spill lemonade on that quilt I promise you you'll wish you hadn't," a voice snapped behind her. With a gasp Sarah dropped the quilt and spun around. Mrs. Compson stood scowling in the doorway, her hands on her hips.

"Mrs. Compson — I thought you were with Matt —"

"I don't remember inviting you in here," the older woman interrupted. Sarah jumped aside as Mrs. Compson strode to the fallen quilt and slowly bent to pick it up. She straightened with an effort, folded the quilt carefully, and returned it to the sofa. "You may wait for your husband outside," she said over her shoulder. "That is, if you can be trusted to find your way to the back door without wandering about?"

Wordlessly, Sarah nodded. She left her glass in the kitchen sink and hurried through the foyer. *Idiot,* she berated herself as she pushed open the back door. Taking the back steps two at a time, she walked as quickly as her heels would allow to the pickup. She climbed into the passenger seat, rested her elbow on the open window, and chewed on her thumbnail. Was Mrs. Compson angry enough to cancel the contract? If Matt lost his new job because Sarah had offended one of his company's clients, she'd never forgive herself.

Thirty minutes later Matt appeared from around the south wing. Sarah watched as he walked over to the back door and knocked. The door swung open almost immediately, but from the truck Sarah could not see inside the house. She fidgeted in her seat as Matt and the unseen old woman conversed. Finally, Matt nodded and raised his hand in farewell. The door closed, and Matt walked down the steps, back to the truck.

Sarah tried to read his expression as he climbed into the cab. "I thought you were going to wait inside, honey. What are you doing out here?" he asked with a cheerful grin, then continued without waiting for an answer. "You should've seen the grounds."

"I wanted to," Sarah mumbled.

If Matt heard, he was too caught up in his enthusiasm to think of a response. Instead, as they drove back to town he described the sweeping front lawn, the gardens gone wild, the orchard, and the creek that ran through the estate grounds. Ordinarily, Sarah would have been intrigued, but now she was too worried about what he would say when she told him she had been snooping about in his client's home.

She waited until after dinner, when the anxiety finally became too much. "Matt," she ventured as she stacked plates in the dishwasher. "What were you and Mrs. Compson talking about right before we left?"

Matt rinsed their knives and forks and turned off the tap. "Nothing important," he said, placing the utensils in the silverware basket. "She wanted to know what I thought of the north gardens, and she said she'd see me tomorrow."

"So she didn't cancel the contract?"

"No. Why would she do that?"

Sarah hesitated. "Well, actually, I was kind of poking around her house and she caught me."

He looked wary. "Poking around?"

"It's not as bad as it sounds. I went into her sitting room and touched a quilt. She got all mad about it." Sarah couldn't look at him. "I was afraid she'd switch to another landscaper."

Matt chuckled and turned on the dishwasher. "You worry too much. She didn't cancel the contract." He held out his arms for her.

She slipped into his embrace and sighed

with relief. "I guess I should've stayed in the kitchen, but I was bored. I wanted to see something of the house, since I didn't get to see the grounds."

"I'll be there all summer. I'll show you around some other time."

"As long as Mrs. Compson doesn't find out." Sarah was in no hurry to see her again. "Tell me, Matt, how come this rude old lady gets a beautiful mansion and the lovely quilt and the gardens while a nice couple like us only gets half of a run-down duplex? It's not fair."

Matt pulled away and studied her expression. "I can't tell if you're joking or not. Would you really want to be like her, living all alone in that big place with no family or even a dog to keep you company?"

"Of course not. Obviously the place hasn't made her happy. I'd rather be with you in a tiny little shack than alone in the biggest mansion in the world. You know that."

"That's what I thought." He held her tightly.

Sarah hugged him — and wanted to kick herself. How much longer would it take before she learned to consider her words before blurting them out? The same habit hurt her in job interviews, and if she didn't overcome it soon, that hypothetical little shack might be their next address.

Chapter 2

The next morning Sarah sat at the breakfast table leafing through the newspaper and wishing that, like Matt, she needed to get ready for work. She heard him moving about upstairs, and from the noises coming through the wall she knew that some of the six undergraduates who rented the other half of the duplex were also preparing for the day. Each morning it seemed as if everyone but Sarah had a place to go, a place with people who needed them.

"So instead you'll sit here and whine. That'll help," she muttered. She sipped her coffee and turned the page, though she hadn't read a word on it. Someone next door turned on the stereo, loud enough for the bass line to throb annoyingly at the edges of her perception but not so loud that Sarah could justify pounding on the wall. She knew from experience that the low drone would go on hiatus at noon, then resume somewhere between six-thirty and seven in the evening and persist until midnight. Sometimes the pattern varied on weekends, but not by much.

The noise probably wouldn't have bothered her if she weren't already in such a foul mood. Unemployment had stopped feeling like a vacation more than a month earlier, ever since she realized that few of the *Waterford Register*'s Help Wanted ads even remotely applied to her. And after eight weeks of unemployment, four unremarkable interviews, and more unanswered application letters than she could stomach, Sarah half feared she'd never work again.

Matt bounded down the stairs and into the room. He paused behind her chair to squeeze her shoulder before continuing on into the kitchen. "Anything?" he called over the sound of coffee pouring into his travel mug.

"I don't know. I haven't looked through the classifieds yet."

"You used to read that section first."

"I know. It's just that I found this really interesting article about —" She glanced at the largest headline on the page. "The Dairy Princess. They just picked a new one."

Matt appeared in the doorway and grinned. "You expect me to believe you're so interested in the new Dairy Queen that you forgot to look at the classifieds?"

"Not Dairy Queen, Dairy Princess." She folded the newspaper, rested her elbows on the table, and rubbed her eyes. "Dairy Queen's an ice cream parlor. A Dairy Princess is . . . well, I guess I don't know what a Dairy Princess is."

"Maybe you should call Her Majesty and see if she's hiring any accountants to help her count cows."

"Gee, you're just bursting with humor today, aren't you?"

"Yep, that's me. Matt McClure, comedian." He reached over to stroke her shoulder. "Come on, Sarah. You know that if you keep looking, you'll definitely find a job you like. I'm not saying it'll be easy or quick, but it will happen."

"Maybe." Sarah wished she could be so sure.

Matt glanced at his watch. "Listen, I don't want to leave when you're feeling so bad —"

"Don't be silly." Sarah stood up and pushed in her chair. "I'm fine. If you took off work every time I got a little down pretty soon you'd be as unemployed as I am."

She followed him to the door and kissed him good-bye, watching through the screen until he drove away. Then she ordered herself to return to the table and the prematurely discarded newspaper. After fifteen minutes of scrutinizing the pages, she felt some hope rekindling. Two new ads announced positions requiring a bachelor's degree in a business or sales field. She carried the newspaper and a fresh cup of coffee upstairs to the small second bedroom they used as an office. Maybe she should adopt Matt's philosophy. Maybe all it took was hard work and a bit of luck. If she stuck with it, she'd surely find a good job sometime before she reached retirement age.

Her Job Hunt disk sat next to the computer, where she had left it the last time she worked on her résumé. She made a few revisions, printed out a couple of copies, then showered and dressed. Within an hour she was waiting at the bus stop for a ride downtown.

Waterford, Pennsylvania, was a town of about 35,000 people, except when Waterford College was in session and the population rose by 15,000 young adults. The downtown bordered the campus, and, aside from a few city government offices, consisted mainly of bars, faddish restaurants, and shops catering to the students. The local residents knew they owed their livelihoods to the transient student population, and although they were grateful for the income, many resented the dependence. Sometimes the town's collective resentment erupted in a flurry of housing and noise ordinances, and the students would strike back with boycotts and sarcastic editorials in the school newspaper. Sarah wasn't sure which group she sided with. The students treated her like a suspicious member of the establishment, and the locals assumed she was a despicable student. She tried to compensate by being polite to everyone, even their rowdy neighbors and the occasional shopkeeper who eyed her as if she might make off with half of the inventory, but it didn't seem to help.

She got off at the stop closest to the post office, carrying her job application materials in her backpack. The day was humid and overcast. She scanned the gray clouds and quickened her pace. In the past few weeks she had learned the hard way that summer rainstorms in her new hometown were as brief and drenching as they were sudden. She would have to hurry if she wanted to stop at the market and catch the bus home without getting soaked.

The errand at the post office took only a few minutes, and after picking up some groceries, Sarah still had ten minutes until the next bus would arrive. She strolled down the street to the bus stop, window-shopping and listening for thunder.

When a patch of bright colors caught her eye, she stopped for a closer look. Her eyes widened in admiration as she studied the red-and-green quilt hanging in the shop window. Eight identical diamonds, each composed of sixteen smaller diamonds, formed a large, eight-pointed star. The arrangement of colors created the illusion that the star radiated outward from its center. Between the points of the star, tiny stitches created intricate wreaths in the background fabric. Something about the quilt seemed familiar, and then she remembered why; its pattern was similar to the quilt she had seen the day before in Mrs. Compson's sitting room.

Studying it, Sarah wished she knew how to make something so beautiful. She had always loved quilts, loved the feel of the fabric and the way a quilt could make color blossom over a bed or on a wall. She couldn't see a quilt without thinking of her grandmother and without feeling a painful blend of love and loss. When Sarah was a child, her family made the long drive to Grandma's small house in Michigan's Upper Peninsula only twice a year, once in summer and once at Christmas. The winter visits were best. They would bundle up on the sofa under two or three of Grandma's old quilts, munch cookies, sip hot chocolate, and watch through the window as snow blanketed the earth. Some of Grandma's creations still decorated Sarah's childhood home, but Sarah couldn't remember ever seeing her mother so much as touch a needle. If quiltmaking was a skill handed down from mother to daughter, her mother must have been the weak link in the chain. Grandma surely would have taught her if she had wanted to learn.

Sarah looked overhead for the sign bearing the shop's name, and laughed in surprise when she saw the words GRANDMA'S ATTIC printed in gold letters on a red background. She checked her watch, gave the bus stop one last quick glance, and entered the shop.

Shelves stacked high with bolts of fabric, thread, notions, and other gadgets lined the walls and covered most of the floor. Celtic folk music played in the background. In the middle of the room, several women stood chatting and laughing around a large cutting table. One looked up from the conversation to smile at her, and Sarah smiled back. She made her way around the checkout counter to the front window and discovered that the quilt was even more beautiful up close. She tried to estimate how the quilt would fit their bed.

"I see our Lone Star charmed another new visitor inside," a pleasant voice broke in on her thoughts. Sarah turned and found the woman who had smiled at her standing at her elbow. She looked to be in her mid-fifties, with dark, close-cropped hair, ruddy skin, and a friendly expression.

"Is that what it's called, a Lone Star? It's beautiful."

The woman casually brushed pieces of thread from her sleeve as she joined Sarah in admiring the quilt. "Oh, yes, it's lovely, isn't it? Wish I could take the credit, but one of our local quilt artists made it. It's queen-sized, entirely hand-quilted."

"How much do you want for it?"

"Seven hundred and fifty dollars."

"Thanks anyway," Sarah said, not entirely able to keep the disappointment out of her voice.

The woman smiled in sympathy. "I know — it's a lot, isn't it? Actually, though, if you took that price and calculated an hourly wage from it, you'd see that it's a bargain."

"I can believe that. It must've taken years to make."

"Most people stop by, hear the price, then head straight to some discount store for a cheap knockoff." The woman sighed and shook her head. "People who don't know quilts can't detect the obvious differences in quality of materials and workmanship. Mrs. Compson's lucky to get what she can for those she displays here."

"Mrs. Compson?"

"Yes, Sylvia Compson. She's been staying up at Elm Creek Manor since her sister died two months ago. Temperamental as hell — I had to install an awning outside before she'd agree to display her quilts in the window. She's right, of course. I'd hate to have one of her pieces fade from the sunlight. She has two quilts in the American Quilter's Society's permanent collection in Paducah."

"That's good, right?"

"Good? I'd be glad just to have something accepted in the AQS annual show." The woman chuckled. "I thought every quilter around here knew about Sylvia Compson."

"I've met Mrs. Compson, but I'm not a quilter. I do love quilts, though."

"Is that so? You should learn how to quilt, then."

"Watch out, everyone, Bonnie's about to make another convert," one of the women called out from the cutting table.

"Run for it, honey," another warned, and they all burst out laughing.

Bonnie joined in. "Okay, I admit I have a vested interest. Satisfied?" She pretended to glower at the others before turning back to Sarah. "We do offer lessons, um . . . ?"

"Sarah. Are you the Grandma from the sign?"

"Oh, no," Bonnie said, laughing. "Not yet at least, thank God, although I do get asked that a lot. There's no Grandma. There's no attic, either. I just liked the name. Kind of homey, don't you think? As you already heard, my name's Bonnie, and these are some of my friends, the Tangled Web Quilters. We're sort of a renegade group separate from the local Waterford Quilting Guild. We take our quilting — and ourselves — very seriously." Her tone suggested that the remark was only half true. She handed Sarah a photocopied calendar. "Here's a schedule if you're interested in the lessons. Is there anything else I can help you with?"

Sarah shook her head.

"Well, thanks for stopping by. Come back anytime. Now, if you'll excuse me, I need to get back to that crowd before Diane hides my rotary cutter again." She smiled and returned to the cutting table.

"Thanks," Sarah answered, folding up the paper and tucking it into her backpack. She left the store, ran half a block to the bus stop, and climbed on the bus just as heavy drops of rain began to pelt the sidewalk.

Chapter 3

 Sarah's heart leaped when she returned home to find the answering machine's light blinking. A message. Maybe Waterford College had called about that admissions counselor job. She let her packages fall to the floor and scrambled for the button. Or maybe it was from Penn-Cellular Corporation. That would be even better.

"Hi, Sarah. It's me."

Matt.

"I'm calling from the office, but I was up at Elm Creek Manor this morning, and — well, I guess it can wait until I get home. Hope you don't have any plans for tomorrow. See you tonight. Love you."

As the tape rewound, Sarah left her backpack on the hallway floor and brought the groceries into the kitchen. What was it that could wait until he got home? She considered phoning Matt to see what was going on, but decided not to interrupt his work. Instead she put away the groceries and went into the living room. She opened the sliding door just enough to allow a breeze to circulate through the duplex, then stretched out on the sofa and listened to the rain.

What should she do now? She'd done the laundry the day before and wouldn't have to start dinner for a while. Maybe she could call one of her friends from school. No, at this time of day they would all be working or busy with their graduate school classes and research.

Funny how things had turned out. In college she had been the one with clear goals and direction, taking all the right classes and participating in all the right extracurricular activities and summer internships. Her friends had often remarked that their own career plans seemed vague or nonexistent in comparison. And now they were going places while she sat around the house with nothing to do.

She rolled over on her side and stared at the blank television screen. Nothing would be on now — nothing good, anyway. She almost wished she had some homework to do. If only she had picked a different major — marketing, or management, maybe. Something in the sciences would have been even better. But in high school Sarah's guidance counselor had told her that there would always be jobs for accountants, and she had taken those words to heart. She had been the only freshman in her dorm who knew from the first day of classes what major she was going to declare at the end of the year. It had seemed so self-indulgent to ask herself if she enjoyed accounting, if she thought she would find it a fulfilling career. If only she had listened to her heart instead of her guidance counselor. Ultimately, though, she knew she had no one but herself to blame now that she had no marketable job skills beyond bean counting.

Suddenly exasperated with herself, she shoved the whining voices from her mind. True, she didn't have a job, but she didn't have to mope and complain like the voice of doom. That was what her mother would do. What Sarah needed was something to keep herself occupied until a job came along. Moving into the duplex had kept her too busy to worry for a couple of weeks; maybe she could join a book club or take a course up at Waterford College.

Then her thoughts returned to the quilt she had seen in the shop window earlier that day. She jumped up from the sofa and retrieved her backpack from the hallway. The quilt shop's class schedule was still there, a bit damp from her rainy walk home from the bus stop. Sarah unfolded it and smoothed out the creases, studying the course names, dates, times, and prices.

Her heart sank. The costs seemed reasonable, but even reasonable expenses were too much when she hadn't seen a paycheck in more than two months. Like so many other things, quilting lessons would have to wait until the McClures were a dual-income family. But the more Sarah thought about it, the more she liked the idea. A quilt class would give her a chance to meet people, and a handmade quilt might make the duplex seem more like a home. She would talk to Matt about it. Maybe they could come up with the money somehow.

She decided to bring it up over supper that evening. "Matt," she began. "There's something I've been thinking about all day."

Matt took a second helping of corn and grinned. "You mean my phone message? I'm surprised you didn't ask about it sooner. Usually you hate it when I keep you in suspense."

Sarah paused. She had forgotten all about it. "That's right. You said you had to talk to me about something."

"First, though, do you have any plans for tomorrow?"

Something in his tone made her wary. "Why?"

"Yes or no?"

"I'm afraid to answer until I know why you're asking."

"Sheesh. So suspicious." But he put down his fork and hesitated a moment. "I spent the day up at Elm Creek Manor inspecting the trees. Not a trace of Dutch elm disease anywhere. I don't know how they managed it."

"I hope you didn't get caught in the rain."

"Actually, as soon as the thunder started, Mrs. Compson made me come inside. She even fixed me lunch."

"You're kidding. She didn't make you cook it yourself?"

"No." He chuckled. "She's a pretty good cook, too. While I was eating, we kind of got to talking. She wants you to come see her tomorrow."

"What? What for? Why would she want to see me?"

"She didn't say exactly. She said she wanted to tell you in person."

"I'm not going. Tell her I can't come. Tell her I'm busy."

Matt's face assumed the expression it always did when he knew he was about to get in trouble. "I can't. I already told her you'd come in with me tomorrow morning."

"Why'd you do that? Call her and tell her — tell her something. Say I have a dentist appointment."

"I can't. She doesn't have a phone, remember?"

"Matt —"

"Think of it this way. It's a lot cooler out there than in town, right? You could get out of this heat for a while."

"I'd rather stay home and turn on the air-conditioning."

"Oh, come on, honey, what would it hurt?" He put on his most effective beseeching expression. "She's an important client. Please?"

Sarah frowned at him, exasperated.

"Please?"

She rolled her eyes. "Oh, all right. Just, please, next time, ask me before you commit me to something."

"Okay. Promise."

Sarah shook her head and sighed. She knew better.

The next morning was sunny and clear, not nearly as humid as it had been before yesterday's rainstorm. "Why would she want to see me?" Sarah asked again as Matt drove them to Mrs. Compson's home.

"For the fourth time, Sarah, I don't know. You'll find out when we get there."

"She's probably going to demand an apology for snooping around her house." Sarah tried to remember the exchange in the sewing room. She'd apologized when Mrs. Compson caught her, hadn't she? "I don't think I actually said I was sorry. I think I was too surprised. She probably dragged me out here to give me a lecture on manners."

Her stomach twisted into a nervous knot that tightened as the truck pulled into the gravel driveway behind the manor.

"You could apologize before she asks you to," Matt said as he parked the truck. "Old people like apologies and polite stuff like that."

"Yeah. I hear they also love being referred to as 'old people,' " Sarah muttered. She climbed out of the truck and slammed the door. But maybe Matt had a point. She trailed behind him as he led the way to the back door.

Mrs. Compson opened it on the first knock. "So, you're here. Both of you. Well, come on in." She left the door open and they followed her into the foyer.

"Mrs. Compson," Matt called after her as she walked ahead of them down a wide, dimly lit hallway. "I was planning to work in the orchard today. Is there anything else you'd like me to do first?"

She stopped and turned around. "No, the orchard is fine. Sarah may remain here with me." Matt and Sarah exchanged a puzzled glance. "Oh, don't worry. I won't work her too hard this morning. She'll see you at lunchtime."

Matt turned to Sarah, uncertain. "Sound okay to you?"

Sarah shrugged and nodded. She'd assumed that Mrs. Compson would want her to come in, make her apology, and leave, but if the woman wanted to drag things out . . . Sarah steeled herself. Well, Mrs. Compson was an important client.

With one last, uncertain smile, Matt turned and left the way they came. Sarah watched him go, then faced the old woman squarely. "Mrs. Compson," she said firmly, trying to sound regretful but not nervous, "I wanted to apologize for going into your sitting room with my lemonade and

52

touching your quilt without permission. I shouldn't have done it and I'm sorry."

Mrs. Compson gave her a bemused stare. "Apology accepted." She turned and motioned for Sarah to follow.

Confused, Sarah trailed behind her as they approached a T intersection and turned right into an adjoining hallway. Wasn't that enough of an apology for her? What else was Sarah supposed to say?

The hallway opened into a large foyer, and Sarah slowly took in a breath. Even with the floor-to-ceiling windows covered by heavy draperies, she could tell how splendid the entryway could be if it were properly cared for. The floor was made of black marble, and to Sarah's left were marble steps leading down to twelve-foot-tall heavy wooden double doors. Oil paintings and mirrors in intricately carved frames lined the walls. Across the room was a smaller set of double doors, and a third set was on the wall to their right. In the corner between them a wooden staircase began; the first five steps were semicircular and led to a wedge-shaped landing from which a staircase climbed to the second-story balcony encircling the room. Looking up, Sarah could see another staircase continuing in a similar fashion to the third floor, and an enormous crystal chandelier hanging from the frescoed ceiling far above.

Mrs. Compson crossed the floor, carefully descended the marble steps, and waving off Sarah's efforts to assist, slowly pushed open one of the heavy doors.

Sarah followed her outside and tried not to gawk like a tourist. They stood on a wide stone veranda that ran the entire length of the front of the mansion. White columns supported a roof far overhead. Two stone staircases began at the center of the veranda, gracefully arcing away from each other and forming a half circle as they descended to the ground. The driveway encircled a large sculpture of a rearing horse; a second look told Sarah that it was a fountain choked with leaves and rainwater. Only that and the road leading from the driveway interrupted the green lawn that flowed from the manor to the distant trees.

Mrs. Compson eyed Sarah as she took all this in. "Impressed? Hmph." She stepped inside and reappeared with a broom, which she handed to Sarah. "Of course you are. Everyone is, the first time they see the place. At least they used to be, when we used to have visitors, before the estate went to pieces."

Sarah stood there uncertainly, looking from the broom to Mrs. Compson and back.

"At least you came dressed for work, not like last time." Mrs. Compson gestured, first waving her arm to the north end of the veranda and then to the south. "Take care of the whole thing, and do a thorough job. Don't neglect the dead leaves in the corners. I'll be back later." She moved toward the open doorway.

"Wait," Sarah called after her. "I think there's been a mistake. I can't sweep your porch."

Mrs. Compson turned and frowned at her. "A girl your age doesn't know how to sweep?"

"It's not that. I know how to sweep, but I —"

"Afraid of a bit of hard work, are you?"

"No, it's just that I think there's been a misunderstanding. You seem to think I work for Matt's company, but I don't."

"Oh. So they fired you, did they?"

"Of course not. They didn't fire me. I've never worked for Matt's company."

"If that's so, why did you accompany him that first time?"

"It was on the way. He was driving me

home from a job interview."

"Hmph. Very well, then. Sweep the veranda anyway. If you're looking for work, I'd say you've found some. Just be glad I didn't ask you to mow the lawn."

Sarah gaped at her. "You know, you're really something." She threw down the broom and thrust her fists onto her hips. "I tried to apologize, tried to be polite, but you're just the rudest, the — the — if you had asked nicely I might have swept your porch as a favor to you, and to Matt, but —"

Mrs. Compson was grinning at her.

"What's so funny? You think being rude is funny?"

The old woman shrugged, clearly amused, which only irritated Sarah more. "I was beginning to wonder if you had any backbone at all."

"Believe me, I do," Sarah said through clenched teeth. She spun around and stormed down the nearest staircase.

"Wait," Mrs. Compson called. "Sarah, please, just a moment."

Sarah thought of Matt's contract, sighed, and stopped on the bottom step. She turned around to find Mrs. Compson preparing to come down the stairs after her. Sarah then realized there was no handrail, and the stone wall was worn too smooth for a secure grip. Mrs. Compson stumbled, and instinctively Sarah put out her arms as if to steady her, though she was too far away to make any difference if Mrs. Compson fell.

"All right," Sarah said. "I'm not going anywhere. You don't have to chase me."

Mrs. Compson shook her head and came down the stairs anyway. "I really could use some more help around here," she said, breathing heavily from exertion. "I'll pay you, of course."

"I'm looking for a real job. I went to college. I have a degree."

"Of course you do. Of course you do. But you could work for me until you find a better job. I won't mind if you need to leave early sometimes for job interviews."

She paused for a reply, but Sarah just looked at her, stone-faced.

"I don't know anybody else, you see," Mrs. Compson continued, and to Sarah's astonishment, her voice faltered. "I'm planning to sell the estate, and I need someone to help me collect my late sister's personal belongings and take an inventory of the manor's contents for auction. There are so many rooms, and I can't even imagine what could be in the attic, and I have trouble with stairs."

"You're going to sell the estate?"

The old woman shook her head. "A home so big and empty would be a burden. I have a place of my own, in Sewickley." Her lips twisted until they resembled a wry smile, but it looked as if she were out of practice. "I know what you're thinking. 'Work for this crotchety old thing? Never in a million years.'"

Sarah tried to compose her features so that her expression wouldn't give anything else away.

"I know I can be difficult sometimes, but I can try to be —" Mrs. Compson pursed her lips and glanced away as if searching for the proper adjective. "More congenial. What would it take to persuade you?"

Sarah studied her, then shook her head. "I'll need some time to think about it."

"Very well. You may remain here or in the kitchen if you like, or feel free to explore the grounds. The orchards are to the west, beyond the barn, and the gardens — what remains of them — are to the north. When you've decided, you may join me in the west sitting room. I believe you already know where that is." With that, she turned and made her way up the stairs and into the manor.

Sarah shook her head in disbelief as she watched Mrs. Compson go. When she said she needed some time to think about the offer, she'd meant a few days, not a few minutes. Then again, she had already made up her mind. Wait until Matt heard about this. As soon as he stopped laughing Sarah would get him to take her home, and with any luck she'd never have to see that strange old woman again.

Her eyes scanned the front of the manor. Mrs. Compson was right; she was impressed with the place. Who wouldn't be? But she doubted she could tolerate an employer like Mrs. Compson in order to work there. She was impressed, not masochistic. She walked around the tree-lined north side of the building and the west wing. She walked briskly, but it still took her ten minutes to reach the barn and another five to reach the orchard, where she found Matt retrieving some tools from the back of the pickup.

"You aren't going to believe this," she greeted him. "Mrs. Compson needs someone to help her get the manor ready for sale and she wants to hire me."

But Matt didn't burst into laughter as she had expected. Instead he set down his tool kit and leaned against the tailgate.

"That's great, honey. When do you start?"

For a moment Sarah was too surprised to do anything but blink at him. "When do I start?"

"You're going to help her, aren't you?"

"I wasn't planning to," she managed to say.

"Why not? Why wouldn't you want the job?"

"It should be obvious. She hasn't been exactly nice to me, as you very well know."

"Don't you feel sorry for her?"

"Of course I feel sorry for her, but that doesn't mean I want to spend every day working with her."

"That's got to be better than moping around the house all day, right?"

"Not necessarily. If I'm sweeping porches around here, I won't be sending out résumés and going on interviews."

"I'm sure you could work something out."

"Matt, you don't get it. I've invested years in my career. I think I'm a little over-qualified for cleaning up a house."

"I thought the whole idea was to start fresh."

"There's starting fresh and then there's starting over at the very bottom. There are limits."

Matt shrugged. "I don't see any. Honest work is honest work."

Sarah stared at him, perplexed. He had always been the first to point out that her career was her business, but now here he was practically pressuring her into a job that didn't even require a high school diploma. "Matt, if I take this job, my mother will have a fit."

"Why does it matter what your mother thinks? Besides, she wouldn't care. If anything, she'd be glad you're helping out an old lady."

Sarah started to reply, then held back the words and shook her head. If he only knew. She could almost hear that familiar chorus of shrill "I told you so"s already. If she took this job, she'd prove that her mother had been right all along when she'd insisted that leaving State College for Matt's sake would send Sarah's career into an inevitable spiral of downward mobility.

Then suspicion crept into her thoughts. "Matt, what's going on?"

"Nothing's going on. What do you mean?"

"First you brought me out here after my interview. Then, without checking with me first, you promised her that I'd come see her. You didn't look at all surprised when I told you she offered me a job, and now you're pushing me to take it. You knew she was going to offer me this job, didn't you?"

"I didn't know for sure. I mean, she hinted, but she didn't come right out and say it." He looked at the ground. "I guess I like the idea better than you do."

Exasperated, Sarah struggled for something to say. "Why?"

"It would be nice if we worked at the same place. We'd get to see more of each other."

"That might be part of it, but what else?"

Matt sighed, took off his cap, and ran his fingers through his curly hair until it looked even more unruly than usual. "You're going to think I'm being silly."

Silly was more benign than the adjectives Sarah considered using. "Maybe, but tell me anyway."

"Okay, but don't laugh." He tried to smile, but his eyes were sad. "Mrs. Compson, well, she reminds me of my mom. Same mannerisms, same way of dressing; she even looks kind of the same. Except her age, of course. I mean, I know she's probably old enough to be our grandmother . . ."

"Oh, Matt."

"It's just that, well, my mom's probably out there all alone somewhere, and I'd like to think that if some young couple had a chance to look out for her they'd take it."

If your mother's out there alone, it's her own fault for running out on you and your dad, Sarah thought, pressing her lips together to hold back the automatic response. She went to him and hugged him tightly. How could Matt remember his mother's mannerisms? Mrs. McClure had left when he was only five years old, and although Sarah would never say so, she suspected Matt knew his mother only from photographs.

Matt stroked her hair. "I'm sorry if I was being pushy. I didn't mean it. I should've come right out and told you what I was thinking."

"Yes, you should have."

"I'm sorry. Really. I won't do it again."

Sarah almost retorted that she wouldn't give him the chance, that she'd be on her guard for the rest of their marriage, but he looked so remorseful that she changed her mind. "Okay," she said instead. "Let's just forget it. Besides, you're right. It would be nice if we worked at the same place."

"We might not run into each other much during the day, but at least we can have lunch together."

Sarah nodded, thinking. She'd wanted the chance to do something different with her career, and this job was certainly different. Besides, it would only be for a few months at most. It would help fill up the days and take her mind off her unsuccessful job search.

Then she remembered the quilt she'd seen on her first visit to the manor, and found another reason to take the job.

"So what do you say?" Matt asked.

"The house is gorgeous, and it's so much cooler out here, too, like you said." Sarah took Matt's hand and squeezed it. "I'm going to go back there right now and tell her I'll take the job, okay?" She turned and started back for the manor.

"Okay," Matt called after her. "See you at noon."

As she walked, Sarah decided that the situation had enough advantages to outweigh Mrs. Compson's eccentricities. She could always quit if things didn't work out. Besides, she knew the perfect way Mrs. Compson could pay her. She hurried up the back steps and knocked on the door.

Immediately, Mrs. Compson opened it. "Have you decided?" She pursed her lips as if she expected bad news.

"I'll take the job, on one condition."

Mrs. Compson raised an eyebrow. "I already planned to feed you."

"Thank you, but that's not it."

"What, then?"

"Teach me how to quilt."

"I beg your pardon?"

"Teach me how to quilt. Teach me how to make a quilt and I'll help you with your work."

"Surely you don't mean it. There are several fine teachers in Waterford. I could give you some names."

Sarah shook her head. "No. That's the deal. You teach me how to quilt, and I'll help you take inventory and prepare the manor for sale. I've seen your quilts, and —" Sarah tried to remember what Bonnie had said. "And you're in the QAS permanently. You ought to be able to teach me how to quilt."

"You mean AQS, but that's not the point. Of course I could teach you. It's not a question of my ability." The old woman eyed her as if she found her quite inscrutable, then shrugged and extended a hand. "Very well. Agreed. In addition to your wages, I'll teach you how to quilt."

Sarah pulled her hand away an instant before she would have been grasping Mrs. Compson's. "No, that's not what I meant.

The lessons are my wages."

"Goodness, child, have you no bills to pay?" Mrs. Compson sighed and looked to the heavens. "Don't let these somewhat dilapidated conditions deceive you. My family may not be what it once was, but we aren't ready to accept charity quite yet."

"I didn't mean to imply that."

"Yes, yes. Of course you didn't. But I simply must insist on some sort of payment. My conscience wouldn't give me a moment's peace otherwise."

Sarah thought about it. "Okay. Something fair." She wasn't about to take advantage of someone who was obviously lonely, no matter how rude she was.

They settled on a wage, but Sarah still felt that she was receiving the best part of the bargain. When they shook on it, Mrs. Compson's eyes lit up with triumph. "I think you would have held out for more if you knew how much work there is to be done."

"I'm hoping that I'll have a real job before long."

Mrs. Compson smiled. "Forgive me if I hope not." She held open the door, and Sarah went inside. "Would you really have swept the veranda for free if I had asked you nicely?"

"Yes." Sarah thought for a moment and decided to be honest. "Maybe. I'm not sure. I'll do it now, though, since I'm on the payroll."

"Let me know when you're ready for lunch," Mrs. Compson said, as Sarah continued down the hallway toward the front entrance.

Chapter 4

As she had promised, Sarah swept the veranda. When every dead leaf had been gathered up and even the corners were surely neat enough to win Mrs. Compson's approval, most of the morning still stretched ahead of her. She decided to move on to the staircases, and swept twigs and leaves and crumbling fragments of mortar to the ground as she descended each curving step. Often she had to stoop over and pull up weeds and tufts of grass that had grown in the spaces between the gray stones. She hadn't noticed the cracks and the scrawny pale shoots earlier, and she reminded herself to tell Matt about them. From the looks of things, he might need to replace some of the mortar, maybe even some of the stones on the lower steps.

As she worked, the manor's shade and a gentle southwest breeze kept the worst of the sun's heat from troubling her. And as noon approached, she felt her thoughts un-snarling until she realized with a start that she was enjoying herself. If her mother could see her now. Sarah pictured her mother's reaction when she learned the truth about her daughter's new career, and had to smile.

At lunchtime, Sarah returned to the kitchen to find Matt setting the table and Mrs. Compson stirring a bowl of tuna salad. While they ate, Mrs. Compson quizzed them on their morning's accomplishments, nodding in satisfaction at their replies. When Matt tried to show Mrs. Compson some preliminary sketches of the north gardens, though, she gave them only the barest of glances, nodded, and abruptly rose from her seat.

Matt and Sarah exchanged a puzzled look. Did that nod mean she liked Matt's ideas or not? "Here, we'll help clean up," Sarah said, standing.

Matt jumped to his feet and began collecting the dirty plates. "No, you two go on. I'll take care of it."

Mrs. Compson stared at him. "You'll take care of it?"

"Sure." He grinned and carried the dishes to the sink. "Don't worry. I won't drop anything."

"I should hope not." Mrs. Compson turned to Sarah. "Well, I suppose this would give us more time to talk about quilts later. But first, Sarah, come with me."

Sarah kissed Matt good-bye and followed Mrs. Compson out of the room. They passed a closed door directly opposite the kitchen entrance and turned down the long hallway. Along the way Mrs. Compson stopped at a small closet to retrieve a bundle of dust rags, which she deposited in Sarah's arms before moving on.

"We'll start upstairs," Mrs. Compson announced as they turned right at the T intersection. "Or rather, you'll start upstairs."

Sarah trailed after her into the front foyer. "Where do these doors lead?"

Without breaking her stride, Mrs. Compson pointed to the double doors on the right. "Banquet hall. No mere dining room for Elm Creek Manor." She pointed to the other set of doors, directly in front of them and to the left of the wedge-shaped steps leading into the corner. "Ballroom. At one time the entire first floor of this wing was devoted almost exclusively to entertaining." She reached the staircase, grasped the railing, and led Sarah upstairs. "We'll begin in the library. It's directly above the ballroom."

"What's above that?"

"The nursery. Oh, I know what you're thinking. Why on earth would any family need a nursery so large? Well, I agree. It's much larger than necessary."

Sarah nodded, wondering what an acceptable size for a nursery would be. As they continued up the stairs, she considered offering the older woman her arm. She suspected she'd be reprimanded for the attempt, though, and decided not to risk it.

Halfway to the second floor, Mrs. Compson paused on the step, breathing heavily. "As for the rest of it," she said, waving a hand in no particular direction. "Bedrooms, each with its own sitting room."

"Why so many?"

"This was supposed to be a family house — several generations, aunts, uncles, and cousins, all living together happily under one roof. Hmph."

"Which room's yours?"

Mrs. Compson glanced at her sharply, then continued her climb. "I have my sitting room downstairs."

"You mean you sleep on the sofa? Aren't the bedrooms furnished?"

Mrs. Compson said nothing. Sarah bit the inside of her upper lip in a belated attempt to restrain the question. When they reached the top step, Mrs. Compson let out a relieved sigh and turned left down another hallway. "My sister saved everything," she finally said as they passed several closed doors on either side. When the hallway widened and dead-ended at another set of double doors, Mrs. Compson stopped. "And I do mean everything. Old magazines, newspapers, paperbacks. I want you to help me sort the rubbish from anything salvageable."

With her lips firmly pursed, Mrs. Compson swung open both doors, and they entered the library. The musty, cluttered room spanned the width of the south wing's far end. Dust specks floated lazily in the dim light that leaked in through tall windows on the south-, east-, and west-facing walls. Oak bookcases, their shelves stacked with books, knickknacks, and loose papers, stood between the windows. Two sofas faced each other in the center of the room, dusty lamps resting on end tables on either side of both, a low coffee table turned upside down between them. More books and papers were scattered on the floor near the large oak desk on the east side of the room. Two high-backed, over-stuffed chairs stood near a fireplace in the center of the south wall, and a third chair was toppled over onto its side nearby.

Sarah sneezed.

"God bless you." Mrs. Compson smiled. "Let's open these windows and see if we can clear out some of the dust with some fresh air, shall we?"

Sarah set the dust rags on the desk and helped her carefully swing open the windows, which were made of small diamond-shaped pieces of glass joined with lead solder. Some of the panes were clear, but others were cloudy with age and weathering. Sarah leaned her head and shoulders out of one of the south windows. She could see the roof of the barn through the trees.

She smiled and turned back to her new employer, who was trying to set the over-turned chair onto its feet. "Where do you want me to begin?" she asked, hastening to help.

"Begin wherever you like. Just see that you get the job done." Mrs. Compson brushed the dust from her hands. "Separate all of the old newspapers into a pile for recycling, and do the same for the magazines. Loose papers may be recycled — or discarded, if you think it best. Gather the old paperbacks somewhere. Later we can box them and donate them to the public library, if they're in suitable condition. I'd like to keep the hardcover books, at least for now. Those you may dust off and return to the shelves."

"Waterford Library may have to open up a new branch for all of this," Sarah remarked, scanning the shelves. "Your sister must've liked reading."

The older woman gave a harsh laugh that sounded more like a strangled cough. "My sister liked reading junk — the cheapest romances, the most trivial tabloid magazines. In her later years she saved newspapers, too, but I don't think she actually read them. No, she just piled them up here, creating a fire hazard, leaving them for someone else to clean up later." She shook her head. "The finer books were my father's. And mine."

Sarah felt her cheeks grow warm. Apparently it was time to stop bringing up Mrs. Compson's family. "Well, I guess I'll get started, then," she said.

Mrs. Compson gave her a brisk nod. "You may work until four, then meet me in the sitting room and we'll discuss your quilting lessons."

Sarah breathed a quick sigh when Mrs. Compson left the library, relieved to have escaped another scolding. Mrs. Compson didn't seem to think very much of her sister. Or maybe she was so grief-stricken that she couldn't bear to think about her and that was why she seemed so abrupt. Sarah stooped over to pick up some scattered newspaper pages, vowing to keep her mouth shut more often.

Even with the windows open, the library was a dusty, stuffy place to work. As Sarah sorted through the clutter, she found several fine leather-bound volumes which she carefully dusted and returned to the cleaned shelves. When she found the piles of yellowed newspaper taking up an entire bookcase in the northeast corner of the room, she leafed through them eagerly. Newspaper clippings from the manor's earlier and happier years would tell her more about the people who used to live there. To her disappointment, however, Sarah soon realized that none of the papers dated from earlier than the mid-1980s. As she continued to work, she began to believe that Mrs. Compson's dismissive critique of her late sister's reading habits had been accurate.

At four o'clock Sarah heard Mrs.

Compson calling her from the bottom of the stairs. She arched her back, stretched, and wiped her brow on a clean corner of a dust cloth. There was still a lot of work to be done, but even Mrs. Compson would have to agree that Sarah had made a noticeable dent in it.

She hurried downstairs, where Mrs. Compson greeted her with an amused look. "There seems to be more dust on you than there was in the entire library."

Sarah hastily wiped her palms on her shorts and tucked in her blouse. "No, don't worry. There's plenty more dust up there for anyone who wants it."

Mrs. Compson chuckled and motioned for Sarah to follow her down the hallway. "How much did you accomplish today?"

"I took care of everything that was on the floor and finished the bookcases on the north and west walls. I closed the windows, too, in case it rains tonight. Do you want to look through anything before it's recycled?"

"Did you follow my instructions? Were you careful?"

"I think I was, but it's your stuff. I'd hate to throw out anything you might miss later. Maybe you should look through the piles just the same."

They entered the kitchen. "No need for

that. Anything I ever wanted from this place isn't here for the taking." Mrs. Compson gestured to the sink. "When you've cleaned yourself up a bit, join me in the sitting room."

Sarah washed her hands and face, then hesitated in the sitting room doorway. Mrs. Compson was pulling some quilts from a cedar chest and draping them on the sofa. Open books were piled on an end table. Mrs. Compson turned and spotted her. "Well, are you coming in or aren't you? It's all right. You've been invited this time, not like that first day."

"I was kind of hoping you'd forgotten about that."

"I never forget."

Sarah figured the older woman probably never forgave, either. She entered the room and walked over to the quilts. The fabric seemed worn and faded, even faintly stained in some places, but the quilting stitches and the arrangements of tiny pieces of cloth were as lovely as the newer quilts she had recently seen. Gingerly she traced the pattern of a red-and-white quilt with a fingertip. "Did you make these?"

"All of them. They're old."

"They're beautiful."

"Hmph. Young lady, if you keep saying

things like that I might just have to keep you around." Mrs. Compson closed the cedar chest and spread one last quilt on the sofa. "They shouldn't be stored in there. Contact with wood can damage them. But Claudia was too scatterbrained to remember such simple things." She sighed and eased herself onto a chair beside the end table. "Not that it really matters. These quilts were made to be used, and to be used up. I thought they might at least give you some ideas, a place to start."

Claudia — she must be her sister, Sarah thought as she pulled a chair closer to Mrs. Compson's.

"The last time I taught someone to quilt — why, it must have been fifty years ago," Mrs. Compson said, as if thinking aloud. "Of course, she never truly wanted to learn. I'm sure you'll do much better."

"Oh, I really do want to learn. My grandmother quilted, but she died before I was old enough for her to teach me."

Mrs. Compson raised an eyebrow. "I learned when I was five years old." She put on her glasses and peered at one of the books. "I thought you could best learn by making a sampler. Mind you, I plan to teach you the traditional way, hand piecing and hand quilting. You shouldn't expect to

78

finish your quilt this week or even this year."

"I know it'll take time. I don't mind."

"There are many other perfectly acceptable modern techniques that make quilting faster and easier." She indicated the sewing machine with a jerk of her head. "I use some of them myself. But for now, hand piecing will do."

Sarah looked at the small machine in disbelief. "You can sew on that toy sewing machine?"

Matt had an expression very much like the one Mrs. Compson wore then, one he usually assumed when Sarah called an amaryllis a lily or when she called everything from mulch to peat moss dirt. "That's no toy. That model isn't manufactured anymore, but it's one of the finest sewing machines a quilter can own. You shouldn't judge things by their size, or by their age."

Chastened, Sarah changed the subject. "You said I should make a sampler?"

Mrs. Compson nodded. "How big do you want the finished quilt to be?"

"Big enough for our bed. It's queen-size."

"Then you'll need about twelve different blocks, if we use a straight setting with sashing and borders instead of setting the blocks on point. Then we'll attach wide strips of your background fabric between the blocks and your outer border so you have plenty of space to practice your hand quilting stitches." Mrs. Compson handed Sarah one of the books. "Pick twelve different blocks you'd like to try. There are more patterns in these other books. I'll help you find a good balance."

With Mrs. Compson's guidance, Sarah selected twelve blocks from the hundreds of patterns in the books. Mrs. Compson explained the difference between pieced blocks, ones that were made from seaming the block's pieces together, and appliquéd blocks, which were made by sewing figures onto background fabric. Mrs. Compson encouraged her to choose some of each style for her sampler. The time spent choosing, reconsidering, and rejecting blocks passed quickly, and before Sarah knew it, it was half past five. She had selected twelve blocks that varied in style, appearance, and difficulty, and Matt was standing in the sitting room doorway smiling at her.

"How's quilt school going?" he asked, crossing the room and giving Sarah a hug.

Sarah smiled up at him. "I'm getting my homework assignment as we speak."

"Yes, Sarah has decided to become a student again," Mrs. Compson said as she jotted down some notes on a pad. She tore off the top sheet and handed it to Sarah. "This is a list of the fabrics and other tools you'll need to complete the quilt top. We'll worry about the other materials later. Do you know the quilt shop downtown?"

"I've been there once."

"Ask someone there to help you select the items from this list. Bonnie Markham is the owner. A very pleasant woman. She'll know what to do."

Sarah nodded, remembering the friendly, dark-haired woman. She scanned the list, then folded the paper and placed it in her pocket. "I'll see you on Monday, then."

Mrs. Compson escorted them to the door, and Sarah and Matt drove home.

The answering machine's light blinked a welcome when they entered the duplex. Sarah's stomach flip-flopped as she ducked around Matt and reached for the playback button.

"This is Brian Turnbull from Penn-Cellular Corporation."

Sarah closed her eyes and suppressed a groan.

"I'm trying to reach Sarah McClure regarding the résumé you sent us. If you're still interested in the position, give me a call today before five so we can set up an interview."

Sarah glanced at the clock in dismay. It was already almost six.

"If you can't reach me before then, I'll be back in the office first thing Monday morning." He quickly recited his telephone number and hung up.

"Doesn't that just figure?" Sarah muttered, snatching up the phone. "The only day I'm not around, and that's the day he calls."

"He might still be there. You could try."

Sarah was already dialing the number. She reached an answering machine and hung up without leaving a message. "If only I'd been here. What if he thinks I'm not interested? By now he could have offered the job to someone else."

"Hey, relax," Matt said, rubbing her shoulders. "He said you could call on Monday, right? Why would he say that if he wasn't interested?"

Sarah shook her head. "This is a sign."

"It's not a sign."

"It is, too. It's a very bad sign."

"Sarah, you're overreacting. You shouldn't —" Matt broke off and sighed, shaking his head and furrowing his brow in exaggerated helplessness. "I'll tell you what. First, we make supper. I'm starved."

Sarah's anxiety began to wane. "And then what?"

"Then we clean up."

"Then what?"

"Then," he said, dropping his hands to her waist and pulling her into a hug. "You forget all about work for a while." He kissed her and smiled, his eyes twinkling with mischief.

Sarah smiled back. "Why wait until after supper?"

Chapter 5

 Over breakfast on Saturday morning, Sarah approached the Help Wanted ads with more confidence than she had felt in weeks. Now that she could count on her job with Mrs. Compson for a regular paycheck, she didn't need to find the perfect career right away. Besides, she'd rather spend the summer exploring Elm Creek Manor than crunching numbers in some climate-controlled office cubicle.

Sarah found three new ads for accounting positions, and she took them as a sign that her luck had changed at last. Usually she struggled to choose the perfect words for her cover letters, but today her fingers flew over the keyboard. On a whim she changed the typeface on her résumé from Helvetica to New Century Schoolbook, since it looked more optimistic and might make a better impression. At ten o'clock she and Matt drove downtown to the post office, where she sent her résumés on their hopeful journeys. Then, while Matt drove off to complete some errands of his own, Sarah hurried down the sidewalk to Grandma's Attic.

The store was more crowded than it had been on her first visit. Several customers browsed through the aisles, studiously comparing different bolts of fabric or leafing through the books and quilt patterns near the front entrance. Sarah spotted Bonnie standing with five other women around the far end of the long cutting table. She was about to approach them when they erupted in peals of laughter. Feeling awkward, she hung back. They didn't seem standoffish, but their friendship was so tangible that Sarah felt like an unwanted eavesdropper. She waved discreetly instead, trying to catch the shop owner's eye without interrupting the lively conversation.

The youngest woman in the group looked her way, smiled, and left the table. She had long, straight auburn hair that was parted in the middle and reached halfway down her back. "May I help you?" she asked as she approached. She seemed several years younger than Sarah, perhaps in her late teens or early twenties.

Bonnie followed close behind. "So, Sarah, you've decided to take the plunge?"

Sarah pulled Mrs. Compson's list from her pocket. "Yes, and I'm supposed to get a bunch of supplies. But I'm not really sure . . . well, like this. I'm supposed to get 'three yards of a medium print.' Does that mean medium as in medium-size?"

"Dark, medium, and light refer to a fabric's value," the auburn-haired girl explained.

"You mean, how much it costs?"

The girl's smile deepened, and a dimple appeared in her right cheek. "Not that, either. Let me start over. Value refers to how dark or light a color is, how much black or white has been added to a hue. You need to have contrasting values in a quilt so the block pattern shows up. It's like if you track dark brown mud all over a light beige carpet. The mud and the carpet have very different values so the footprints really show up. But if you track dark brown mud on a dark blue carpet, you can't see the footprints as much. And if your mom's anything like mine, she won't even notice the stains."

"I heard that, kiddo," one of the women called out from the cutting table. "You know you're not supposed to air my housekeeping foibles in public." She, too, was auburn-haired, but more sturdily built than her slender daughter. She wore a long flowing skirt and several beaded necklaces.

"She isn't telling us anything we don't already know, Gwen," the woman at her side drawled. She was strikingly pretty, tall, thin, and tan, and she wore her short blond hair in curls.

"Besides, Mom, it was for a good cause. I was helping a new quilter."

Gwen shrugged. "Oh. In that case, go right ahead."

The others burst into laughter again. Sarah felt a smile twitching in the corners of her mouth as she watched them.

"It looks like Summer has everything under control, so why don't I leave you in her capable hands?" Bonnie suggested. "She knows as much about quilts as anyone here."

"Not exactly. I'm still learning, too," Summer replied, but she looked pleased as she motioned for Sarah to follow her to the closest aisle of fabric bolts.

After searching through cotton prints of every imaginable pattern and color, Sarah found a medium value print she liked, a paisley pattern in shades of red, blue, cream, and brown. Then Summer showed her how to match other fabrics to the colors in the first print. At first Sarah selected all floral designs, but Summer explained that different prints — some large, some airy, some geometric, some tone-on-tone, and others multicolored — would give the finished quilt a more interesting texture.

"There's so much to think about," Sarah said, overwhelmed. "I didn't think making a quilt would be easy, but if the shopping's this difficult, I can't imagine what the sewing will be like."

"It gets easier, but I know what you mean," Summer confided, lowering her voice. "When my mom first started teaching me how to quilt, I felt the same way. But don't tell her I said so. She's convinced I was a child prodigy, and I'd hate to ruin my image."

Sarah laughed and agreed. It felt good to have a friendly person to talk to again. With a pang, she suddenly realized how much she missed her friends from State College. They used to talk and laugh and have a good time no matter where they were or what they were doing. Even trips to the Laundromat could be fun with them, and no terrible workday or argument with her mother could withstand their power to commiserate and comfort. Bonnie and the other women around the table acted as if they had a friendship like that. As Summer helped her find the other items on Mrs. Compson's list, Sarah wished that she and Summer were friends and that Summer would take her over there and introduce her to the other women. They all looked so cheerful, so comfortable together.

"Are you taking one of Bonnie's classes?" Summer asked as they carried the bolts to the other end of the cutting table. She unrolled the first bolt and began to cut the fabric.

"No, Sylvia Compson is going to teach me."

Summer stared at her, scissors frozen in mid-cut. "Sylvia Compson is your quilt teacher? No way."

At that, the conversation at the other end of the table broke off, and the women looked their way. Their expressions varied from mild surprise to outright astonishment. A woman of Asian heritage broke the silence. "She always quilts alone — at least, that's what they say." She held a baby in a carrier on her back, and as she spoke she absentmindedly removed a lock of her black hair from the child's fist.

The oldest woman, petite and white-haired, shook her head. "I believe Judy's right." Her blue eyes were wide with amazement behind pink-tinted glasses. "She doesn't teach anymore, and hasn't for a very long time, as far as I know."

"Looks like you've got yourself some competition, Bonnie," the blond woman beside Gwen added.

"I'm glad for it," Bonnie protested. "She's so talented. It's wonderful that she's passing along that gift."

"It's about time she stopped being so stuck up," the blond woman muttered. "She'll take all the ribbons all right, but she won't join a guild."

"Knock it off, Diane." Gwen elbowed her in the side. Diane's mouth opened in protest, but she said nothing else.

"Not everyone's a joiner," Judy said. "Besides, she hasn't been back in town very long, only since Claudia passed away. Who knows? Maybe she belonged to a guild back in — wherever she was."

"Sewickley," Sarah said.

Six pairs of eyes fixed on her.

"Are you from Sewickley, too?" the oldest woman asked. "Are you a friend of hers? Can you tell us how she's doing? I'm Mrs. Emberly. Mrs. Compson wouldn't mind if you told me — in fact, I suppose she'd expect me to ask. Are you a relation?"

"Well, no, I mean, I'm not a relation. I work for Mrs. Compson. But I'm not from Sewickley. I'm from State College." Sarah tried not to fidget. "I don't really know Mrs. Compson all that well —"

"Ah, yes. State College." Gwen grinned. "Of course, that means you must be a Penn State grad."

"That's right. I just moved to town."

"Have you signed with a team yet or are you still a free agent?"

Sarah's brow furrowed in puzzlement.

Summer came to her rescue. "What Mom's trying to ask is, did you already join the Waterford Quilting Guild or are you still looking for a bee?"

"I guess I'm still a free agent, not by choice, but —"

"Then you can join our group," Summer exclaimed. "I mean, if you want to. If you're not too busy."

"I'd love to. But I'm just a beginner. Is that okay?"

"We were all beginners once," Gwen assured her. She introduced the other women, who smiled at Sarah as Gwen went around the circle.

Gwen explained that the 100-member Waterford Quilting Guild met once a month on the college campus to discuss guild business and activities, and broke up into smaller groups for weekly quilting bees. "The Tangled Web Quilters started out as one of those bees, but eventually we stopped going to the guild's monthly meetings. I for one got tired of all the bureaucracy, electing officers for this, selecting a committee for that . . . all that nonsense takes up valuable quilting time. You're more than welcome to join us if you like, if your Thursday evenings are free."

"You'll enjoy yourself, Sarah," Bonnie said. "Bring something to quilt and be prepared to tell us your life story."

Diane grinned. "Or, as we usually say, 'Stitch and Bitch.' "

They all laughed.

"Don't tell her that," Mrs. Emberly said, struggling to hide a smile. "She'll think we're horribly rude."

"No, not at all," Sarah assured her. The Tangled Web Quilters were more like her State College friends than she ever could have suspected.

Summer finished cutting Sarah's fabric while Gwen wrote down some information about the next week's quilting bee. Sarah paid for her supplies, said good-bye to her new friends, and left the store. Swinging her shopping bag cheerfully, she walked up the street to the coffee shop where Matt was going to meet her for lunch. For the first time since they'd moved to Waterford, the downtown seemed the warm, friendly place their real estate agent had promised.

"This Diane sounds like she's jealous of Mrs. Compson," Matt said after Sarah told him about her morning.

"Oh, I'm sure she's nice enough. They all seemed very nice." Sarah regarded him closely and tried to suppress a grin. He looked ready to leap to Mrs. Compson's defense if he heard another word against her.

"While you were at the quilt shop I picked up a car phone from work," Matt went on. "I thought we could use one since we're going to be spending a lot of time out at Elm Creek Manor."

"That's a good idea."

"Maybe we should try to talk Mrs. Compson into having a phone installed. Not for us, for her, in case she has an accident or something. I can't figure why she wouldn't have one already." Suddenly he frowned and looked puzzled. "What? Do I have crumbs on my face or something?

What are you grinning at?"

"You," Sarah teased. "You're so cute, the way you're so concerned about Mrs. Compson. It's like you've adopted her or something."

Matt looked embarrassed. "You make me sound like a Boy Scout."

"I think you're sweet." She reached across the table and squeezed his hand affectionately. "You're right about the phone, too. I wonder what she could do in an emergency. I don't think anyone would hear her if she shouted for help."

"I doubt it. The main road's too far from the house, and not many people use it. Elm Creek Manor's pretty isolated, especially if you don't drive."

"Doesn't she?"

"Think about it. Did you ever see any cars behind the manor? Except for ours, I mean?"

Sarah tried to remember. "No, I don't think so, and she'd probably park as close to the back door as possible, since she has some trouble walking." That thought troubled her. No phone, probably no car, and no one else in the house except when Sarah was working. How did Mrs. Compson get groceries? What if she had an accident?

"No wonder she wants to sell the place and move back to Sewickley." Matt shook his head. "It's too bad. When we finish our work that place is going to be awesome, and she won't be able to enjoy it."

"Yeah. It's a shame." Sarah frowned and tapped her fingers on her coffee cup.

Chapter 6

Before Sarah and Matt left for Elm Creek Manor on Monday morning, Sarah gathered her courage and called Mr. Turnbull at PennCellular Corporation. "Why don't you go upstairs or something?" she said to Matt as she dialed the kitchen phone. "You'll distract me."

"Okay," Matt agreed, but he lingered in the doorway.

After a few rings a receptionist answered and promptly put Sarah on hold. As she waited, she began to feel her throat tightening.

"Don't be nervous," Matt whispered.

Sarah waved him away, but he only took one step out of the kitchen.

"Turnbull here," a gruff voice suddenly barked in her ear.

"Good morning, Mr. Turnbull," Sarah said. She forced some confidence into her voice. "This is Sarah McClure. I'm returning your phone call about —"

"Oh, yes, right. Sarah McClure." Papers shuffled in the background. "You applied for a job in our public relations office, correct? Quite a nice résumé you sent in."

"Thank you."

"I'm a Penn State grad myself, you know. 'Course, that was before your time. I see you took advanced auditing. Is Professor Clarke still teaching it?"

"Yes. I mean, as far as I know she is. I had her years ago."

"Liked her lectures, hated her exams." Mr. Turnbull chuckled. "Well, let's see here. I've been going over your background, and you know something, Sarah? You really seem more suited for a job in our accounting department."

Sarah's heart sank. She tried to think of an appropriate response.

"Now, it just so happens we have an entry-level opening there, too," Mr. Turnbull went on. "It hasn't even been advertised yet. What do you say? Interested?"

"Well, sure, but I'm also very interested in the other —"

"Good. Then some of the folks in the accounting department want to meet you and talk about it. How about some time this week?"

"That would be great, thanks."

"How about tomorrow, say, about one o'clock?"

So soon? "That sounds fine." Sarah knew she ought to say something else, something impressive, something brilliant, but the words eluded her.

Mr. Turnbull raced through directions to his office as Sarah scrambled to write them down. "See you tomorrow, then."

"Thank you, Mr. Turnbull. I'm looking forward to meeting with you. I'll see you tomorrow. Thanks again."

Matt had been studying her expression throughout the conversation, and he stepped back into the kitchen when Sarah hung up the phone. She groaned, closed her eyes, and slumped against the kitchen wall. "It couldn't have been that bad," Matt said, incredulous. "You weren't on the phone long enough to do that much damage."

"I should've practiced what I was going to say. God, won't I ever get this right?" She thumped her head against the wall.

"Well, hitting your head on the wall isn't going to help."

"He's not considering me for the PR job."

"What do you mean? Didn't you just

schedule an interview?"

"For an accounting job. Every time I tried to talk about the PR job, he steered the conversation back to accounting."

"You're meeting with him tomorrow, right? Talk about it then."

"No, I blew it. Talk about terrible first impressions. Maybe I should call him and cancel."

Matt laughed. "Oh, sure. That'll make an even better impression." He crossed the room and put his hands on her shoulders. "Give yourself a break, Sarah. So you were a little nervous. That doesn't mean you blew it. I bet everyone he talks to gets nervous, probably more than you did. He must've liked how you sounded or he wouldn't have offered you the interview, right?" He stooped down until his eyes were level with hers, and gave her a playful grin. "Am I right? Tell me I'm right."

Sarah managed the barest hint of a smile in return. "Okay, maybe you're right. I guess he could've hung up on me. And he's Penn State alumni. He had Professor Clarke."

"Well, there you go. Turnbull likes Professor Clarke, and Professor Clarke likes you, right? You're a shoo-in."

"I don't think it's that simple, Matt."

"You never know." He gave her a quick kiss, then picked up his wallet and keys from the counter. "Come on, let's get going. Mrs. Compson might not be too thrilled if we're late."

Sarah snatched up her bag of quilting supplies, threw on her raincoat, and hurried after him to the truck. By the time he dropped her off behind Elm Creek Manor, she was about fifteen minutes late. She tried to avoid the biggest puddles as she ran from the gravel driveway to the back steps.

Mrs. Compson was waiting in the foyer. "You're late," she said before Sarah had a chance to say hello. "I didn't think you were coming."

"I'm sorry, Mrs. Compson." She took off her raincoat and shook the rain from her hair. "I had to make an important phone call, and their office didn't open until eight."

"At eight you were supposed to be here working, not at home making phone calls."

"I said I'm sorry. It won't happen again."

"Hmph." Mrs. Compson sniffed, relenting a little. "I suppose you forgot to buy your quilting materials."

"Everything's right here." Sarah showed her the bag.

"Did you wash and press the fabric?"

"Just as you told me."

"Hmph. Well, I suppose you might as well continue with the library this morning until lunchtime." Mrs. Compson took the bag and walked toward the kitchen. "Leave your shoes here. It won't do to have you tracking mud everywhere."

Sarah made an exasperated face at Mrs. Compson's back. That woman had a real gift for overreacting. She knew that Sarah's search for a real job had to be her first priority. If Mrs. Compson had a phone like normal people, Sarah could have come to work on time and called from there. She jerked off her shoes, and the chill from the cold tile floor crept into her toes. Muttering complaints under her breath, she pulled up her socks and padded down the hallway.

"Was my quilt still in the window of Grandma's Attic?" Mrs. Compson asked when Sarah passed the kitchen. She was sitting at the table, peering through her glasses at a newspaper.

Sarah paused in the doorway. "It was still there Saturday morning."

Mrs. Compson frowned and shook her head. "Maybe it's time for them to take it down. I doubt if anyone will buy it. I should just stick it in the cedar chest with the others."

"Oh, no, they should leave it up. It's so pretty. Someone will buy it soon, I'm sure."

Mrs. Compson looked up then, her face uncertain. "Do you really think so?"

"I'd buy it, if I could."

"You're a sweet girl to say so, but I have my doubts. It just seems like people don't care about things like quilters anymore."

Sarah thought about Bonnie, Summer, and the other Tangled Web Quilters. "I don't know. I think a lot of people care about quilts."

Mrs. Compson smiled halfheartedly. "That's not what I said." She sighed and returned to her newspaper.

Sarah watched her for a moment, then turned and went upstairs to the library. She didn't feel like a sweet girl. She wished she could be more like Matt — always accepting people, never making snap judgments, giving people the benefit of the doubt instead of getting angry over the least little thing. Maybe Mrs. Compson had overreacted, but Sarah had been late for work, if only by a few minutes. She felt a tiny prick of guilt on her conscience, more for her angry reaction to Mrs.

Compson's behavior than for her tardiness.

Mrs. Compson had left three empty cartons, a ball of twine, a can of furniture polish, and a pile of clean rags on the floor next to the desk. Since the wind was blowing from the south, Sarah opened the windows on only the east wall so she could get some fresh air without soaking the hardwood floor or the Persian carpet that covered its center. Then she began her day's work by filling the cartons with Claudia's old paperbacks and tying up bundles of newspaper with the twine. The library was pleasantly cool that morning, and Sarah hummed cheerfully as she worked, listening to the rain outside. Sometimes a low peal of thunder would toll far off in the distance, making the windows tremble and the lights flicker.

At noon she heard Mrs. Compson's slow step from the end of the hallway. Sarah set down her dust rag and hurried to open the library door. Mrs. Compson stood there with a tray loaded with sandwiches, fruit salad, and a pitcher of iced tea.

"You didn't need to come all the way up here." Sarah took the tray and carried it to the coffee table. "I would've come downstairs."

"I thought I might like to see how you're

coming along up here instead." Mrs. Compson looked around, nodding in satisfaction as she joined Sarah in the center of the room. "Yes, you're doing a fine job. This place looks almost as I remember it." She gingerly lowered herself onto the sofa, and a cloud of dust rose.

Sarah made a mental note to beat the cushions after lunch. She sat on the floor on the other side of the table and poured herself a glass of iced tea.

"I thought I'd join you for lunch," Mrs. Compson said. "If you don't mind the intrusion."

"It's no intrusion. I'd like the company." Sarah poured a second glass and handed it to her employer. She took a sandwich from the top of the pile and placed it on the delicate china plate Mrs. Compson set before her. The plate was almost translucent, with scalloped edges trimmed in gold and a rearing stallion etched in the center. "You know, I've noticed this horse emblem all over the place," Sarah mused, forgetting her earlier vow to resist prying into Mrs. Compson's life. "There's the fountain in the front of the manor, and the same horse is etched on the china, and it's embossed in gold on the desk —"

"Compson is my married name." Mrs.

Compson sipped her iced tea. "Oh, yes, of course. You're new to Waterford. You haven't heard, I suppose, of Hans Bergstrom? Or of Bergstrom Thoroughbreds?"

Sarah shook her head.

"What do you know of horses?"

"Not much."

"Hans Bergstrom was my great-grandfather." Mrs. Compson rose and went over to the desk. She ran a hand over the emblem of the rearing stallion. "In his time he raised the finest horses in the country. I never knew him, except from my parents' stories, but he must have been a remarkable man. All Bergstrom men were remarkable men."

I remember one story in particular. Out of all the stories this house holds, it's my very favorite.

My great-grandfather was the youngest son of a rather well-to-do family in Germany from a small city near Baden-Baden. I say the family was from Baden-Baden, but that's not entirely true. Hans's grandfather moved there from Stockholm when he married a German girl. And you'd think that would be enough moving about for one family, but you'd be wrong.

I suppose Hans Bergstrom was a lot like his grandfather — never one to stay in one place. His parents wanted him to go into the clergy, but he would have none of that. He wanted to seek adventure and fortune in America. When he was a young man, perhaps only a few years younger than you, he boarded a ship and emigrated without his parents' permission, without even informing them of his journey. Only his eldest sister knew, and she told no one until his ship was a week at sea.

Before long he made his way to Pennsylvania and began to use his knowledge of horse breeding and raising in other men's employ, saving every spare cent he could. He had a plan, you see, to establish his own stables someday and to breed the finest horses anywhere, new world and old alike.

When he was ready, he found this land and built a small house on the western edge of the property, where the orchard grows today. Such a confident man he was, brash even, so certain he was of his future success. He wrote to his family back in Germany to urge them to join him here, but only his eldest sister, Gerda, agreed to make the journey. She was unmarried, and very sensible, but not afraid to take a few risks.

When Gerda's ship was scheduled to arrive, Hans traveled to New York City to meet her. And this is the part of the story I like best. When he arrived at Immigration, he found a small knot of men talking excitedly and waving their arms about and carrying on as men always do when they argue. Never one to keep his nose in his own business, Hans nudged one man and asked him what was going on.

"They've got a girl there," the man told him. "Folks say she's been loitering here for three days now."

"I heard a week," another man interjected.

The first man shrugged. "Either way, they want her gone. They're trying to figure out what to do with her."

Intrigued, Hans pushed his way to the center of the crowd, and there he discovered the prettiest girl he had ever seen. Oh, she looked exhausted, to be sure, but with her green eyes and brown hair — well, I've seen her portrait, and I tell you she must have been a vision. She sat on top of a shining new treadle sewing machine cabinet, ankles crossed, hands folded primly in her lap, brave chin up, for all the world as if she were sitting on a throne. A couple of steamer trunks rested on the floor beneath her feet, and beside her three men in uniforms debated her future as if she had no say in the matter — which, I suppose, she probably didn't. She ignored them with all the dignity she could muster.

After questioning some others in the crowd, Hans learned that this young woman was from Berlin and that she was supposed to have been met there three days before by the man who had promised to marry her. She had spent her life savings on her passage to America and on the sewing machine with which she hoped to earn her keep, had gambled everything on that scoundrel's promise. The officials did not know what to do with her. She had no other family in the country, and spoke no English, and had no one to sponsor her now that her good-for-nothing fiancé had betrayed her. Most of the men were all for bundling her back on board the next ship for Germany, but she refused to budge. She wouldn't disobey them, but she wouldn't allow herself to be meekly driven away, either.

Now, if I had been that young woman, I would have planted my feet, looked those men straight in the eye, and dared them to try to put me on board a ship when I didn't want to go, but times were different then. I suppose my day was as different from hers as yours is from mine.

Then one of the officials threw up his hands in exasperation. "Well, unless one of you lot wants to marry her, I'm all for tossing her on the next ship east, sewing machine and all!"

"I'll marry her," my great-grandfather said, stepping forth from the crowd. He turned to the beautiful girl sitting on top of her sewing machine and greeted her in German.

She blinked in astonishment at the sound of her own language coming from an American. She became even more surprised when he translated what he had told the men.

"I'd marry you today and consider myself a lucky man," Hans said in German. "But it would be wrong for me to expect you to decide under these circumstances. Besides, I'd like to think that my bride chose me for myself and not because her only other option was deportation."

The beautiful girl smiled at that.

"We'll tell these men that you're my bride," Hans continued. "What they don't know won't hurt them. You can live with my sister and me as long as you want. Maybe in a year or two, you'll tell me that you truly will be my bride. Or maybe you'll find another fellow. I hope you'll choose me, but I want you to know what you're getting before you say yes."

She smiled and gave him her hand. "Perhaps you'll give me your name first, and we can discuss marriage later. In a year or two."

It turned out that she needed only six months to make up her mind. They fell in love, and that speeded her decision. Sometimes I wonder if she fell in love first with Hans's dream, with its hopes and challenges, and then with the man himself. Or perhaps her love for the man grew into love for his dream. I suppose I'll never know.

Well, I suppose you've figured out by now that the beautiful girl was my great-grandmother, Anneke. She and my great-grandfather were married eight months after they met, and Gerda was the maid of honor. As the years passed they established Elm Creek Manor and spent their lives working tirelessly until Bergstrom Thoroughbreds was recognized everywhere as the pinnacle of excellence. Even today the world's finest horses can be traced back to this land.

My great-grandparents raised their children here, and when the children married, their spouses lived here as well with their children. Some moved away, but when my father married he brought my mother here. I remember having fourteen young playmates close at hand when I was a child. It was a wonderful, happy time.

"Then what happened?" Sarah prompted. Why had Mrs. Compson sounded so sad at the end? And what had happened to change everything? The manor was all but abandoned now, unrecognizable as the happy place Mrs. Compson had described.

"The manor thrived. My father continued the tradition my great-grandfather had begun, as did my husband and I, for a time." Mrs. Compson sighed and went to an east-facing window. She pulled the curtain back and gazed outside. "But that was all a very long time ago, and things are much different now. Much of the land we once held has been sold off, and all that is left of Great-Grandfather Bergstrom's dream is this house, a handful of acres, beautiful horses scattered around the world —" Mrs. Compson's voice caught in her throat. "And memories. But I suppose that will have to be enough. Sometimes it's too much."

Sarah wanted to say something, but could only watch as Mrs. Compson stared outside at the rain. In the tightness of the older woman's shoulders and in the bowing of her head, Sarah thought she could see the surface of a grief she could not understand.

Mrs. Compson turned and crossed the room. "Bring the tray down with you at three, will you?"

"Aren't you going to finish your lunch?"

"No thank you, dear. I'm not hungry after all. I'll see you downstairs this afternoon." She left the room, shutting the library door behind her.

Frowning, Sarah started to finish her lunch. Then she set down her sandwich and pushed the plate away. What could have happened to the Bergstrom family to make Mrs. Compson so unhappy?

Sarah went to the window where Mrs. Compson had been looking out at the storm. If there were answers in the rain-drenched lawn, the distant trees tossing their green boughs in the wind, and the pool of the rearing horse fountain rapidly filling with rainwater, Sarah couldn't see them.

Chapter 7

At three o'clock Sarah carried the tray downstairs to the kitchen and joined Mrs. Compson in the sitting room. The well-lit room was snug and cheerful in spite of the storm outside. Mrs. Compson had draped Sarah's fabric over the sofa and was studying it when Sarah greeted her.

"You have a good eye for color, Sarah."

"One of Bonnie's employees helped me match things up." Sarah picked up one of the quilting books and flipped through the pages. "Are we going to start quilting today?"

"If you mean quilting as in the whole process of making a quilt, yes. If you mean quilting as in sewing through the three layers of the quilt, no." Mrs. Compson pushed her sewing machine against the wall and beckoned Sarah to join her at the table. "We'll begin by making templates for your first block, the Sawtooth Star."

"Templates?"

Mrs. Compson found the block's diagram in a quilt book. "We transfer the pieces of the block from the drawing to this clear plastic. Then we cut out the template, place it on the wrong side of our fabric, and draw around it. Cut a quarter of an inch around the drawn line, and you have your first quilt piece."

"Why don't we cut on the line?"

"The drawn line is your sewing line. The extra quarter inch is the seam allowance."

"Oh." Sarah wasn't sure she understood, but she sat down and took the sheet of plastic Mrs. Compson handed her. A grid of fine red lines covered it. "Should I just trace it out of the book? It looks too small."

"That's quite correct," Mrs. Compson said. "If you simply traced the pieces, your finished block would be six inches square, only half the size we need. Many books and magazines provide actual-size drawings, but we will need to enlarge this one."

She showed Sarah how to use the author's half-scale diagram and the grid on the plastic sheet to create a template of the correct size. With Mrs. Compson's help, Sarah soon created four templates: a small square, a larger square, a small isosceles right triangle, and a larger isosceles right triangle.

As Sarah worked, a memory tickled in the back of her mind. Whenever she looked at the Sawtooth Star diagram, she felt as if she were missing something obvious, something important, something she ought to see but didn't. She tried to shake the feeling, but it lingered.

"Now for the tracing." Mrs. Compson selected Sarah's medium blue print and her cream background fabric from the pile on the sofa. She instructed Sarah to cut one larger square and eight smaller triangles from the blue, and to cut four small squares and four larger triangles from the cream. When Sarah had finished, Mrs. Compson arranged the pieces on the table so that the different shapes formed a star.

The persistent sense of familiarity tugged at Sarah as she studied the pieces. "I've seen this before."

"Of course you have. You chose this block yourself."

"No, that's not it." Sarah thought hard, and then it was as if a blurry image suddenly shifted into focus. "I had a quilt like this once." As she said the words, she could almost see the pink-and-white quilt her grandmother had made for her eighth birthday.

She could still remember the way her mother's mouth had tightened when Sarah unwrapped the present. "Good Lord, Mother," her mother had said. "You didn't need to do that. I just bought her a new bedspread two months ago."

"A granddaughter deserves a handmade quilt. It was a joy to make."

"She'll just spill something on it and ruin it."

"No, I won't. I promise," Sarah had said, running her small hand over the quilt.

"Don't you like the bedspread we picked out together?"

Sarah had looked up then, startled by the warning tone in her mother's voice. "Y-yes." She hesitated. "But I like the quilt, too."

"Which one do you like better?"

"Don't ask her that," Grandmother had murmured.

"No, no. Don't worry about offending me, Mother. I want to know. Come on, Sarah. The truth."

"I like —" Sarah remembered looking from her mother's hard eyes to her grandmother's sad ones. "I like the quilt best."

"Figures." Her mother stood up. "I

guess that's what you hoped to hear, right, Mother?"

"It isn't a contest."

"Easy for you to say. You won." Her mother took the quilt and stuffed it back into the box. "Sarah will take good care of it, won't you, Sarah?" She carried the box away without another word.

Grandmother held out her arms then, and Sarah climbed into her lap. She squeezed her eyes shut against the tears, but they fell anyway.

Even now, so many years later, resentment washed over her. She pushed the memory away. "My grandmother made me a Sawtooth Star quilt when I turned eight."

"Is that so?"

"Uh huh." Sarah stared at the quilt block. "I wasn't allowed to use it, though. My mother said it was too fancy for every day, so she kept it in a box in her closet. I was only allowed to use it when Grandmother came to visit."

"I see." Mrs. Compson gave her a knowing look. "So your mother was the fussy type, with plastic on the furniture and all that, hmm?"

"No." Sarah moved two of the block pieces closer together and studied them.

"She wasn't like that about anything except this quilt." She wondered where it was now. Still on the floor of her mother's closet, probably. "I had forgotten all about it. Funny, isn't it, that out of all of those blocks you showed me, I would pick this one?"

"Not necessarily. Perhaps you chose this block because some part of you never forgot your grandmother's quilt and never stopped missing it."

"Do you think so?"

"Or perhaps the gift wasn't a Sawtooth Star quilt but a Dove in the Window or a Sunbonnet Sue. Or maybe it wasn't a quilt at all, but a doll or a pretty dress. Memory can be a tricky thing sometimes."

The thought made Sarah uneasy. "So you think I'm remembering something that never happened?" That didn't make sense. She could picture herself holding that quilt, running her hand over its softness and delighting in the bright colors.

"Certainly not. Something happened, some conflict with your mother, some tension between her and her own mother. But whether it was over a Sawtooth Star quilt or something else entirely, I couldn't say."

Sarah frowned. Mrs. Compson's explanation was no comfort. She rearranged some of the block pieces and glowered at them. "These corners — they don't match up right."

Mrs. Compson tapped her wrist. "Stop fiddling with the pieces. You're forgetting about the seam allowances again. Once the pieces are sewn together, everything will match up just fine and you'll see how pretty the block will be." She opened a small tin container full of pins. "Now you'll learn how to hand piece."

Sarah knew how to sew on a button but nothing more complicated than that, so she listened carefully as Mrs. Compson explained what to do. Following Mrs. Compson's directions, she picked up a cream triangle and a blue triangle, placed the right sides facing each other, and pinned them together along the sewing line. Then she took the threaded needle Mrs. Compson handed her, tied a small knot at the end of the thread, and sewed a running stitch from the beginning to the end of the line, removing the pins as she came to them. After tying a second knot and trimming the extra thread, she creased the seam flat with a fingernail.

"Now, if you do that several thousand times, you'll have a quilt top," Mrs. Compson remarked.

Sarah continued to work, with Mrs. Compson looking over her shoulder and giving advice. When Sarah had finished all the straight seams and had joined several units into rows, Mrs. Compson explained how to sew through seams when joining rows together. Although Sarah's piecing became faster and more accurate with every seam, Matt arrived before she was able to finish the block. She put the pieces and her sewing tools into her backpack so that she could continue sewing at home.

The rain had stopped, and the usual heat and humidity had returned. On the drive home, Sarah told Matt the little Mrs. Compson had revealed about her family and the history of Elm Creek Manor.

"I wonder what went on here to ruin everything," Matt said when she finished.

"Me, too. For a moment I thought she was about to tell me, but just when she opened up, she got all upset and left. I can't figure it out. From what she said, they had everything. Literally. A family, a home, enough money to take care of everything. Why would someone want to leave all that?"

"You're asking the wrong guy."

Sarah barely heard him. "I wonder," she mused. "Claudia or someone must have done something terribly wrong to Mrs. Compson for her to break off all ties with her family."

"Sometimes people break off all ties even when the family does everything right."

Sarah started in realization. "Matt, honey, I didn't mean —"

"Can we drop it, please?"

"But I didn't mean that your mother left because you —"

"I said, can we drop it?"

Sarah watched him as he stared grimly out at the road in front of them. A long moment passed in silence.

"Matt?"

"What."

"Mrs. Compson came back to Elm Creek Manor. You never know, maybe —"

"No, I do know. If my mother was coming back, she would have done it a long time ago. Don't treat me like I'm five, okay?"

Stung, Sarah sat back in her seat and stared out the window. When they reached their duplex she jumped out of the truck and ran inside. She hurried upstairs and took a long shower, rinsing her stinging eyes again and again. She finished reluctantly and lingered in the steam, not knowing how to avoid her husband in such a small home.

When she finally pulled on her robe and went to the bedroom, Matt was sitting cross-legged on the bed, looking miserable.

Sarah tried to ignore him as she put on a T-shirt and cotton shorts.

"Sweetheart, I'm sorry I snapped at you."

Sarah didn't answer. She found some socks in her drawer and sat down on the bed to pull them on.

"Sarah, I'm really sorry."

"I didn't mean anything," she muttered, looking at the floor. "I was only trying to make you feel better."

"I know." He touched her gently on the shoulder.

"I always make things worse."

"No you don't."

"Yes, I do. I don't mean to, but I do. I always say the exact wrong thing at the worst possible time."

"That has nothing to do with it. I just don't like talking about my mother."

"Okay." Sarah thought for a moment. "But in the truck I wasn't talking about your mother. I was talking about Mrs. Compson's sister."

"You were talking about people going away."

"Oh, right." Sarah turned to face him and gave him a small smile. "So let me make sure I have this straight. I shouldn't talk about families, or people going away, or mothers —"

"We can talk about your mother if you want."

"Please, no. Anything but that." Sarah flopped onto her back on the bed and closed her eyes.

"You know, you really ought to give your mother a break."

Sarah groaned and threw an arm over her face. "Please don't start." They'd had this discussion many times before, and neither one ever altered the other's opinion. Ever since Sarah's mother started dating again, three months after Sarah's father died, every conversation between Sarah and her mother turned into an argument. Sarah's solution was to avoid contact as much as possible, even though it was obvious how much this disappointed Matt. He probably thought that if not for Sarah's attitude, they could all be one big happy family. If he only knew what Sarah's mother said about him when he wasn't there to hear.

Sarah sighed. "I won't talk about your mother anymore tonight if you don't talk about mine."

Matt chuckled. "Okay. Deal."

Sarah reached out for his hand and pulled him down beside her. She rested her head on his shoulder and breathed in his scent of grass and earth and sunlight.

Her family, Matt's, Mrs. Compson's — none had lasted. She searched her memory and concluded that she knew only a few families that weren't obviously screwed up. And those few probably just hid it better.

She held Matt closer. He was her family now. They would make their own family, one that didn't hurt.

Chapter 8

As she worked in the library the next morning, Sarah tried to concentrate on reorganizing the bookshelves instead of worrying about her upcoming job interview with PennCellular. After sorting the last pile of books, papers, and loose pages, she carried the newspaper bundles downstairs. Later she and Matt could load them into the truck and leave them in the recycling bin near their duplex.

With most of the clutter removed, the library took on a more dignified air. Sarah looked around, satisfied with her work. If she and Matt ever bought a house, she would love to have a room just like this one, full of books, with comfortable sofas to curl up on and a cheery fire in the fireplace in the winter. Before they could buy a house, though, Sarah would have to have a job. A real job.

Sarah sighed and gave up. It was no use;

every random thought led her back to the job interview no matter how hard she tried to keep busy. Working at Elm Creek Manor was fine for now, but she had to find something with a future. If only she had a relative or a friend of the family who could help her get her foot in the door somewhere. But she had no such connections, and it wasn't likely that she'd make any in Middle of Nowhere, Pennsylvania.

At noon Sarah changed into her interview suit and went to the sewing room to tell Mrs. Compson she was about to leave. The older woman set her quilt aside and scrutinized Sarah's outfit. "Stand up straight," she admonished. "You want them to think you have confidence, don't you? They won't want to hire someone who slouches."

Sarah wished all she had to worry about was her posture.

Matt dropped her off a good fifteen minutes early, which she thought was just about right: early enough to make a good impression but not so early that she seemed desperate. "Maybe you are desperate, but Brian Turnbull doesn't need to know that," Sarah muttered to her reflection as she pulled open the glass door.

A receptionist near the entrance greeted

her and directed her to a small waiting room. Some of the men sitting there glanced up as she entered, then returned to their newspapers and magazines.

She took the last empty seat and tried to get a look at the other applicants without being too obvious. They were all men, which was odd enough in itself, but they were also in their late forties to mid-fifties, surely too experienced for the kind of work Sarah was qualified to do. They wore expensive and expertly made suits. Dismayed, Sarah fingered the hem of her off-the-rack suit jacket and felt her cheeks starting to burn. She could have sworn Turnbull had said the position was entry-level. This interview was going to be a nightmare.

The man in the next chair turned to her and smiled. "Are you here for the cost accounting interview?"

Sarah nodded. "Yes."

"We all are." The man shifted in his seat and rubbed his palms on his fine pinstriped slacks. The large rings on the fourth finger of each hand glistened as he gestured to the occupied chairs. "Look at all these folks, and the opening hasn't even hit the papers yet."

"I guess a lot of people want to work here."

"A lot of people want to work, period." He leaned back and rested his right ankle on his left knee. His hair and mustache were thick and dark, sprinkled heavily with gray throughout. "Did you just graduate from college?"

Sarah smiled. "I'll take that as a compliment. Actually, it's been a while."

"Oh. You look younger." He let out a heavy sigh. "An accounting major?"

"That's right."

"There sure are a lot of you out there, aren't there?"

Sarah looked him squarely in the eye. "I'm not sure I know what you mean."

"Nothing. I don't mean anything." His smile appeared forced. "Just . . . there seem to be more accounting majors every year."

Sarah shrugged, wishing she could find a polite way to get out of the conversation. "I guess so. It's an interesting field, I guess, and it's a pretty stable career choice —"

"Stable?" a stocky man seated across from them interrupted. "Haven't you ever heard of downsizing?"

"Bill, is that necessary?" the dark-haired man asked. He turned back to Sarah. "Don't mind him. He gets cranky if he has to go five minutes without a cigarette."

The stocky man glowered and raised his newspaper to block their view of him.

"Sounds like you know him," Sarah murmured.

"We worked a temp job together during tax season. Bill smokes like a chimney, all right. I quit six months ago, myself. Did you know that corporate insurance rates are higher for smokers than for non-smokers?"

Sarah shook her head.

"Well, it's true. That's why I quit. Why hire a smoker when you can save money by hiring a nonsmoker?"

"Can they really do that? Isn't that discrimination?"

"Strictly speaking, they probably aren't allowed to, but they can always find some other excuse to write down. 'You're over-qualified.' Or 'The new owners like to hire their own teams.' Some such nonsense." He sighed. "The point is, why risk it?"

"I see what you mean."

"I worked for the largest corporate insurance company in Pittsburgh for twenty years, and I know what I'm talking about."

Everyone looked up as a tall woman in an elegant tailored dress appeared at the door. "Thomas Wilson?" she announced.

The dark-haired man picked up his

leather briefcase and stood. "Nice talking with you. Good luck." He extended his hand.

Sarah shook it. "Thanks. Good luck to you, too." He followed the woman out of the room.

Her nervousness suddenly returned in full force. She selected a magazine from the pile on a nearby table and tried to concentrate on an article about HMOs. Occasionally the elegant woman would return and call out the name of another applicant, who would rise and follow her out of the room.

Finally, it was Sarah's turn.

When they left the waiting room, the woman greeted Sarah with a firm handshake and a pleasant smile. "It's good to meet you, Sarah. I'm Marcia Welsh, Director of Personnel."

"It's nice to meet you, too." Sarah was surprised to hear that her voice sounded far more confident than she felt.

Marcia stopped at a door bearing a sign that read CONFERENCE ROOM. She opened the door and let Sarah enter before her.

The conference room was roughly the same size as the waiting room, but it was almost completely filled by a large table. The four men and the woman sitting on the other side wore conservative business attire and stern expressions. Marcia closed the door and took a seat between two of the men. She gestured to a lone chair on Sarah's side of the table. As Sarah sat down, the man closest to her poured a glass of water from a crystal pitcher and pushed it across the table to her.

"Thank you," Sarah said. He ignored her.

"Well, let's get started," the man in the center began. "I'm Brian Turnbull, owner and CEO of PennCellular Corporation." He reeled off the others' names and titles so quickly that Sarah had no hope of catching them. She did get the impression that the group included the company's top executives and representatives from the accounting department, but no one, it seemed, from public relations.

"It's nice to meet you." Sarah stood and tried to reach across the table to shake their hands, but she couldn't quite make it. Embarrassed, she quickly sat down. Marcia smiled understandingly, but the others showed no reaction.

Brian Turnbull began by asking her the same questions she always heard at these interviews: what made her decide to go to Penn State, what she had accomplished at her last job, what did she think her strengths and weaknesses were, and so on. She recited the answers she had prepared in advance, taking care to make eye contact with everyone around the table. They seemed satisfied with her answers, so Sarah's anxiety began to ebb.

Then the man who had poured the water set down his pen and pushed his pad away. "Enough of this beating around the bush. How are your math and reasoning skills?"

Sarah started, not because the question was difficult but because until then no one but Mr. Turnbull had addressed her. And Mr. Turnbull had been much nicer. "I feel that they're quite good," she replied, trying to look confident. "As you can see from my résumé, I have a three-point-nine GPA in my accounting courses and experience in —"

"Yes, yes, I can see the résumé. That doesn't answer my question."

Sarah hesitated. Why did he look so annoyed? "Well —"

"Can you, for example, tell me how many grocery stores there are in the United States of America?"

"How — how many grocery stores?"

"Yes. How many grocery stores. You can include convenience stores if you need to water it down."

Sarah stared at him. "Grocery stores. Sure." She decided to take a drink to buy some time. She watched as her hand lifted the glass in slow motion to her lips. It trembled dangerously, and for an instant she imagined it sending a shower of water in all directions. She tried to smile as she carefully returned the glass to the safety of the tabletop. "I was probably sick the day they taught that."

No one smiled.

Okay, wrong answer. "I guess I could try to figure it out."

"Try." The man on the end shoved his pen and pad at her.

"Okay, well, the population of the United States is about a quarter of a billion, right?"

No response.

"Okay, a quarter of a billion." She scribbled the number on the pad, her heart sinking when she realized they weren't going to give her a single hint. The interviewers' silence made her nervous, so she described the steps in the problem aloud as she worked through them on paper. First she estimated the number of aisles in a typical grocery store, then the amount of time an average customer spent in line. As she used those numbers to calculate the number of customers per store per day, she knew her figures could be off by several thousand or by several hundred thousand, but there was nothing she could do to verify them.

She plowed on doggedly, since she had no other choice. As she worked, her nervousness hardened into anger. It was an unfair question, one with no relevance to the job she sought, one she had no chance of answering accurately. She had researched PennCellular, she knew everything there was to know about the latest trends in the profession — but none of that made any difference. All they cared about was this ridiculous grocery store tally.

The man on the end rolled his eyes and shook his head when Sarah had to double back to correct a mistake; she had been working with the number of people in the country rather than the number of families, which was a more appropriate figure since usually one person did the shopping for their household. She tried not to let the man's disdain bother her, but she felt her cheeks growing hot and she wished she had never come. She raced through the last calculations. The sooner she finished, the sooner she could leave.

"Okay," Sarah said at last. "If we have

sixty-two million five hundred thousand shoppers —"

"That's a pretty big 'if,' " the man on the end muttered.

Sarah took a deep breath, fighting to keep the tremor out of her voice. "If that's how many shoppers we have, we would need, um . . . four thousand, one hundred thirty-three and a half grocery stores. Except there wouldn't be a half of a grocery store, so let's say four thousand, one hundred and thirty-five." She stared at the figure. "That doesn't sound right. It seems like there should be more than that." She bit her lip and looked at the man on the end. "Is that right?"

He straightened in his seat, indignant. "How should I know?"

Sarah gaped at him. "But —"

"Well, I guess that should pretty much do it," Turnbull said. "Do you have any questions?"

"Huh?" Her eyes were still fixed on the man on the end.

"Do you have any questions about PennCellular or the job?"

Questions — she had to ask some questions about the job. Frantically she searched her memory for the list she had prepared. Where was it? "Cell phones," she blurted out. "You sell cell phones?" It sounded like a tongue twister. You sell cell phones by the sell shore.

Turnbull looked puzzled. "Yes, of course we do. I thought you knew that."

"Oh, I did. I was just checking. Maybe you sell something else, too."

"No, just cell phones." He paused and studied her. "Anything else?"

"No — no, I don't think so."

"Well, then, we're all set." Turnbull rose and the others jumped to their feet. Sarah stood, her legs trembling. He reached across the table and shook her hand. "You'll be hearing from us either way in a few weeks. Thanks for coming. Ms. Welsh will show you out."

Sarah nodded. "Thank you." She felt numb. Marcia led her to the exit and bid her good-bye.

Sarah spotted the truck in the parking lot and almost ran to it. "Thank God you're here." She took her seat and leaned back, closing her eyes.

Matt started the truck. "I've been here a while. They sure kept you long enough."

"I spent most of that time in the waiting room. That was the most bizarre interview I've ever had." She told him what had happened, not omitting a single strange or embarrassing detail.

When she finished, Matt shrugged. "Sounds to me like you handled everything just fine."

" 'Just fine'? I sounded like I never made it past high school algebra." Then she thought of something else and slapped a palm to her forehead. "Damn."

"What?"

"I calculated how many grocery stores there need to be, not how many there are."

Matt glanced away from the road to look at her. "That doesn't really matter, though, right?"

"What do you mean? Of course it matters. It's a completely different issue."

"Maybe he's interested in how you tackled the problem, not in whether you got the right number. It's not like he could check your answer, right? Maybe he was also trying to see how you respond to pressure."

"Do you really think so?"

"Well, sure."

"Then it's worse than I thought."

"Oh, Sarah." He chuckled and shook his head. "I'm sure you did as well as anyone else they talked to. Probably better."

"Think so? You didn't see the waiting room. All those older men, with all that experience. How am I suppose to compete with them?"

"They probably wonder how they're supposed to compete with someone younger who won't expect as much money and won't be thinking about retirement in five or ten years."

Sarah looked out the window and said nothing. True, she did wonder why anyone with their experience would be interested in an entry-level job and why they would be out of work in the first place. But those men surely wouldn't be out of work for long, not with their backgrounds. Everyone else who passed through that waiting room that day would probably have another job before she even had another interview.

Chapter 9

Two days later, Sarah finished her work in the library and was ready to move on to the next cleaning and inventory assignment. But not right away. First, she wanted to continue her quilting lessons. She took the stairs two at time and hurried to the sitting room.

"Fine work," Mrs. Compson remarked, studying Sarah's finished Sawtooth Star block with a critical eye. "These stitches are a bit crooked here, but not so bad that you need to rip them out. Fine work for a beginner."

"What's next?"

"You'll need to make templates for your next block, the Double Nine Patch. This block is still rather simple since it has no curved seams or set-in pieces, but it can be tricky. Some of the pieces are small and there are many places where the seams must match up perfectly or the design will be ruined." As Sarah took a seat, Mrs. Compson handed her the template drafting supplies.

The Double Nine Patch block, Mrs. Compson explained, was one of many quilt blocks based on a three-by-three grid; they were called nine patches because a single large square was divided by the grid into nine smaller squares. In the Double Nine Patch, the smaller squares in the corners and in the center were further divided into nine even smaller squares.

This time Sarah made two square templates, one large and one small. She cut four of the bigger squares from the cream background fabric, then used the smaller template to make twenty-five little squares from the dark red fabric and twenty from the cream.

"The first quilt I ever made was a Nine Patch," Mrs. Compson remarked, picking up some quilting of her own to work on while monitoring Sarah's progress. "Not a Double Nine Patch, a Nine Patch. It looked like a checkerboard in all different colors."

Sarah looked up from pinning two of the tiny squares together at the corners. "Did someone give you lessons like you're giving me?"

"Hmph. My sister and I learned together, and our lessons were hardly this pleasant. Nothing ever went smoothly when Claudia and I were in the same room. See now, I think that's where my mother went wrong. Instead of teaching us at the same time she should have taught Claudia first, a few years earlier, when I would have been too young to care." She shook her head and sighed. "Perhaps that would have made a difference."

"What happened? Will you tell me about it?"

Mrs. Compson hesitated. "If you'll get me a glass of water first."

Sarah jumped up and quickly returned with the glass. Mrs. Compson took a deep drink, then set the glass aside. "Well, then, I'll tell you," she said. "But don't get so distracted that you don't pay attention to your quilting. If your stitches aren't good enough I'll make you take them out."

My sister, Claudia, was two years older than I, but since I was just as smart and almost as big as she was, people treated us as if we were the same age. Claudia was the pretty one; she had our mother's thick brown hair rippling in shining waves down her back, while at that age my darker hair was always dull and wildly unkempt from running around outdoors. All the grownups said Claudia was the very image of Great-Grandmother Anneke, but they respected our ancestors too much to hold any of them responsible for my appearance. I did better with my lessons, but the teachers always liked Claudia best. Everyone did. She was always friendly and cheerful, while I was sulky and sensitive. I imagine it must have been a terrible disappointment to our mother, to have a child like me after doing so well the first time.

The winter when I was five and Claudia was seven, we had a blizzard. It snowed so terribly that we couldn't go to school. Claudia was relieved; she had not learned her lessons for that day and dreaded to disappoint our pretty young teacher, Miss Turner, whom everyone liked. I, on the other hand, fretted for hours, glaring out of the nursery windows and stomping about. What if the other children learned something and I missed it? My mother assured me that none of the other children would be going to school that day, either, but I was not consoled until she promised to teach us something new that day. "But not reading or math," she said, to my surprise. "It's time you two girls learned to quilt."

We had watched Mother sew before, but this was the first time we would be allowed to quilt, like our aunts and Mother's grown-up lady friends. They used to quilt all the time. Some of their quilts may still be around here someplace — up in the attic, perhaps.

So Mother showed us how to quilt, very much how I have shown you, except with scraps from her sewing basket. We scarcely wanted to stop for lunch, we were having so much fun. We carefully selected the prettiest scraps, cut our pieces, and sewed them together. By late afternoon we had each finished several small blocks.

I counted the blocks in my pile, and then those on the floor by Claudia's side. "I have four in my pile, and you only have three," I said.

"Maybe, but I'm almost finished with this one," she told me. She held the unfinished block close to her eye and struggled to tie a knot at the end of a seam.

"But I'm almost done with this one, too. That means I'll have five and you'll have four."

Claudia merely shrugged and yanked on the knot.

"That means I should get to use the quilt first."

At that she finally looked at me. "I'll get to use it first because I'm oldest and that means I'm first."

"I'll get to use it first if I do more of the work."

"Well, maybe you won't do more of the work."

"Well, maybe I will."

"Girls, girls," Mother broke in helplessly. "There's no need to argue. You'll share the work and the quilt equally."

But we paid no attention. As soon as Mother left the room, the race was on. We both scrambled for fabric, fought for the scissors, pieced our blocks with the biggest stitches you've ever seen. Our piles grew, but although I blazed through my sewing, growing angrier and more determined with each seam, Claudia began to grow tired. She rubbed at her eyes and struggled over and over again to poke the same end of thread through the needle's eye. Sometimes she had to take out stitches after sewing the wrong side of one piece to the right side of the other. She began to mutter a little under her breath, and let out a frustrated whine every now and then, but I paid her no mind. My pile of Nine Patches was growing and growing, and I was going to win.

Suddenly she flung down her block and burst into tears. "It's not fair," she sobbed. "You always do everything best. You always beat me. I hate you!" She ran out of the room.

I didn't look up. I kept sewing, but more slowly now. I counted the blocks Claudia had scattered as she ran away. There were six. I had nine, including the one I was still working on.

Mother must have heard my sister's outburst, because moments later, she entered the room. "Sylvia, what's going on here?"

"Nothing, Mother. I'm just sewing, like you told us to." The picture of innocence and obedience, I was.

Mother shook her head, troubled. "Claudia's in her bedroom, crying. Why is that?"

I shrugged, not lifting my eyes from my sewing.

Mother sighed and sat down on the floor beside me. "Sylvia, my little girl, what am I going to do with you?"

I shrugged again. My eyes began to fill with tears.

"I want you to go and tell your sister you're sorry, and I want you to play nice from now on."

"But I didn't do anything," I protested.

145

All I had done was sew faster and better than Claudia had done. I hadn't called her any names or hit her or pulled her hair. Was I supposed to sew slowly just because Claudia did? That wasn't right.

Mother frowned at me, a sad and disappointed frown. I felt simply awful. She never looked at Claudia that way.

I trotted down the hallway to Claudia's bedroom. She lay facedown on the bed, her sobs muffled by a pillow.

"Claudia?"

"Go away."

"Mother said to say I'm sorry, so . . . I'm sorry I sewed faster than you."

"Go away." She sat up and wiped her nose on her sleeve. "You're just a mean, awful brat. Go away."

Then I started to cry, and I hated crying in front of other people. "I said I was sorry. Claudia?" But she'd flung herself onto the bed again. I backed out of the room and softly closed the door.

She didn't come out for supper, and I could hardly swallow a bite myself. All through the meal my parents and my aunts and uncles — and even Grandpa — frowned sternly at me as if I were the worst little girl in the world. My cousins just stared at me wide-eyed and wondering, whispering to each other.

Claudia didn't speak to me for the remaining two days we were snowed in. When school resumed, she finally forgave me and let me help her with her spelling.

She never touched those Nine Patch blocks again. I put hers with mine and finished the quilt a few months later. I offered it to Claudia, but when she said sleeping under it would give her nightmares, I gave it to my cousin, who had just turned four and had dark, unruly hair like mine.

"Claudia did finally learn how to quilt, of course," Mrs. Compson said. "She made a somewhat acceptable green-and-white Irish Chain quilt for Grandpa when she was eight."

"Whatever happened to the Nine Patch quilt?"

"I don't know. I imagine it's long gone. A four-year-old can quite literally love a quilt to pieces."

"Did you and Claudia ever quilt together again?"

"Hmph." Mrs. Compson stood up and walked to the window. "Of course we did. But not for a long time. Maybe I'll tell you about that another day."

Sarah certainly hoped so. If Mrs.

Compson told her more about her life at Elm Creek Manor, Sarah might learn why she had left and what had happened to her family.

"Matthew is here." Just as Mrs. Compson spoke, Sarah heard the truck pull up behind the manor. She set her quilt block aside and they went to meet him in the kitchen, where he gratefully accepted the glass of lemonade Mrs. Compson offered.

"The orchards are in much better shape than I expected," he told Mrs. Compson after taking a deep drink and wiping his brow. "From what you first told me, I thought the trees hadn't been tended for years."

"They haven't been tended *well* for years," Mrs. Compson corrected. "But my sister did manage to hire help and make a bit of a harvest every year, as far as I know."

"With some care, you should be able to get a good harvest this year, too. I can't do the work alone, though. I'll need you to sign off on the additional expense."

"Certainly. That should be no trouble."

Matt finished his drink and set the glass in the sink. "I don't think Waterford College has an agriculture program. It's too bad we aren't closer to Penn State. Ag majors would manage this place for you as interns, pretty cheap, to get the experience and to run tests. You know, new organic fertilizers, cultivation methods, things like that."

"That's a great idea," Sarah said. "We aren't too far away. You had to travel farther than this for your internship, and I took a whole semester off for mine."

Mrs. Compson nodded. "It may indeed be something the new owners should consider."

Sarah's heart sank. Just for that moment, she had forgotten that Elm Creek Manor was going to be sold.

"Dear, is anything wrong?"

"No — no, Mrs. Compson. I just remembered that — I forgot my quilting stuff." Sarah returned to the sitting room and collected her sewing tools and quilt block pieces. Matt was watching her worriedly when she came back, so she gave him a bright smile to reassure him.

On the way home Sarah thought about the library she had worked so hard to restore. Somebody else would probably come along and change everything, putting wall-to-wall carpet on the beautiful hardwood floor, covering up the fireplace with ugly wallpaper, and doing other things, worse things that would give any decorator with taste nightmares. Sarah frowned and stared out of the truck window. Maybe Mrs. Compson wouldn't find a buyer. How many people in Waterford had that kind of money anyway?

Then Sarah felt a stab of guilt. If Mrs. Compson wanted to sell her home, it wasn't right for Sarah to hope she'd fail. But she couldn't ignore the fact that Mrs. Compson's success meant no more visits to Elm Creek Manor, no more job, no more quilting lessons, and no more interesting stories about Claudia and the Bergstroms. The best she could hope for was that buyers wouldn't appear for a long time and that the new owners would appreciate Elm Creek Manor as much as the Bergstroms once had.

The day's mail did nothing to improve her mood. She received two rejection letters, both from jobs she'd thought she had a reasonable chance of getting. And there was a postcard. The photograph showed an enormous cruise ship anchored in a serene tropical bay. "Having a wonderful time, Darling," her mother had written on the back. "Uncle Henry sends his love."

Uncle Henry. Unbelievable. If she were a

child, Sarah might have tolerated calling her mother's many boyfriends Uncle, but not now. Even the title boyfriend seemed inappropriate.

Sarah crumpled up the postcard and threw it away before Matt noticed.

Chapter 10

Since the library was finished, the next morning Mrs. Compson and Sarah began working on a bedroom suite near the library. "We'll keep the furniture in the rooms until the auction," Mrs. Compson said. "We'll probably discard nearly everything else, though."

The furniture in these rooms, Mrs. Compson explained, was from Lancaster and had been handmade by Amish craftsmen. Sarah ran her hand over the dresser's smooth wooden surface. A blue-and-rose Lone Star quilt, faded but still lovely, was draped over the bed. Net curtains hung across a thin metal rod over the large window in the east wall. A door on the left led to a dressing room, where she spotted a dusty overstuffed sofa with wood armrests carved to resemble a swan's profile, and a small vanity with a cracked mirror.

"These were my Aunt Clara's rooms," Mrs. Compson said. She removed the quilt from the bed, gave it a quick shake, and folded it carefully. "She died of influenza when she was only thirteen."

"I'm sorry."

"Oh, don't be. It was a very long time ago. I barely remember her. Almost everyone I've ever known is dead now, and you can't feel sorry all day long." Mrs. Compson placed the quilt on the floor. "Let's start a 'save' pile and a 'throw away' pile, shall we?"

"I hope that's the 'save' pile," Sarah said, indicating the quilt. "You wouldn't throw it away after spending so much time on it, would you?"

"Of course not! But I didn't make this quilt. Claudia did." She bent over and unfolded a corner so that the pattern was visible. "See how the corners of these four diamonds don't meet? That's a sure sign of Claudia's piecing every time."

"I take it this isn't a quilt you two worked on together?"

"Certainly not." Mrs. Compson sniffed indignantly. "I would've made her take out those stitches and do them over, and if you match your points as poorly, I'll do the same to you."

Sarah grinned. "Don't worry. I know better."

"As indeed you should." Mrs. Compson opened a closet and began to sort through the clutter. "See if there is anything worth saving in the dresser. This room should be easy to finish. It hasn't been used in a long time."

Sarah pulled open two empty drawers before she found one half full of worn handkerchiefs, scarves, and a few pieces of costume jewelry. "When did you and Claudia finally start quilting together again?"

"Oh, let's see." Mrs. Compson tapped her chin with a finger. "Why, it must have been to make the baby quilt. Yes, that's right."

Before we worked together on that project we both still quilted, just not together. The summer after the Nine Patch fiasco we both had quilts in the state fair, and we both won blue ribbons in the girls' competition. The following summer I won a blue ribbon and Claudia took second. My, she was furious. She told me, when Mother and Father couldn't overhear, that the judges gave me the ribbon only because I was younger. I stuck my tongue out at her, which, naturally, Mother saw. At first she said I would not be allowed to ride, as a punishment, but Father was so proud of my riding so well at such a young age that he convinced Mother to relent. I won a ribbon in riding, too, my first ever. That probably made Claudia even angrier. She was afraid of horses, and Father teased her about it.

When I was seven and Claudia was nine, Mother and Father had such wonderful news. We were going to have a new baby brother or sister —

"You never mentioned another brother or sister."

"You never asked."

"I thought it was just you and Claudia."

"Well, now you know differently. Are you planning to interrupt anymore, or may I continue?"

"Sorry. No more interruptions. Please go on."

"Very well."

As I was about to explain, when I was seven and Claudia was nine, Mother and Father told us they were going to have another child. We were thrilled. Claudia couldn't wait to help Mother take care of the new baby, and I was looking forward to having a new playmate. We were busy preparing for many months. One of the rooms was made over for the baby, and of course, the baby would need a quilt.

Claudia said that she should be in charge of making the baby's quilt because she was the oldest. I said I should get to be in charge because I was the better quilter. "If that's the way you're going to be, I'll make the quilt all by myself," Claudia announced.

Naturally, I piped up that I would make my own quilt for the baby, too. Then we began to argue over whose quilt the baby would use first, and Claudia said hers, since she was the oldest. My, how that argument infuriated me. Claudia would always be the oldest, and there was nothing I could do about that, so she would always use age to justify everything, from who had to help Cook with the dishes to who got the best scraps from Mother's basket.

"I know," I suggested. "How about this: the baby will use first the quilt that's finished first?"

Well, that just made her angry. I thought it might, which is why I suggested it.

As the argument escalated, Mother decided we should both work on the quilt together. We pouted, but with Mother watching, we had to agree. We decided that I would pick out the block pattern and Claudia could pick out the colors. I selected the Bear's Paw; there would be many triangle points to match, but since there were no curved seams or set-in pieces, Claudia couldn't mess it up too badly. And then it was Claudia's turn.

"Pink and white, with a little bit of green."

I screwed up my nose. "What if it's a boy?"

Claudia folded her arms. "I like pink, white, and green, and I get to choose, remember?"

"But what if it's a boy?"

"It's a baby. It won't care."

"If he's a boy he'll care. Let's pick something else."

"You picked the pattern. I get to pick the colors. You can't pick everything."

"Compromise, girls." That was Mother. She shook her head and gave me that disappointed smile again. In all those years I don't think Claudia ever received one of those looks.

I looked away. "Okay," I said to my sister. "Then you pick the pattern and I'll pick the colors."

Claudia beamed at Mother. "Then I pick Turkey Tracks."

Just for a moment, my heart seemed to beat more quickly, and I gasped. "I don't think that's a very good idea."

"What's wrong now?"

"Yes, Sylvia, what's wrong?" Mother looked surprised. "You've made blocks like it before."

"She doesn't think I can make it, that's what's wrong." Claudia glared at me. "But I can, as good as you, too."

"Sylvia, is that so?" Mother asked.

I shook my head no.

"What is it, then?"

"Turkey Tracks." My voice held a fearful tremor as I said the name. "It's also called Wandering Foot, remember? Remember what Grandma used to say?"

Mother and Claudia stared at me. Then Claudia began to giggle. "That's just a silly superstition, silly."

Even Mother smiled. "Sylvia, you shouldn't let Grandma's old stories worry you so. I think it's a lovely pattern."

I bit my lip. I didn't like being laughed at, and I didn't like being called silly, but I still knew it wasn't a good idea. It would have been better to make a pink quilt and hope Mother had a girl than to do this.

"How about if we make the Bear's Paw instead?" I said. "We can use pink if you want."

Claudia shook her head. "No, I like this idea better."

"Come now, what colors would you like?" Mother beckoned me over to her scrap basket.

I took all the blue and yellow pieces from the overflowing basket. If we had to make a Wandering Foot quilt, and I didn't see any way out of it, then at the very least I was going to make it from my lucky colors.

I think it was about two months later when we finished the quilt. It was very pretty, but I still had misgivings. And a few months after that, in January, Mother had a baby boy. Father named him Richard after his brother who died in the Great War, and we all adored him.

Mrs. Compson finished cleaning out the closet and stood, rubbing her lower back. For a moment Sarah only watched her, puzzled. "I don't understand," she finally said.

"Don't understand what?"

"The quilt pattern. What was wrong with Turkey Tracks?"

"Oh." Mrs. Compson sat on the bed, her thin figure barely compressing the mattress. "Some people think that by changing a block's name you get rid of the bad luck, but I know that bad luck isn't so easily fooled. Turkey Tracks is the same pattern as Wandering Foot. If you give a boy a Wandering Foot quilt, he will never be content to stay in one place. He'll always be restless, roaming around, running off from home to who knows where — and I can't even begin to tell you what that pattern will do to a girl." She shook her head. "What a silly choice. Claudia should have known better."

Sarah nodded, but secretly she sympathized with Mrs. Compson's mother. She wouldn't have pegged Mrs. Compson as the superstitious type, especially over something like a quilt.

Mrs. Compson studied Sarah's expression and frowned. "Now, I'm not superstitious, mind, but why take unnecessary chances? Life will give you plenty of necessary ones on its own. And I was right, too, as it turned out. But that's no consolation. I would have preferred for Claudia to be right this time."

"What do you mean? The superstition came true?"

Just then she heard voices downstairs.

"My hearing isn't what it used to be, but that sounds like Matthew. Let's go see if I'm right." Mrs. Compson rose and left the room.

Sarah followed, wishing Mrs. Compson had answered her question. But it was a stupid question anyway. A quilt pattern couldn't bring bad luck, unless . . . Annoyed and exasperated with herself, Sarah shook her head as if to clear it of such illogical thoughts.

Chapter 11

Matt and another man Sarah recognized from Exterior Architects were waiting just outside the front entrance. "We didn't want to track mud all over the place," Matt explained as his friend gestured sheepishly at their muddy work boots. "We're going to head on in to town to grab some lunch. Is there anything you need us to do for you while we're there?"

"You needn't go into town. I'll make lunch for you."

"There're six of us, ma'am," the other man said. Joe, that was his name. "We don't want you to go to any trouble."

"Even so. What a poor hostess your friends will think me."

"Not at all." Matt grinned. "Besides, for what our boss charges you, we should be making *you* lunch."

"Is that so? Very well, then. In that case, I won't insist. As for your offer to run errands for me, thank you, but no. The grocery store delivers weekly and I don't need anything else right now."

"If you ever do, just ask." Matt gave Sarah a quick kiss, and he and Joe left.

Mrs. Compson turned to Sarah. "Perhaps we should be thinking about lunch ourselves."

"Do you want me to finish upstairs first?"

"Leave it until tomorrow. I'd prefer to work on our quilts for a while. In fact, I believe I feel like seeing the old gardens. Would you like to take our lunch and our quilting outside?"

"Oh, I'd love to. I haven't seen the gardens yet."

"Don't expect much. I doubt if they've been tended for a long time. I should have been to see them before now, if only to tell Matthew what to do there."

They went to the kitchen and packed a small wooden basket with sandwiches, fruit, and a plastic jug of iced tea. Mrs. Compson fetched an old quilt and a wide-brimmed hat from the hall closet while Sarah collected the quilt blocks and the tackle box Mrs. Compson used to store her sewing tools. Then Mrs. Compson led her down the hallway toward the front foyer, but instead of turning right toward the front entrance, they turned left. Several doors lined the hallway until it ended at an outside door at the corner of the L-shaped manor. The door opened onto a gray stone patio surrounded by lilac bushes and evergreens. At the edge of the patio, a stone path continued north into the bushes.

Mrs. Compson paused in the center of the patio. "Out of all the lovely places on the estate, this was my mother's favorite. In fair weather, she would have her afternoon tea out here. It was so pleasant in springtime when the lilacs were flowering. She called this place the cornerstone patio."

"Why did she call it that?"

"You wouldn't need to ask if these bushes were properly pruned. Here, help me with this." She went to where the edge of the patio met the northwest corner of the manor and struggled to push the branches aside. Sarah hurried to help her.

"See there?" Mrs. Compson pointed to a large engraved stone at the base of the building.

Sarah pushed through the branches and kneeled on the stone patio so that she could read the carved letters. " 'Bergstrom 1858.' Was that when the manor was built?"

"Yes, but only the west wing, of course. Hans, Anneke, and Gerda laid that cornerstone with their own hands. My grandfather was only a toddler then, and my great-aunt was not yet born." Mrs. Compson sighed. "Sometimes I picture them, so young and hopeful and brave, laying the foundation of Elm Creek Manor, and of the Bergstrom family itself. Do you suppose they ever dreamed they would accomplish so much?"

Sarah thought for a moment. "From what you've told me about them, I think they probably did. They sound like the sort of people who dreamed big and had the fortitude to match."

Mrs. Compson looked thoughtful. "Yes, I believe you're right." Then her gaze swept around the patio, taking in the tangled bushes, the weeds growing up between the stones, and the peeling paint on the door. "I suppose they never thought their heirs would neglect what they had worked so hard to build."

Sarah rose and brushed off her knees. "I think they'd understand." She let the branches fall back into place in front of the cornerstone.

"Hmph. That's kind of you, dear, but I don't even understand, and I'm one of those neglectful heirs myself. Come along, now." She continued across the patio to the stone path, which disappeared into the surrounding bushes. In another moment, the foliage hid her from view.

Sarah pushed after her, only to find herself standing on the lawn on the north side of the building. She spun around, but could not see the patio or the door through the thick brush. The other day when she had passed this side of the manor while mulling over Mrs. Compson's job offer, she had not even suspected an entrance was there.

"What's keeping you?" Mrs. Compson called. She had already crossed the lawn and was waiting where the stone pathway continued into the woods. Sarah followed her down the shaded, meandering path until it broadened and opened into an oval clearing surfaced with the same gray stone. In the foreground were four round planters, each about fifteen feet in diameter and three feet high; the lower halves of their walls were two feet thicker than at the top, forming smooth, polished seats where visitors could rest. The planters, which now held only rocky soil, some dry branches that might once have been roses, and weeds, were spaced evenly around a black marble fountain of a mare prancing with two foals. Beyond them was a large wooden gazebo, paint peeling and gingerbread molding sagging dejectedly. Through the wooden slats Sarah could see terraces cut into the slope of a gentle hill on the other side, but their supporting stones had long since fallen away, allowing the beds to erode. As Sarah watched, a bird flew from inside the roof of the gazebo, alighted on the mare's head, then flitted away.

Mrs. Compson draped the quilt over the nearest planter's seat and sat down. "It used to look much nicer than this," she said dryly. Sarah nodded, thinking that her employer had a gift for understatement. They unpacked the basket and ate their lunches in silence. As usual, Mrs. Compson only nibbled at hers. Most of the time she sat with her hands clasped in her lap as she looked around the garden. Occasionally her lips would part as if she were about to speak, but then she would sigh and press them together again, shaking her head in regret and disappointment.

"You should have seen it when I was a girl," she finally said as Sarah packed up their leftovers and trash. "The planters were full of roses and ivy, the fountain would sparkle, the terraces held bulbs that bloomed with every variety of lovely blossom. What a shame. What a shame."

Sarah touched her arm. "Matt can restore it. You'll see."

"It never should have been allowed to fall into such disrepair in the first place. Claudia could have easily afforded a gardener — a whole staff of gardeners. She should have had better sense."

"Mrs. Compson, why do you want to sell the manor? I know it needs some fixing up, but it could be such a wonderful place again, and Matt and I will help."

"I could never be happy here. Even if it were as beautiful as it once was, it could never be what it was supposed to be. You couldn't possibly understand, a child your age."

She frowned so gloomily that Sarah looked away. Certainly the garden needed a lot of work, but Matt had restored places in even worse disrepair. If Mrs. Compson just gave him a chance —

"Besides, I already have a buyer."

Sarah whirled on her. "You what?"

Mrs. Compson studied the stone bench beside her. "A local real estate company has already expressed a great deal of enthusiasm. A gentleman from University

Realty visited me Tuesday afternoon, while you were at your interview. Of course, we haven't agreed to any terms yet, but I'm sure we'll strike a fair bargain." Mrs. Compson surveyed the garden with a critical eye. "That's why I'm investing so much in the restoration, to increase the estate's value."

"I see."

"Now, don't sound so dejected, Sarah. I'll be here all summer. That's plenty of time to teach you how to quilt."

"But what will you do after that?"

"Sell the manor, auction off the contents, and return to my house in Sewickley. Don't look so surprised. You do recall why you were hired, don't you?" Abruptly, she rose. "If you're finished eating, I have something else to show you."

Sarah followed her to the gazebo. The steps creaked tiredly, as if they would have collapsed except it required too much effort. Wood benches resembling rectangular wooden crates lined the walls of the octagon-shaped structure.

Mrs. Compson pointed to the top of each bench in turn, and cocked her head to one side. "What do you think?"

Sarah peered closer. Inlaid in the middle of each seat was a pattern of interlocking multicolored wood rectangles fitted around a small center square. Some benches had a yellow center square — yellow pine, perhaps — while the rest had a red center square. The colors might have been vivid once but were now weathered and faded. Sarah traced one of the blocks with a finger. "This pattern looks familiar, but I can't place it."

"It's a quilt pattern called Log Cabin. Supposedly it was invented to honor Abraham Lincoln, but that might just be a myth. According to tradition, the quilter should always put a red square in the middle, to symbolize the hearth, or a yellow square, to represent a light in the cabin window."

"It's pretty."

"That's true, but there's more. Look carefully."

Sarah carefully examined each bench in turn, not sure what she should be looking for. Then she saw it. "This one," she said, pointing. "Its center square is different. It's black."

"Good girl." Mrs. Compson nodded. "Lift up the bench."

"It lifts up?" Sarah grasped the edge of the bench. She saw no hinges, nothing to distinguish it from the other benches.

"Carefully, now. Lift up the edge and slide it back."

The wooden seat creaked in protest and stuck, but Sarah jimmied it lose. As she eased it away from her, the wooden slats folded into a hidden recess beneath the bench, almost like a rolltop desk. "What in the world —" The seat had covered some kind of opening. Sarah saw narrow boards nailed in a column, like a ladder leading down from a child's treehouse.

"In the Civil War era, Elm Creek Manor was a stop on the Underground Railroad," Mrs. Compson explained in a conspiratorial tone. "A Log Cabin quilt with a black center square was a signal. If an escaped slave saw a log cabin quilt with black center squares hanging on the washline, he knew it was safe to knock on the door."

"But wouldn't bounty hunters or whatever see the quilt, too?"

Mrs. Compson regarded her with mock astonishment. "Why, who pays attention to women's work? Laundry, hanging on the line? Sorry, we can't be bothered. We're out doing important man things."

Sarah bent forward, trying to make out the ground below in the darkness. "So people would see this design on the bench and know it was a hiding place. This is amazing. Does it go underground?"

"Just deep enough so that one can stand comfortably beneath the gazebo. My grandmother told me that every evening someone would come out to check if anyone was in the hiding place and see to their needs. Then when it was safe, they could be brought inside the manor."

"I'm going to check it out." Sarah sat on the adjacent bench and swung her legs through the opening.

Mrs. Compson placed a hand on her elbow. "I wouldn't if I were you. Who knows what could be down there now — snakes, rabid squirrels — better let Matthew take care of it."

Quickly, Sarah withdrew her legs, then pulled the seat back to cover the opening. If a rabid squirrel had made the hiding place its home, she didn't want Matt to go down there, either. She rose and dusted off her hands, "You can't tell me there's anything this interesting in some house in Sewickley."

"How would you know? You've never been there," Mrs. Compson replied, but then she sighed. "Very well, I won't pretend to think Elm Creek Manor is any less wonderful than I know it truly is. But Sarah, my dear, don't wish for excitement.

Interesting doesn't always mean good. Sometimes the most ordinary things are the ones we learn to miss the most." Mrs. Compson sighed again more deeply, placed her hands on the gazebo rail, and looked out over the garden. "Why don't you fetch our things, and we'll quilt for a while until it's time for you to go."

Chapter 12

 That evening Sarah went to her first Tangled Web Quilters' meeting. As she drove downtown, she realized that this was the first time she had gone out in the evening without Matt since they moved to Waterford. Driving without him made her feel strange, as if she had forgotten something at home but couldn't remember what.

She found a parking spot across the street from Grandma's Attic, picked up the white cardboard box of chocolate chip cookies she had baked after work, and left the truck. She was halfway across the street before she remembered her quilting supplies. Exasperated, she went back for them. She'd been less nervous going to PennCellular the other day. The Tangled Web Quilters had already invited her to join their group, and since they hadn't said anything about a trial membership, she had no reason to be so anxious. Just because they were the only people in Waterford who wanted to be her friends . . .

Her thoughts went to Mrs. Compson as she walked down the alley between the building that held Grandma's Attic and a similar three-story building next door. Didn't Mrs. Compson have any friends? She never spoke of any, and no one ever came to visit her while Sarah was there. The last time Sarah had been at Grandma's Attic, Diane had hinted at some kind of conflict. Maybe tonight Sarah could get her to explain more. Diane would probably enjoy talking about it — if Gwen let her.

She found the back door; it was unlocked, as Bonnie had promised. Just inside the door there was a steep, narrow staircase, which Sarah climbed to the second-story landing while balancing her bag of quilting supplies on top of the box. She knocked on the only door.

It swung open on the second knock, and Bonnie stuck her head into the hallway. "Welcome, new member," she cried, and her eyes widened when she spotted the box in Sarah's arms. "Ooh, what did you bring?"

"Chocolate chip cookies. I can't supply much in the way of quilting advice, but at least I can bring snacks."

"And we love you for it. You can never have too many snacks, not with this crowd." Bonnie took the box out of Sarah's arms and led her into the house. "Hey, everybody, Sarah's here."

Mrs. Emberly, Gwen, Judy, and Diane greeted her from their places around a kitchen counter covered with goodies. Judy was holding her baby.

"I guess that means we're just waiting for the kid," Gwen said, helping herself to a brownie.

Judy put on a puzzled frown and looked from her baby to Gwen. "You mean Emily?"

"No, you nut. I mean my kid."

"I bet she loves it when you call her that," Diane said.

"She doesn't mind."

Mrs. Emberly smiled. "I hope when I'm not around you don't call me 'the old lady.'"

"No, we call you Lady Emberly of the Perfect Stitches."

"What do you call me?" Diane asked.

"You don't want to know."

The door slammed, and Summer rushed

in, breathless. "Sorry I'm late," she said. "I had to finish typing a paper."

"It's nice of you to join us at all, instead of going to the bars like all the other students," Diane said.

Summer rolled her eyes. "Not all students live and die for beer." She put an arm around Sarah's shoulders. "I'm glad you're here. If we bring down the average age of the group, they won't be able to treat me like the baby anymore."

"You'll always be my baby," Gwen said.

"That's different. That, I expect."

Everyone laughed.

"You're not the youngest, anyway," Judy reminded her, giving Emily a little pat on her diapered bottom and carrying her into the other room to her playpen.

Sarah picked up a red plastic plate from the counter and joined the others in selecting treats. Carrying her plate and the bag of quilting supplies in one hand and a cup of diet soda in the other, she followed Summer into the living room.

A breeze came in through the two large windows along the north wall, carrying with it the sounds of cars passing and people laughing on the street below. The Markham home seemed like an extension of Grandma's Attic; a rose-and-hunter-green quilt hung above the sofa on the wall opposite the windows, and there was an old treadle sewing machine near the doorway. Sarah wished she could see the other rooms. She had expected a home above a store to be — well, she wasn't exactly sure what she had expected, but she hadn't expected a regular middle-class home.

She found a seat in an armchair next to a upright piano at the far end of the room. Gwen and Summer sat side by side on a loveseat to her left, between the windows. Bonnie carried a rocking chair in from another room and placed it in the corner between Gwen and Sarah.

When Mrs. Emberly entered, Judy jumped up from her place on the sofa beside Diane. "Here, take my seat."

"No, no, that's all right," Mrs. Emberly said, settling beside her in an armchair identical to Sarah's. "This is comfortable. And I like being next to Emily."

Emily looked up and smiled when her name was spoken. She shook a plastic ring of keys at the older woman and squealed.

"I guess Emily wants you there, too," Judy said, laughing.

"Just think, Judy," Diane said. "Fifteen more years and she'll want real keys, and a car to go with them."

Judy pretended to shudder. "Don't remind me. I have enough to think about between now and then." She reached into a tote bag and brought out a small quilt in primary colors.

From across the room, Bonnie looked on in interest. "How's that coming?"

"Not bad, though I wish I had more time to work on it. At this rate it won't be done until Emily's in first grade."

"So I guess you won't be entering it in the Waterford Summer Quilt Festival after all," Summer said.

"No, but I don't mind. My Log Cabin will be there."

Mrs. Emberly reached over to stroke the quilt. "Didn't I tell you the Jacob's Ladder would be prettier than a Wandering Foot?"

Sarah almost dropped her block. "You shouldn't make a Wandering Foot quilt for Emily."

The others looked at her and smiled.

"I'm only teasing her, honey," Mrs. Emberly said. "How did you learn about that old superstition? I thought only senior ladies like me believed them anymore."

Sarah felt her cheeks growing warm. "I don't believe it, exactly. Mrs. Compson told me about it."

Everyone's hands froze over their work. The room went quiet.

After a moment Mrs. Emberly resumed sewing. "Oh. Of course."

The others exchanged glances and continued quilting.

Summer met Sarah's gaze for the briefest instant before turning to Mrs. Emberly. "What's that you're working on? Is it something new?"

"No, just another Whig Rose block, same as last time."

"Can I see it?"

Mrs. Emberly smiled as Summer came over and sat down on the floor by her feet. She took the block from the older woman and held it up for the others to see.

Gwen shook her head in admiration. "Beautiful. How are you going to set them?"

"Oh, I haven't decided yet. I have to make six more blocks first. Maybe I'll use a Garden Maze setting."

"What's that?" Sarah asked.

"You sew dark strips around each block, and then you sew the blocks to each other, separated by light strips."

Sarah tried to picture it and couldn't.

Mrs. Emberly smiled. "I'll bring a photo next time."

"That's at my place," Diane told Sarah. "I'll draw you a map if you want."

"Sure, thanks."

"Won't you guys be too tired from quilt camp to have a bee that night?" Summer asked.

Gwen rolled her eyes. "Right, kid. We'd better just sit around in our rocking chairs recuperating."

"What's quilt camp?" Sarah asked.

"Next week a few quilt instructors are running a three-day session of workshops and seminars in the Poconos," Bonnie said. "It's a fun way to get together with lots of other quilters, learn some new techniques, stuff like that."

"That sounds like fun."

"Everyone's going but you, me, and Bonnie," Summer said. "And Emily. I have classes."

"I wish I could go," Bonnie said. "But someone has to run the store. Besides, Craig and I are trying to watch the money, what with all three of the kids in college."

Sarah figured that if Bonnie couldn't afford it, she certainly couldn't either.

"You guys'll have to take good notes and share them with us when you get back," Summer said.

"It'll cost you." Diane nudged Summer

with her foot. "Hey, you're on the wrong side of the room."

"Huh?" Summer rose and returned the appliqué block to Mrs. Emberly.

"This is where the real quilters sit. You belong over there with the machine people."

Gwen turned to Bonnie and Sarah, shaking her head in sorrow. "Her mind has finally gone."

"No, look," Diane said. "Mrs. Emberly, Judy, and I always sit on this side of the room, and you, Bonnie, and Summer always sit over there."

"I sit here because I want to be near Emily's playpen," Judy said.

"And I sit here because it's next to the lamp and away from the window," Mrs. Emberly added.

Gwen grinned. "So much for your theory."

"And excuse me, but I resent that comment about real quilters." Summer made a face and returned to her seat beside her mother.

"Oh, come on," Diane protested. She looked to Mrs. Emberly and Judy for support. "We all know that true quilts are made entirely by hand."

Bonnie sighed. "Here we go again."

"That's tradition. Hand piecing, hand quilting. It's not that machine quilts aren't pretty, but they aren't true quilts. Even if you hand quilt a machine-pieced top, it's not the same."

Gwen set her sketch pad and colored pencils aside. "Diane, I do believe that's the most ridiculous thing I've ever heard you say."

"You only think that because you're a machine person. Come on. I know I'm not the only one who feels this way. Judy?"

"Don't drag me into this."

"Back me up here."

"I would if I agreed with you, but I don't. The only reason I hand piece and hand quilt is because I work with computers and lab equipment all day. The last thing I need is another machine in my life."

Diane groaned. "You're no help."

"Sorry."

"Looks like you're outnumbered," Gwen said.

Diane looked around the room, glaring. "You all know I'm right." She stood, snatched up her plate, and stomped out of the room.

Shocked, Sarah watched her go. The others were smiling and shaking their heads. As Mrs. Emberly and Judy struck up a conversation on the other side of the room, Sarah turned to Gwen. "Should we go after her?"

"Why would we do that?"

"Because . . . because she feels bad."

"Oh, it's all right," Gwen said. "This happens at least twice a month."

"Really?" Sarah craned her neck and tried to see into the kitchen.

"Sure. You'll get used to it."

"I thought you guys were friends."

"We are friends."

"But —"

"We are friends. All of us. We accept each other the way we are. Friends don't demand that you overhaul your entire personality. They know your faults and love you anyway. That means we tolerate Diane's moods — and my tendency to make speeches."

Sarah smiled. "I think I'm catching on."

"Good." Gwen picked up her sketch pad and resumed coloring a quilt pattern. "Hmm . . . I wonder what we're going to have to tolerate about you?"

Sarah laughed.

"So what are you working on, Sarah?" Bonnie asked.

"I'm working on a Double Nine Patch block now." She took the Sawtooth Star block out of her bag and held it up. "I finished this one on Tuesday."

"How pretty," Summer said.

Gwen motioned for Sarah to hand her the block. "Time for inspection." Sarah passed it over, and Gwen scrutinized the seams. "Not bad." She passed it to Summer. As the block went around the circle, each person complimented Sarah on her piecing skills.

"Your first quilt block ever," Mrs. Emberly said when it was her turn. "This is quite an occasion. I must say this looks much better than my first block did."

"Mine, too," Diane said as she came back into the room. "I chopped off all the tips of my triangles and the block buckled in the middle." She sat down and gave Sarah a searching look. "So I guess the lessons are going well?"

Everyone looked at Sarah, and from their expressions she could tell that each had been wondering the same thing. "They're going great. Mrs. Compson is a really good teacher."

"See, ladies, I told you it would be all right," Mrs. Emberly admonished them. She turned to Sarah. "She taught me how to quilt — or tried to, rather. I wasn't the best student back then and our lessons didn't go well. That was years ago, though, and I've learned a trick or two since."

"Of course you have," Bonnie said. "Your appliqué is the best of everyone here."

The others chimed in their agreement.

Sarah told them about her lessons, but she mentioned nothing about Claudia or the other Bergstroms she had come to know through Mrs. Compson's stories because it would have been like divulging a secret. She also told them about the Wandering Foot superstition and the meaning of the Log Cabin pattern with a black center square, but here, too, she omitted the personal details about Elm Creek Manor.

"I've heard those stories before," Gwen said. "I came across them in my research when I was planning the syllabus for my history of American folk art course." She hesitated for a moment. "Sarah, are you and Mrs. Compson friends?"

"I think so. At least, I think we're getting there."

"Do you think Mrs. Compson would be interested in visiting my class sometime as a guest lecturer?"

"I don't know. She likes to talk about quilts, but —"

"Sylvia is a teacher — or, rather, she was," Mrs. Emberly broke in. "She has a degree in art from Carnegie Mellon. Perhaps she'd enjoy talking to students again."

Gwen turned to Sarah. "What do you think?"

"I can ask," Sarah said. "The worst she can do is say no, right?"

Mrs. Emberly sighed. "No, she can do far worse than that."

"What do you mean?" Sarah asked, surprised.

"Nothing," Bonnie said quickly. "So, what are you all going to enter in the Waterford Quilting Guild's Summer Quilt Festival?"

"There's no need to change the subject," Mrs. Emberly told her, then turned to Sarah. "Sylvia and I had a falling out a long time ago."

"She's had a falling out with most of the quilters around here," Diane muttered.

Mrs. Emberly silenced Diane by patting her wrist. "I won't pretend it doesn't still trouble me, but I don't like to talk about it."

Sarah nodded, uncomfortable. She was growing fond of Mrs. Compson, but knew how abrasive the older woman could be sometimes.

"I do miss Elm Creek Manor, though. It was so lovely once."

"She's going to sell it," Sarah responded automatically, immediately regretting it when she saw Mrs. Emberly's shocked expression.

"What do you mean?" Judy asked.

Sarah shrugged, wishing she could just drop it. Maybe Mrs. Compson didn't want anyone to know. "She said University Realty may buy the estate."

Summer and Gwen exchanged a quick look.

"University Realty manages my apartment building," Summer said.

Her mother nodded. "All of their holdings are student apartments. That's what they do. They're in property management, not home sales."

"You don't think —" Mrs. Emberly looked around the circle. "You don't think they'd take that lovely manor and turn it into a student apartment building, do you?"

"If they do, I'm going to enroll next semester," Diane said.

"Now, don't you worry about anything." Bonnie shot Diane an exasperated look before turning back to Mrs. Emberly. "We don't know that she'll sell it to them — or to anyone, for that matter. And think about how impractical it would be to turn Elm Creek Manor into an apartment building. They'd have to spend a fortune."

"I suppose." But Mrs. Emberly still looked doubtful.

"I probably heard her wrong," Sarah said. "She probably meant some other company."

Mrs. Emberly tried to smile, then busied herself with her appliqué.

Gwen quickly changed the subject, and before long the earlier spirit of the gathering returned. Mrs. Emberly remained quiet, however, and Sarah noticed her deep frown of concern. She looked as worried as Sarah felt. Sarah understood that the students had to live somewhere, but did they have to live in Elm Creek Manor?

Chapter 13

Mrs. Compson spent the next morning sorting through documents in the library while Sarah worked alone in Aunt Clara's suite. It took all the self-discipline she had to keep from dashing down the hallway and confronting Mrs. Compson with her worries about the future of Elm Creek Manor. She knew, though, that if she burst out with her questions, the older woman would just purse her lips and walk away.

Not long after lunch Sarah finished the suite, which gave her the perfect excuse to join Mrs. Compson in the library. The older woman was sitting at the desk behind a stack of yellowing papers, one hand resting on the arm of her chair, the other holding up a water-stained document.

When Sarah lingered in the doorway Mrs. Compson looked up and peered at her over her glasses. "Finished already?"

Sarah nodded. "What should I work on next?"

"Leave the work for now. I'll finish up here and then we can have a quilt lesson." Her gaze returned to the paper.

"What's that?" Sarah asked, pointing at the paper and walking over for a closer look.

"Don't point, dear. It's nothing of your concern, just the family accounts. Claudia was never a good bookkeeper, and she became even more careless after her husband passed." She shook her head and pushed the chair away from the desk. "She and Harold made a mess of things, though it's not their fault alone."

"Maybe I could help. I know something about accounting."

"That's right. You do indeed, don't you?" Mrs. Compson rose and returned the document to the top of the pile. "How is your search for a *real* job going, by the way?"

Only Sarah's faint blush showed that she realized Mrs. Compson's emphasis was a teasing imitation of her own. "I have another interview Monday morning. I meant to tell you about it. It's in the morning so I won't be in until after lunch, if that's okay."

"You don't sound particularly enthusiastic."

Sarah shrugged.

Mrs. Compson smiled. "Well, don't get discouraged. You need to be confident. Show them what you've got. Something will come along."

"Sometimes I wonder."

"Now, none of that. You'll have plenty of time for self-pity when you're old and gray, like me."

"You're not old."

"Oh, I'm not, then? How very interesting. I'll have to remember that." She patted Sarah's arm. "Now, dear, I'm only teasing you. Surely you must be used to that by now."

"Not as used to it as I'm going to be, I bet."

Mrs. Compson laughed. "You can take it like the best of them, can't you?" She motioned for Sarah to follow her out of the library. "How are you coming with the Double Nine Patch?"

Sarah followed her down the hallway and to the stairs. "I finished it last night. There's a group called the Tangled Web Quilters, some people I met at Grandma's Attic. They get together and quilt once a week, and they asked me to join them."

"How nice."

"You could come next week, too. It would be fun."

Mrs. Compson shook her head. "They didn't invite me."

"But I'm a member now. They invited me, and I'm inviting you."

"That's not the same thing and you know it. I used to belong to the local guild — Claudia, too. We started going to meetings with my mother when we were young girls, and sometimes held quilting bees here. We would set up several quilt frames in the ballroom and everyone would come over, and we would have such a grand time." Mrs. Compson paused on the bottom step, her eyes distant. Then she sighed and continued across the marble floor and down the hallway leading to the west wing. "But we left the guild when the other women showed us we weren't welcome."

"What did they do?"

"Hmph. Their feelings were obvious, believe me. Even Claudia noticed."

"When was this?"

"Oh, I don't know. Fifty years ago, give or take."

"Fifty years? But — well, don't you think it's time to give it another chance, maybe? The Tangled Web Quilters are really nice. You'd have a good time. Besides, they're a different group, not the Waterford Quilting Guild."

"Now, dear." Mrs. Compson stopped outside the kitchen and placed a hand on Sarah's arm. "No more of this. The local quilters made it clear I was not welcome, and until they let me know they've changed their minds, I must assume their feelings haven't altered. I'd rather quilt with you or alone than with a group of strangers who don't want me among them in the first place. Now, are we agreed?"

Sarah opened her mouth to protest, but Mrs. Compson's expression silenced her. She nodded instead, reluctantly.

They went to the sitting room, where Sarah was struck by the feeling that something was different about the room. She looked around for a moment before realizing that the neatly folded pile of sheets and pillows Mrs. Compson usually kept on the sofa was gone.

Mrs. Compson noticed her staring at the sofa. "I decided to move back into my old room, if you must know," she said crisply, before Sarah even spoke a word.

Mrs. Compson leafed through a pattern book and found Sarah's third quilt block, Little Red Schoolhouse. For this block Sarah needed to make templates for several rectangles in different sizes, a parallelogram, and another four-sided figure. When she had cut pieces using all but the last template, Mrs. Compson showed her how to "reverse a template" by tracing around it to make one piece, then flipping the template over and tracing around it again to make its mirror image.

When Sarah had finished piecing some of the straight seams, Mrs. Compson showed her how to set in pieces, sewing a third piece of fabric to two others that met at an angle. Sarah attached the new piece to the first by sewing a straight seam into the angle where the three pieces would meet. Then she pivoted the new piece around her needle until the next edge was aligned with the edge of the second piece, and continued her running stitch to join them. She hoped Mrs. Compson was right and that setting in pieces would become easier each time she did it.

Once satisfied that Sarah could manage on her own, Mrs. Compson began to work on one of her own quilts. "Richard used to call this block the Little Red Playhouse," she remarked, smiling as she worked her needle in tiny stitches through the smooth layers held snugly in her quilting hoop.

"Why did he call it that?"

"Probably because Father once built him a little playhouse painted red, near the gardens, where the stables and exercise rings were. Richard loved to watch Father work with the horses, and this way Father could keep him near enough to watch without fearing for his safety."

"Where was it? Near the gazebo?"

"Oh, no. Near the edge of the old gardens, on land that was sold off a long time ago to build the state road." Mrs. Compson rested the quilt hoop in her lap. "My, how we all doted on that child. We had to, of course, to try to make up for losing Mother."

"You lost your mother? Did she — was it when she had Richard?"

"No, thank God. Not until a few years later, when I was ten and Richard was three. At least he had that little time with her."

"I'm sorry." The words sounded hopelessly inadequate.

Mrs. Compson slipped the silver thimble from her finger and handed it to Sarah. "This was Mother's. She gave it to me when she became ill the last time. She gave Claudia another just like it. I suppose she must have known, somehow, that she would be leaving us."

★ ★ ★

Although the way I remember it Mother was a spirited woman, she tired easily. We children knew to keep quiet when she went about the manor pressing her fingers to the side of her head, almost blind from headaches that could last for days. Father worried about her, and often sent an older cousin running for the doctor. Mother tolerated the doctor's orders for bed rest and limited activity only reluctantly; as soon as the headaches passed she would be playing dolls with us on the nursery floor, planning a ball with Father, or exercising the horses. He would protest that she should not work herself so hard, but she would pretend not to hear him, and he would pretend she was fine.

She was not supposed to have any more children, but there it was, and she was so happy that none of the aunts could scold her. I did not know that until much later. At the time, Claudia and I and the cousins were only happy about the news.

The pregnancy was difficult, and Richard arrived almost a month early. We other children were not allowed to see him until he was nearly five weeks old. I overheard some of the older cousins whispering that it was because the grown-ups thought he would die, and that it would be easier for us if we had not seen him. I had such terrible nightmares after hearing that.

But the baby grew stronger, and Mother seemed to be well again. Father was so thrilled to have a son. Not that he didn't love Claudia and me, mind you, but I think a man just feels something different, something special, about a son. At least at first — then the son gets older and the father and son fight like a mother and daughter or a mother and son never would. It happens all the time that way, and I don't know if anyone really knows why.

As I was saying, the baby grew stronger, and Mother seemed healthy for a while, but as Richard learned to walk and talk and play, Mother seemed to weaken, almost to fade away. First she stopped riding, then even quilting became too much for her, and then one morning the rest of us woke but Mother did not.

How dark and lonely Elm Creek Manor became then. I don't like to think about it, when I can help it.

We all went on, as people always have to, but it was difficult. Mother's passing left an enormous emptiness in our lives. Claudia and I tried to take Mother's place raising Richard — with our aunts' help, of course. How he managed to become such a dear boy instead of a spoiled brat . . . well, I surely don't know. Between the two of us, Claudia and I made sure he never wanted for anything. What a pair of young mother hens we were.

Father, too, indulged him, just as he had always indulged Mother, I suppose. When Richard demanded to be allowed to ride alone when he was barely tall enough to bump his head if he walked under the horse, Father would hold him on the back of a tired old mare and walk them slowly around the grounds. Richard had little patience for school as he grew older, and when I tried to tutor him he would dash off to explore the barn, or run away to the orchard to see if the apple trees were blossoming.

Such a headstrong, mischievous boy. But he had such a kind heart, that one. Once, when he was in his third or fourth year of school, a new boy came to his class. I would see him every morning when Claudia and I dropped Richard off before walking down the block to our school. It was heartbreaking, really. The boy's clothes looked as if they had not been washed, his eyes looked tired and hungry, and sometimes he would have such awful bruises on his arms. Most of the children avoided him, but Richard became his friend.

Once, at dinner, Richard asked Father if the boy could come and live with us, because his mommy and daddy were mean. Father and Uncle William exchanged looks — you know the kind of looks I mean, the ones they think the children don't see. After dinner they took Richard aside and questioned him. They went out that evening and would not tell the rest of us where they were going.

Later I overheard them talking to my aunts. Very well, if you must know, I crept out of bed and pressed my ear against the library door. Father and Uncle William told my aunts that they had gone to the little boy's house to speak with his father. Father wanted to see the boy, but when his daddy went to check his bed, the little boy wasn't there. His sister spoke up then and said that her brother hadn't been home for two days.

Father grew so angry that Uncle William had to hold him back or he might have hit the man. "How can a man not know whether his eight-year-old son is under his own roof?" he had shouted. They stormed out of the house and went straight to the police, who went back and took the little sister away from those horrible people. But no one knew what had happened to the little boy. He had disappeared.

"Did he run away?" I asked Richard the next morning.

He hesitated, then shrugged. "He didn't tell me he was going anywhere."

I didn't know what to think. The rumors raced around school like wildfire. Some said the little boy had been murdered by his own parents. Others said he had run off to the city. I couldn't bear to believe the former, but I knew he was too young for the latter.

A week later, I woke early and heard someone walking in the hallway past my bedroom. It was not yet dawn. I crept from the bed, tiptoed across the room, and opened the door.

Richard's back was just disappearing around the corner. I crept after him, downstairs to the kitchen, out the side door and down the stone path to the garden. It was a clear evening in early autumn, and my bare toes were chilly as I trailed Richard beyond the gardens to his playhouse. He ducked inside, and I heard soft voices murmuring.

I followed, only to find Richard and the little boy sharing a loaf of bread and a paper sack of apples. They looked up in fright when I entered. The little boy jumped up and tried to run for the door, but I was blocking his way and caught him around the waist. He shrieked and tried to punch me with his fists, but Richard grabbed his wrists.

"No, Andrew, it's Sylvia. She's my sister. Everything's okay now," he said, his voice sounding so much like Father's when soothing a jittery colt. He repeated the refrain until Andrew went limp in our arms.

Our two dogs started barking when Andrew cried out, and soon all the grown-ups were awake. Fine guard dogs, indeed, to be silent until then. Before long we were inside the warm kitchen with quilts wrapped around us, sipping warm milk. I didn't know why they gave me warm milk, since I had not been hiding in a playhouse or sneaking outside every night to care for a friend, but never mind.

Richard later tried to convince me that he hadn't lied to me, not exactly. "I said Andrew didn't tell me he was going anywhere," he argued. "That's true. Andrew didn't tell me that because I already knew."

I told him he intended to deceive me, and that was as bad as a lie. He was quite abashed and said he would never lie to me again.

But that tells you what kind of boy Richard was: good intentioned but so very impulsive. His instinct was to help his friend the only way he knew how. It never occurred to him that the grown-ups could help Andrew more than Richard himself could.

Who knows what might have happened if I had not found them in the playhouse that night. As usual, Richard's luck rescued him in the end.

"What happened to Andrew?" It was Matt, leaning against the wall near the sitting room doorway. Sarah had not heard him arrive.

"The police came for him. He and his sister were taken to live with an aunt in Philadelphia. Richard saw him again, but not until they were young men. His parents moved away, and I don't know what became of them. Good riddance." She sighed and stood up, making a tsking sound with her tongue when she saw how little piecing Sarah had finished. "No more stories. It distracts you from your quilting."

"No, don't say that. I can sew and listen at the same time. Really."

"Hmph." Mrs. Compson shook her head, but a slow smile crept across her face. "One more chance. I'll be watching carefully next time, mind you." She rose and left the room, returning with a brown leather purse. She took out a checkbook and a pen and filled out one of the checks. "Here," she said, tearing the check from the book and giving it to Sarah. "Your wages. I'll see you Monday."

Sarah was about to put the check away when she noticed something odd. "This can't be right."

"Not enough for you? Hmph."

"No, that's not it." In her head Sarah calculated her wages for the number of hours she had worked. "Mrs. Compson, you overpaid me. I think you accidentally paid me for the hours we spent quilting, too, not just the hours I worked."

"Accident has nothing to do with it." Mrs. Compson zipped her purse shut and folded her arms.

"But that's not fair to you. That's not what we agreed." Sarah tried to return the check, but Mrs. Compson shook her head and refused to listen. Instead she guided Matt and Sarah out the back door. As they drove away, they spotted her on the back porch, watching them go.

Chapter 14

Sarah had all weekend to finish the Little Red Schoolhouse block, and — despite Matt's attempts to distract her — to worry about her upcoming job interview. This time, she resolved, she was going to be perfect. She would answer every question with intelligence and charm. Sure, it had been years since she'd attended those job interview seminars at Penn State, but she remembered the most important tips. And hadn't her professors told her that with each interview she would improve?

Several of them had, and every so often she felt like giving them a call and asking them when she could expect this improvement to kick in.

"How do you feel?" Matt asked as she finished her breakfast on Monday morning.

"Not bad, considering that I've done this about a million times. Now I'm really an expert at interviewing." She was also becoming all too familiar with the variety of ways employers delivered rejection.

Hopkins and Steele was a small public accounting firm two blocks away from Grandma's Attic. The secretary greeted her and led her down a carpeted hallway. "The nine-o'clock was a no-show," she confided in a whisper. They stopped in front of a windowless door, and the secretary gestured for Sarah to sit in a nearby armchair. "They'll come out for you when they're ready."

About five minutes after the secretary left, the door opened. "Sarah?" a tall, balding man asked. He shook her hand and led her into the office, where another man sat at a round table. The first man pulled out a chair for Sarah, then took his own seat.

The interview was more casual than Sarah had anticipated. Mr. Hopkins and Mr. Steele were good-humored and friendly, and Sarah felt she responded to their questions well. She even remembered to ask a few questions to demonstrate her interest in the position. By the time the interview ended, Sarah felt she had made her best showing yet.

Afterward, Hopkins offered to show

Sarah out. When they opened the door and stepped into the hallway, they saw a man waiting in the armchair.

"Guess we're running behind," Hopkins said. "Sarah, do you mind finding your own way out?"

"No, not at all."

"Follow this hall all the way down to the receptionist's desk and you'll see the exit. You'll be hearing from us." He smiled, then turned to the man in the armchair. "If you'll give us a minute to regroup, we'll be right with you."

"Thank you," Sarah said. Hopkins nodded and shut the door, and she turned to leave.

"Well, hello again," the man in the armchair said.

Sarah looked at him closely. Where had she seen him before? "Oh . . . hi."

"Tom Wilson. From the PennCellular waiting room? Hey, we really have to stop meeting like this. Although I guess it had to happen, so many accountants and so few jobs, and all."

"Yes, of course. How are you?"

He shrugged. "Oh, you know. Same old, same old." He grimaced and jerked his head toward the closed office door. "How was it in there?"

"Oh, fine. Very nice people."

"Good, good. You must have done really well for them to keep you late like that. That's a good sign. You must have impressed them."

"Really? Do you think so?"

"Well, sure. My appointment was for ten, and here it is quarter after. They wouldn't run overtime for just anybody."

Sarah felt a small spark of hope. "You know, I think it went well, too. They really seemed interested in me. I almost wish —" She bit her lip.

"Wish what?"

"Nothing."

"Come on, what?"

"It's just —" She glanced at the office door to assure herself that it was still closed. She lowered her voice. "It's just that I was hoping to find something outside of accounting. I mean, I know that's where all my experience is, and I know I can do the work, but —" She searched for the words.

"But what?"

"I don't know. I guess I just wanted to try something different, something, well, more interesting. No offense." He was an accountant himself, after all.

He chuckled. "None taken. But why are

you applying for jobs you don't want?"

"It's not that I don't want them. I need a job, and I'll be grateful for whatever I get. I just wanted to try something else, maybe something I would enjoy more. You know, explore my options. Except I don't seem to have any options. Like with PennCellular? I really wanted to apply for the opening in their PR department, but they wouldn't even give me a chance. One look at my accounting degree and that was that."

He shrugged. "At least you're getting the interviews. And you're still young. You have plenty of time to switch careers if you want. Me, on the other hand — well, like they say, you can't teach an old dog new tricks. They call us displaced workers. There's so many of us we even have our own buzzword. Can you believe that?"

Sarah couldn't decide what to say, so she shook her head.

"Besides," he continued, "who's going to hire a guy like me who wants to be paid what he's worth and knows more about the boss's job than the boss does? Not like some green college kid who —" Suddenly his gaze shifted over her left shoulder.

Sarah heard the door open behind her and Mr. Hopkins speaking to Mr. Steele. "I'd better go," she said. Tom raised his hand in farewell, and she hurried down the hallway to the exit.

She met Matt at the square, a small downtown park near Waterford's busiest intersection. They stopped home for a quick lunch, where Sarah told him about the interview. It had been a long time since she'd had good news to share about her job search, and even longer since she'd left an interview thinking she had a good chance of landing the job.

When she finished, Matt placed his elbows on the table and frowned. "I don't know if it was such a good idea to tell that Tom guy how you felt about the job."

Sarah's smile faded. "Why? I made sure the door was shut first."

"Maybe the interviewers didn't overhear you, but that doesn't mean they won't find out."

"What do you mean? You think he went in there and told them what I said?"

"No, I don't think that, but —"

"Then what do you think?"

"I think you ought to be more careful, that's all. If you want to get a job, you have to be smarter. You can't keep screwing up your chances like this."

"So you think I don't have a job yet because I'm not smart enough or I'm messing up on purpose?"

"That's not exactly how I put it."

"It's pretty close. God, Matt, that was the best interview I've had since we moved here, and all you can do is criticize me."

"You're overreacting. I'm not criticizing you." Matt shoved his chair back from the table and stood. "But if you didn't want my advice, then why tell me about it?"

"I am not overreacting." She hated it when he said that. "I told you about the interview because I thought you might be interested in what goes on in my life, not because I want to be criticized every time I do something."

"How do you expect to improve if you don't get any feedback?"

"I don't see how you know any more about the interviewing process than I do. I managed to find myself a job in State College, remember?"

"Fine. It's my fault you don't have that job anymore, and it's my fault if you can't find a new one. Satisfied?"

"I didn't say it was your fault. Now who's overreacting?"

"I'll be waiting in the truck." Matt grabbed his lunch dishes and stormed into the kitchen. Sarah heard them clatter in the sink, and then the front door slammed.

Red-faced and fuming, she raced after him.

They drove out to Elm Creek Manor in silence. When the truck pulled up behind the manor, Sarah jumped out and slammed the door without a word. The truck sped away, its tires kicking up a shower of dirt and gravel.

Sarah went inside and paused in the back foyer, fuming. He was right, and she knew it. She shouldn't have confided in Tom Wilson. But the other things he'd said were so wrong. He had no right to criticize her for not finding anything yet. Hadn't she left her job in State College for his sake? Matt's new job didn't pay any more than Sarah's old one had, so they weren't any better off financially. Matt was better off — at least, he seemed happier — but what had Sarah gained?

"We should've stayed in State College," Sarah said aloud.

The manor's silence absorbed her words.

She closed her eyes and leaned back against the wall, her stomach tightening. Moving to Waterford had been a mistake. They should have stuck it out in State College a little while longer; surely Matt would have found something. He was more likely to find a job in State College than

Sarah was to find something in Waterford.

She knew this as certainly as she knew that she could never tell Matt how she felt.

It was too late, anyway. She'd made her choice and she had to live with it. It would be a lot easier to live with, though, if Matt appreciated her sacrifice. Sometimes she thought he didn't even realize she'd made one.

She took slow, deep breaths until most of her irritation subsided. She felt the manor surrounding her, comforting and quiet, more like home than the duplex would ever be.

Another quiet minute passed before Sarah opened her eyes and went upstairs.

She found Mrs. Compson in the suite next to Aunt Clara's. She was sitting on the floor on top of a folded quilt and removing faded clothing from the bottom drawer of a bureau.

"I'm here," Sarah said as she came into the room.

"So I see." Mrs. Compson eyed her. "Should I not ask how it went, then?"

"Hmm? Oh. The interview. No, the interview was fine."

"Of course. That explains why you're so cheerful this afternoon."

Sarah almost smiled.

Mrs. Compson set aside a flannel work shirt. "Well, then, since you clearly aren't in the mood for working today, why don't we have a quilt lesson instead?"

"But I haven't done any work yet today."

"True, but I've been working all morning."

Sarah shrugged. "Okay. You're the boss."

"Indeed I am," Mrs. Compson said. She motioned for Sarah to help her to her feet. "You'll be starting a new block today, the Contrary Wife."

Sarah snorted. "Got one called the Contrary Husband instead?"

Mrs. Compson raised an eyebrow. "Do I detect a note of discord? That can't be, not with the two lovebirds."

"Matt was being a pain today. I told him about my interview, and all he could do was pick apart everything I said."

"That doesn't sound like him."

"And I didn't even do anything wrong." Sarah explained what had happened.

Mrs. Compson drew in a breath and grimaced. "I'm afraid I have to agree with Matthew." She raised a hand when Sarah opened her mouth to protest. "With what he said, not with how he said it. He should have been more tactful. But I think he's right to caution you against speaking too freely with others who are competing for the same jobs."

Sarah plopped down on the bed. "I knew you'd take his side."

"Oh, is that what I'm doing? I thought I was merely offering my opinion." Mrs. Compson sat down beside her. "If I am taking his side, it's because he's right. This Tom Wilson didn't need to know how you feel about your profession."

Sarah sighed. Maybe Mrs. Compson and Matt were right. She'd really blown it this time.

"I don't think this Tom Wilson will divulge your secret, however," Mrs. Compson said.

"I hope not, but why wouldn't he?"

"Because he'll seem terribly unprofessional if he does. Why should they believe him, anyway, someone spreading rumors about another applicant?"

"That's probably true."

"However, I do hope you've learned a lesson. Be careful to whom you divulge your secrets. You never know —" Mrs. Compson paused, smiling to herself.

"What? What's so funny?"

"Oh, nothing." Mrs. Compson's smile grew. "I was just thinking about how I met my husband."

"You met him at a job interview?"

"No, no." Mrs. Compson laughed. "But the day we met, he was even less discreet than you were today, much to his later embarrassment."

I told you before how every year at the state fair Claudia and I would show our quilts, and how I would compete in the riding events. Father would show his prize horses and spend hours debating the merits of various breeding and training practices with the other gentlemen. Richard hung on every word; he wanted to be ready for the day he would take over Bergstrom Thoroughbreds. He spent nearly every moment with Father and the horses. Despite my efforts, however, he did not have the same diligence for his schoolwork. I suppose that isn't unusual for a nine-year-old boy.

I was sixteen, and I loved the fair. And I loved to ride. I must have annoyed some of the other girls, since I took first place in every competition I entered. But I didn't care as much about the ribbons and trophies as they thought I did. What I loved was flying like the wind, feeling the horse gather all its strength before soaring over a jump, the delicate power of the flashing hooves and flowing manes — oh, it was wonderful. Seeing the pride in Father's eyes when I won on his horses — well, that was wonderful, too.

One morning I was riding Dresden Rose in the practice ring when I noticed a young man leaning against the fence, watching us exercise, just as he had for the past two mornings of the fair. After returning his greeting with a nod I pretended to ignore him, but it was difficult not to watch him out of the corner of my eye as I rode. It was also rather annoying to have him there again. I had my first competition coming up and needed to concentrate, and I couldn't do so very well with someone staring.

Afterward in the stable, I was brushing Dresden Rose, checking her feed, and murmuring to her encouragingly to build up her confidence for the afternoon's events. Then I heard the stall door open behind me.

I whirled around, startling Rose. The young man from the practice ring stood there grinning at me.

"Beautiful animal," he said.

"Yes, she is," I replied, my voice tinged with irritation. I stroked Rose's neck and spoke soothingly to calm her.

The man reached over to stroke her muzzle. "A Bergstrom?"

"Yes." Then I realized he meant Rose, not me. "Yes, she is."

His admiring gaze turned to me. "You're a fine rider."

My cheeks flushed, although I willed them not to. He was quite handsome, tall and strong with dark eyes and dark, curly hair. I was very aware that there was no one else around, and how I probably looked to him. I was never the beauty Claudia was, but in my own way I was quite pretty back then, or at least he seemed to think so.

"Thank you," I finally managed, half hoping that Richard or Father would suddenly appear, and half afraid that they would.

He moved along Rose's side, and I stepped back involuntarily even though the horse was between us. "Don't worry," he murmured to Dresden Rose as he stroked her neck. "I don't mean you any harm." He ran a hand along her flank, looking her over with a practiced eye. "Do you get to ride Bergstroms often?"

I looked at him in disbelief. "Of course."

"They're supposed to be the finest horses around."

"A lot of people think so."

He grinned at me. "I know I shouldn't admit this, but the best of my family's stable can't match the worst of old Bergstrom's."

"Oh, really?" I was so surprised I almost laughed. "Well, I suppose 'old Bergstrom' would be delighted to hear that."

"I bet he already knows." He had continued around Rose's hindquarters and was now on my side of the stall. "My father has plans, though. He thinks he'll catch up to Bergstrom in a generation."

"Those must be some plans." My voice trembled as he drew closer, and I busied myself with Rose's mane. "Will they work?"

He shook his head. "Not a chance. His ideas are a good start, but they don't go far enough. And you can't get anywhere in this life without taking a few chances."

"My father would agree."

"No, no one will catch Bergstrom for a while yet. But someday I'm going to breed horses that will rival his. Maybe even surpass them."

I raised my eyebrows in surprise and challenge. "Do you really think you can?"

"Oh, sure. Not soon, but someday. I have some ideas." He stepped closer and took the brush from my hand. "May I?" I nodded, and he continued Rose's grooming. "Hard to imagine there could ever be a finer horse than you, though, isn't it?" he murmured in Rose's ear. She nuzzled his face.

"Her name is Dresden Rose."

"And what's yours?"

I paused for a moment. "Sylvia."

He smiled, his eyes crinkling in the corners. "Sylvia. Lovely name."

"Thank you."

"I'm James Compson."

I took in a breath. "One of Robert Compson's sons?" Robert Compson raised horses in Maryland. He was my father's nearest rival.

His smile turned wry. "The youngest of many."

"I see." I reached out for the brush.

He dropped the brush and took my hand in both of his. Startled, I moved as if to pull away.

"Please, don't run off," he said, stepping closer. "It's taken me two days just to get up the courage to speak to you."

"My father will be here soon." My voice shook and I felt very strange, but I didn't back away.

A hurt look flashed in his eyes, and he

released my hand. "Do you want me to leave?"

I shook my head, and then I nodded, and then I just looked at him in dismay. I wanted him to take my hand again, and I wanted him to be gone.

"I'm sorry. This was foolish of me." He opened the stall door and left.

By the time I finished caring for Dresden Rose, my hands had stopped shaking. By the time Father, Claudia, and Richard arrived to help me prepare for the competition, I was able to appear calm. I didn't fool Claudia, though; she knew something had happened, but she wouldn't press me to explain, not with Father and Richard there.

The competition began, and soon it would be my turn. I spotted my family cheering in the spectators' seats, and I grinned as I waved back, my confidence bolstered.

Then, as I looked away from my family and into another part of the stands, my eyes met James's. My stomach flip-flopped. His gaze was so steady and intense, and it so unsettled me, that I sawed on Rose's reins. She whinnied in protest, jolting me back to alertness.

Then it was my turn. "Our fifth competitor," the announcer's voice rang out so that all could hear. "Sylvia Bergstrom."

There was just enough time before I trotted into the ring for me to see James's jaw drop.

"You see, he didn't know who I was."

"Yes, I figured that out," Sarah managed to say through her laughter. "But when he asked for your name, why didn't you say Sylvia Bergstrom instead of just Sylvia?"

Mrs. Compson looked abashed. "I was having too much fun at his expense, I'm afraid." She laughed. "My goodness, how embarrassed he must have been. Can you imagine?"

"But everything worked out fine in the end, didn't it?" Sarah teased. "I mean, you did marry him, right?"

Mrs. Compson smiled. "Yes, I did. So maybe everything will work out just fine for you, too, but I do hope you'll be more cautious."

"I will."

They went downstairs to the sewing room, where Mrs. Compson helped Sarah draft her new templates. As they worked, Sarah realized that most of her anger had faded, but Matt's criticism still stung. Was it because she knew he had been right —

not just about divulging secrets but about everything? Was she subconsciously screwing up her search for a real job?

Sarah thought about it and decided that it couldn't be true. Why would she want to do that, subconsciously or otherwise?

She concentrated on her quilting — and on figuring out a way to get Matt to apologize before she confessed that he'd been right.

Chapter 15

That week Sarah and Mrs. Compson finished the second suite and started a third, working on the manor in the mornings and quilting in the afternoons. On Thursday, Sarah completed the Contrary Wife block and began another, which Mrs. Compson called the LeMoyne Star. Mrs. Compson must have liked the pattern herself, since it appeared in several of the quilts she had taken from the cedar chest.

Thursday was also the day Sarah remembered Gwen's request. "You know that group of quilters I told you about?" she asked as she traced a figure onto the template plastic.

Mrs. Compson kept her eyes on her quilting. "No, I've never made their acquaintance."

"Actually, you do know one of them, Bonnie Markham. But you know what I mean. Do you remember them?"

"How could I remember them if I've never met them?"

Sarah decided to start over. "Last week when I went to the Tangled Web Quilters' meeting, I met a woman named Gwen Sullivan. She's a professor at Waterford College."

"How very nice for her."

"She's teaching a course on the history of American folk art, and she wondered if you might be willing to be a guest speaker."

"Really." Mrs. Compson set down her quilt hoop. "Does she want me to teach the class how to quilt or to teach them about quilt history?"

"I think she wants you to talk about quilt history and folklore and stuff."

"If Gwen is a quilter herself, why does she need me?"

Sarah hesitated. "Well, sometimes it's more fun for the students to listen to someone other than the professor. And you tell good stories."

Mrs. Compson smiled. "Very well, then. You may tell your friend it would be my pleasure to speak to her class."

"Great. Gwen will be glad to hear that." Sarah paused. "You could come to the

Tangled Web Quilters' meeting with me tonight and tell her yourself."

"I don't think that will be necessary. I'm sure you're responsible enough to carry the message."

"Of course I am, but —"

"Then it's settled."

Sarah gave up.

They worked without talking for a few minutes until Mrs. Compson broke the silence with a chuckle. "So I tell good stories, do I?"

"Of course you do. It's too bad you don't like to tell them."

Mrs. Compson looked astonished. "Why, what on earth do you mean?"

"Getting information out of you is like pulling teeth, or — or like setting in pieces."

"That's not so."

"It is too. You started to tell me about James on Monday, and here it is Thursday already and you still haven't explained how you ended up together. I've been wondering about it all week, but you haven't said a word."

"My, all week," Mrs. Compson teased. "If you think that's long, I have to wonder if you have the diligence and perseverance it takes to finish a quilt."

"It's not the same thing and you know it."

"Very well, then. If only to prove that I'm not as reticent as you think."

James avoided me for the rest of the fair that summer. I know, because I looked for him everywhere, but I saw neither hide nor hair of him the rest of the week. I supposed he must have been terribly embarrassed, and perhaps he thought I had been making fun of him by not telling him who I was. And perhaps he felt that he had insulted me by suggesting he could one day challenge Father's business. I wasn't insulted, however; I just knew he was wrong. The very idea — to surpass Bergstrom Thoroughbreds.

In autumn Father was invited to teach a course in the agricultural school at your alma mater, though it was called Pennsylvania State College then. Richard begged and pleaded to be allowed to accompany him. Oh, how Richard wanted to see the world, even at that age. Father refused, saying that he would not have time to care for a young boy and that Richard could not miss school. But he refused so reluctantly — he hated to be away from his son — that Richard must have thought there was still a chance.

He came running out to the garden, where Claudia and I were having a party with some of our friends. It was a picnic of sorts, to say a sad good-bye to the summer and welcome in the new school year. One fellow was especially fond of Claudia, though he was too shy to even look her in the eye, much less speak to her. I used to tease her about him mercilessly, of course. She was not the only one who interested the boys, either. I had two young men who adored me, too, although I was indifferent to them both and had told them so. They still insisted on courting me, though, which I found highly irritating — did they think I didn't know my own mind? Honestly. Since they were determined to pine away rather than heed my words, well, I decided to let them. I used to enjoy watching them glower at each other when I would seem to prefer one more than the other, and would pretend not to notice when they fought for the next dance or the empty seat by my side.

One of the young men was telling a joke when Richard burst into the party. "Sylvia, Sylvia," he cried, tugging at my hand.

"What is it, darling? Are you hurt?"

"No, no." He glared, impatient. I had

228

forgotten that he had made me promise not to call him "darling" in front of the older boys anymore. "I figured out how to get Father to take me with him."

I pulled him onto the gazebo seat by my side. "I thought Father already told you no."

"But we can change his mind. If you come, too, Sylvia, you can look after me. Then Father has to say I can go."

"But what about school?"

"I won't mind missing school."

I laughed. "I realize that, but you have to go to school if you want to run Bergstrom Thoroughbreds someday. And I have to go to school, too, if I want to go to college."

Claudia had been listening in. "Have you forgotten something?" she asked, approaching us from across the gazebo. She stood behind Richard and placed her hands on his shoulders. "I've graduated already, so I wouldn't miss any school. I could look after you."

"But Sylvia and I would have fun." Richard's face assumed its familiar stubborn frown. Claudia pursed her lips, and I shot my brother a look of warning. "We would, too, Claudia, but Elm Creek Manor couldn't get along without you for so long."

You charmer, I thought, as he tried to hide a grin. Good thing Claudia couldn't see his face. "Since Claudia is needed here, and I can't leave school — I'm sorry, Richard, but it doesn't sound feasible."

Richard looked down at the gazebo's wooden floor, crestfallen. "I know you want to go to college, Sylvia. I'm sorry — I didn't think about you missing school. But just think of it — the chance to go somewhere."

I was thinking about it, and as much as I loved my home, I too wanted to see some of the world before I returned to Elm Creek Manor to settle down. "I'm sorry, sweetheart. Maybe when you're older."

"When I'm older. That's what Father said. Everything's when I'm older."

Claudia sighed. "I'm sure they have schools near the college. You could both probably transfer easily enough. It's only for a semester, after all."

Richard brightened. "Do you think so?"

"I don't see why not, if Father agrees. And if Sylvia wants to transfer."

"Of course I want to," I exclaimed. "It would almost be like going away to college myself. Think of all the new things to see and people to meet."

My two young men frowned uneasily at that.

Richard crowed triumphantly and

hopped down from the seat. He grabbed my hand and began to run from the gazebo toward the house, pulling me after him.

We spoke to Father, and without too much wheedling on our part, he agreed. Before long all the arrangements were made. We were to live in a faculty house on campus, and Richard would be able to attend a nearby elementary school. But the best part was that I would be allowed to continue my studies at the college.

My, how I enjoyed those days! I made many new friends, and Richard and I had a grand time exploring the campus. My classes were challenging, but not nearly as difficult as I had thought they would be. I was very proud that I could hold my own with the older students.

Our faculty home, while it could not be compared to Elm Creek Manor, was cozy and snug. Sometimes Father would bring home some of his students or other faculty members for supper, and they would banter and debate every conceivable topic late into the night. Often they discussed the news from Europe, sometimes in hushed tones that I had to strain to hear from the kitchen, sometimes in angry shouts that would make the china rattle in the cupboards. I would usually make some excuse so that I would not have to stay and listen. Even though we Bergstroms had considered ourselves thoroughly American since Great-Grandfather's time, and if we still had any distant relatives in Germany we did not know of them, the stories about Hitler and his politics always filled me with dread. Richard would eavesdrop if I could not find his hiding place and shoo him off to bed first.

One evening, Father came home joking merrily with two students. "Sylvia!" he called. "Come meet our guests for dinner."

In the kitchen, I sighed. I never knew when Father would bring company home until they stood on the doorstep. Wiping my hands on my apron, I hurried to the foyer, where Father and his guests were removing their coats and Richard was peppering them with questions. Then I froze in my tracks.

One of the young men was James Compson.

Father made the introductions. "James says he knows you, Sylvia," he said, bemused. "But I can't imagine how that's possible."

I gave James a sidelong glance. "We met at the fair, Father, last summer. He watched me ride."

"And a fine rider you are." James's eyes crinkled when he smiled, and I found myself smiling back.

I served supper, using a few tricks I had picked up from Cook to stretch the food for three into a meal for five. Throughout the meal, every time I looked up, James would be gazing steadily at me. His eyes were so intense that I could hardly bear to return his looks, but I could bear less turning away from him. I tried to keep my voice steady during the polite conversation, but I admit I was nervous.

"I'm surprised to find you here, Sylvia," James finally said when we were finished eating.

"I'm surprised to find you here as well."

"He won't be here for long," Father said. "He has big plans for himself, don't you, young man?"

"That's right, sir," James said. "I could stay with my family's operation, but with my older brothers in charge, there isn't a lot of room for me. Or for any new ideas."

"You could come work for Father," Richard chimed in. "Couldn't he, Father?"

Everyone laughed. It was clear that Richard admired his new friend very much.

"Perhaps he could." Father chuckled.

"What do you think of that, Sylvia?" James's eyes twinkled with amusement.

"I couldn't possibly say one way or the other. Why on Earth would you consult me about your plans?"

"James always wonders what pretty girls think about him," the other student joked. "It's one of his few redeeming qualities."

"Thanks for nothing," James protested with a grin, elbowing his friend in the side. "I was doing badly enough on my own without your help."

I eyed Father surreptitiously, but his expression suggested nothing. We might have been discussing horse feed for all he seemed to care. I had expected a more outraged response to the obvious flirtation with his daughter being conducted under his very nose. It was indeed puzzling.

After I had cleared away the dishes and had attempted unsuccessfully to put Richard to bed, I went into the other room while the men drank coffee and talked by the fire. I was pretending to study, but in truth I was eavesdropping. I wouldn't have, except I wanted to hear what James would say, and if he would say anything about me.

The conversation quickly turned to politics, and their voices became heated.

"I cannot believe it, not even of that little man," Father's voice boomed from the other room.

"He's right, James. Be reasonable. Think of the Olympic Games," the other student added.

"Berlin was whitewashed for the games. You know it as well as I." James's voice was low, but steady and emphatic. "It was a disgrace. A sham put on for an audience of people who want to be deluded, because we fear another war."

My heart seemed to skip a beat. Another war? I clutched my mathematics textbook with cold and trembling hands. That could not be. Germany was so far away, and no one wanted to get involved in another war so soon, if ever.

"But twelve thousand Jews died for Germany in the Great War," Father protested. "Surely that will count for something."

"I wish I could believe that, sir," James replied. "But I doubt it. Think of the Nuremberg laws. They aren't even a year old and look at what's happened already."

"It's strictly an economic problem," the other student said. "You tell him, Mr. Bergstrom. When their economy improves, the Nazi influence will waver again. Hitler can't last. With all his crazy talk about the

Jews — why, surely he can only stay in power so long spouting nonsensical rubbish like that. He talks like an insane man."

"An insane man that an entire country listens to with enthusiasm," James said. "Haven't you read his writings?"

"God forbid you should fill your minds with such filth," Father broke in.

"Point taken, sir, but a man should know his enemies. I've read them, and it's clear that he fully intends to take over the world, if he can, and this alliance with Italy is only the beginning. There won't be a Jew left in Europe, or the world, if he isn't stopped. And if he isn't stopped soon, now, as his power is still growing, I shudder to think what it will take to stop him later."

A fist pounded on the table, and I jumped. "Germany will not follow Hitler like a newborn colt does its mother," Father shouted. "We are a logical people. We will not so blindly follow a madman."

There was silence.

Then the other student spoke up. "It's a European problem, anyway. It won't affect us here." I could almost see Father nodding. He had said as much before.

"The Great War affected us here," James reminded them.

I set down my book and crept away, my thoughts in turmoil. Was another war like the Great War truly possible? What would this mean for my friends — for James? They were old enough to go to war now, if there were to be a war. I thanked God that Richard was such a young child still. If the worst happened, he would at least be safe. I prayed he would remain so.

The disobedient subject of my prayers was crouched outside the door, listening to every word. I scolded him in a whisper and marched him upstairs.

"Did you hear, Sylvia?" His eyes were shining as I tucked him into bed. "Maybe I could be a soldier like Uncle Richard."

"Yes, and get yourself killed like Uncle Richard." My voice was harsh. I pulled the blankets up to his chin, blinking back tears.

But here I've been going on and on about one evening when you wanted to know how James and I fell in love and married. Well, that was the first of many evenings he spent at our residence that semester. When we returned to Waterford, James wrote me at least once a week, and two years later he asked me to marry him. I made him wait two years more while I attended Waterford College to study art. I fancied myself an artist and wanted to be an art teacher someday, but I left college before receiving my degree. When I was twenty and James was twenty-two, we were married, and James joined our family at Elm Creek Manor.

"Claudia had not yet married," Mrs. Compson added. "My aunts said I should let her marry first since she was the eldest sister, but Father quickly silenced them. He was almost as fond of James as I was, and was eager for him to join the family."

"Was Claudia jealous?"

"No, at least, not always. She would have preferred to be the first to marry, but she rarely complained. Besides, the shy young man from the party — Harold — had found his tongue, and so we all thought her own wedding wouldn't be far behind."

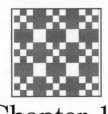

Chapter 16

After work Sarah baked brownies to take to the meeting of the Tangled Web Quilters. She followed Diane's map a few blocks south of campus to a neighborhood populated by Waterford College professors and administrators. The gray stone houses with their sloped roofs and Tudor woodwork looked like scaled-down versions of Elm Creek Manor. Their carefully landscaped front yards heightened the similarity, except that oak trees rather than elms lined the street.

As she parked the truck behind Judy's minivan, Sarah figured that few landscape architects and personal assistants to wealthy recluses lived nearby.

A walkway of red bricks in a herringbone pattern led from the driveway to the front porch. Sarah went up to the house and rapped on the front door with the brass knocker.

The door opened enough for a boy about thirteen years old to look out and study her. "Yeah?" He wore jeans several sizes too big for his slender frame and a baseball cap turned backward. His black T-shirt bore a grinning skull with fire streaming from the eye sockets.

"Hi," Sarah said. She heard the Tangled Web Quilters laughing somewhere inside. "I'm here to see your mom."

He sighed and looked over his shoulder. "Ma!" he bellowed.

Sarah winced and tried not to cover her ears.

The boy turned back to Sarah. "Summer with you?"

"No."

Disappointment crossed his face.

Sarah hid a smile. "She'll be here soon, probably."

He shrugged. "Whatever."

Just then Diane appeared behind him. "Leave her standing on the porch, why don't you," she grumbled to the boy, who rolled his eyes and shuffled away. Diane turned to Sarah and opened the door wider. "I see you've met the pride and joy."

Sarah smiled and went inside. "Just barely. I didn't catch his name."

"Michael. Except these days he prefers

to go by Mikey J." Diane led her along a carpeted hallway and downstairs to the basement. "He's okay, if you ignore the flaming skulls."

"I didn't know you had a son."

"Two, actually. The other's eleven, so he's still relatively normal."

In the finished half of the basement, the Tangled Web Quilters were gathered around a card table covered with snacks. Sarah added her plate of brownies to the lot. "How come every time I see you guys you're always standing next to the food?" she teased, by way of a greeting.

"You better hurry or there won't be anything left for you," Judy retorted. "Serves you right."

A few minutes later Summer burst into the room carrying a large plastic trash bag. "Hi, everybody. Sorry —"

"We know," Diane said. "Sorry you're late."

"I was here on time, but I was upstairs. Mike wanted to show me his new zip drive."

Gwen grinned. "Oh, so that's what the kids call it these days."

"You're sick, Mom. Mike's just a baby."

"Don't tell him that," Diane said. "You'll break his heart."

When everyone had sampled enough treats, they sat down in the sofas and chairs Diane had arranged. Sarah showed the others her new finished blocks, and they praised her progress.

Then Bonnie took a sheet of paper out of her sewing basket. "The president of the Waterford Quilting Guild dropped off a flyer at Grandma's Attic the other day. They're asking for volunteers to help set up for the Waterford Summer Quilt Festival."

"Can't they get their own people to do it?" Diane asked.

"I guess they need more help. Waterford College won't let them set up until the evening before the festival because there's some other display in the library atrium."

Summer shrugged and looked around the circle. "I'll go if some of you go."

"I can help," Sarah said.

"I'll go if it will help me win a ribbon," Diane said.

Everyone chuckled.

"You can have one of mine," Gwen offered.

"Thanks, but I'd rather earn my own, if I live that long."

Summer brushed some cookie crumbs off her lap and unfastened a twist-tie on the garbage bag. "While you guys were off having fun at quilt camp, I was getting some work done." She reached into the bag and pulled out a folded bundle.

"Oh, you finished piecing the Bear's Paw," Mrs. Emberly exclaimed. "Let's have a look at it."

Summer and Gwen each took two corners of the quilt top and held it open between them. Sarah could see where the pattern had earned its name, as it did resemble a bear's footprints. Summer had selected a different solid fabric for each of the twelve blocks, and the vivid colors stood out from the black background fabric. There were three rows of four blocks each, and a border of small isosceles right triangles surrounded them.

"Nice work," Diane said. "You can hardly tell it's machine pieced."

Summer rolled her eyes. "Gee, thanks." Then she turned a hopeful gaze on them all. "I thought maybe since we're all here, you could help me baste it?"

"Baste it?" Sarah asked. "You mean like a turkey?"

The others burst into laughter.

Sarah looked around in surprise. "What? What did I say?"

"I'm so glad you joined the Tangled Web

Quilters, Sarah," Gwen said, wiping her eyes.

"Now, stop teasing the poor girl," Mrs. Emberly admonished. "We were all new quilters once. Sarah, basting stitches are large stitches that hold something in place temporarily."

"You might baste an appliqué to the background fabric so that it stays put while you blind stitch it down," Judy said.

"But in this case, basting means sewing big stitches through the quilt top, batting, and backing fabric so that the three layers don't shift around while you're quilting them," Summer said. "Basting's actually kind of boring."

"A true quilter enjoys all stages of the quilting process," Diane said, and earned herself a chorus of groans.

Gwen shook her head. "You should've been a philosopher, you're so concerned with what's true."

"Well, who says I'm not? Maybe I'm a quilt philosopher."

Diane led them to a Ping-Pong table in another corner of the basement. After removing the net and the dust, Summer and Gwen placed a large piece of black fabric right side down on the table. Summer unrolled a sheet of thin cotton batting on the fabric, enlisting the group's help to smooth out the wrinkles. Sarah then helped her place the quilt top right side up on the batting.

"This is what we call a quilt sandwich," Gwen told Sarah.

Summer showed Sarah how to sew large, zigzag stitches through all three layers of the quilt. "I won't take out the basting until I finish quilting," she explained. "If you don't keep the layers smooth your quilt will be all wrinkly and puckered on the back."

Each of them threaded a needle and began basting a section of the quilt sandwich.

"How was quilt camp?" Bonnie asked.

Summer smiled. "Yeah, tell us all about it and make us jealous."

"Oh, it was even nicer than last year," Mrs. Emberly said.

Gwen, Diane, and Judy joined her in describing quilt camp: the classes they had taken, which nationally famous quilters had turned out to be equally skilled as teachers and which had not, and all the new quilts they were now inspired to make.

"It would have been more fun if you three had been able to come, too," Judy added.

Diane sighed. "It was such a treat to be able to spend the whole weekend quilting, without having to worry about getting somebody's dinner or cleaning house or doing the laundry —"

"Or checking papers or dealing with undergraduates or taking care of the kids," Gwen said. "No offense, Summer."

"None taken, Mom."

"Life is too short to worry about chores when there's important quilting to be done," Mrs. Emberly said, smiling. "Most people I know don't see it that way, though."

Gwen stopped basting and rested her elbows on the table. "Why do you suppose that is?"

Mrs. Emberly shrugged. "A sense of duty, I suppose."

"Or guilt," Bonnie said. "Sometimes people look critically at a woman who spends time on her hobbies when the carpet needs to be vacuumed."

"Yes, but think about it." Gwen rested her chin in her palm. "Who would criticize a male artist who spent the day painting or sculpting instead of mowing the lawn? Nobody, I bet. 'He's an artist; he must paint.' Or sculpt. Whatever. That's what they'd say."

"I think most people don't consider quilting to be art," Sarah said.

The others groaned in protest.

"Heresy," Gwen cried, laughing.

Diane frowned. "Of course it's art."

"I didn't say I feel that way, just that other people might."

"And why is that?" Gwen mused. "Consider that even today there are far more female quilters than male. Is quilting not considered art, then, because it's something women do, or are women allowed to quilt because it isn't considered art? Quilting does have a practical purpose, after all, so it could be said that the women are not creating art but are instead remaining within their acceptable domestic sphere —"

"All right, Professor," Diane broke in. "We aren't in one of your classes."

Sarah wondered how Mrs. Compson would respond to this discussion. "Of course it's art; what a question," she'd probably declare, and then stare down anyone who dared to disagree.

"Well." Bonnie sighed, tying a knot in her basting thread. "As far as I'm concerned, women need art at least as much as men do, even if no one sees their work but themselves. We all need to give ourselves that time and try to ignore other people's criticism if it comes."

"And we need to give ourselves that space," Judy said. "One of the nicest things about quilt camp was that we all had so much room to ourselves, to spread out our fabric and our templates and things without worrying about getting in someone else's way or having a baby crawl on a rotary cutter or needles."

"Time, space, and lots of friends — that's what you need to be a successful quilter," Summer said. She surveyed their work as Mrs. Emberly put the last basting stitch in the quilt sandwich, tied a knot, and cut the thread. "This would have taken me hours, but now it's all done. Thanks, everybody."

For the rest of the evening they worked on their own projects, and Sarah was able to finish the LeMoyne Star block. Gwen took a piece of paper out of her bag and gave it to Sarah. "This will tell Mrs. Compson everything she needs to know about the lecture," she said. "When, where, how long, all that. If she has any questions, though, she can give me a call."

"Thanks," Sarah said, tucking the note into her bag of quilting supplies. She knew Mrs. Compson couldn't and wouldn't call, but Sarah could carry messages if necessary.

Mrs. Emberly had looked up when Gwen mentioned Mrs. Compson. "Sarah, dear, is there any news about the sale of Elm Creek Manor?"

"Nothing as far as I know. Sorry, Mrs. Emberly."

"Oh, that's all right. Perhaps no news is good news. Perhaps she's decided not to sell after all."

"I wish she wouldn't," Sarah confided. "I tried to get her to join the Tangled Web Quilters, but —"

"You did what?" Diane demanded.

Startled, Sarah looked around at the others. Their expressions were guarded. "I — I'm sorry," Sarah said. She felt her face growing warm. "I thought that since I was a member I was allowed to invite others to join. I — I'm really sorry. I should have checked first."

"Please tell me she said no," Diane said.

"Well — yes. I mean, yes, she did say no."

"What a relief."

Mrs. Emberly drew herself up and gave Diane a sharp look. "I disagree. Have some compassion. She just lost her sister, and she's already lost so much in her life. I for one would welcome her into our group, and who here has more cause to exclude her than I?"

Abashed, Diane looked at the floor.

"She's right," Bonnie said. "I'll never forget how you all rallied around me when Craig was in the hospital last year. Whom does Sylvia Compson have?"

"Well, she must have someone," Diane muttered.

"Maybe she does and maybe she doesn't," Gwen said. She turned to Sarah. "You go ahead and ask anyone you want to join. Sylvia Compson or anyone."

The others nodded and murmured their agreement.

Sarah nodded, but felt herself withdrawing from the circle of friends, suspended in the middle between the Tangled Web Quilters and Mrs. Compson. She wanted Mrs. Compson to make friends in Waterford so that the friendships would encourage her to stay at Elm Creek Manor. But Diane — well, Diane seemed to enjoy having a recognizable enemy, a clear boundary between those who were good enough to get in and those who would be excluded. Mrs. Emberly was another mystery. Could she have been one of those Waterford girls who had been jealous of

Mrs. Compson's quilting and riding awards so many years ago?

Sarah sighed to herself. She wouldn't give up. The others seemed willing to welcome Mrs. Compson into the group, though it might be awkward at first. As for Diane, she would just have to get used to the idea.

If Mrs. Compson would agree to join. And if she wouldn't sell Elm Creek Manor and move away.

Chapter 17

The next morning, Sarah and Matt arrived at Elm Creek Manor to find a dark blue luxury car parked in their usual spot.

"Was Mrs. Compson expecting someone today?" Matt asked as they went up the back steps and into the manor.

"She didn't say anything to me. I hope nothing's wrong."

They hurried inside, calling Mrs. Compson's name. Her voice returned an unintelligible reply from somewhere in the west wing. To their relief, they found her seated on an upholstered armchair in the formal parlor, sipping coffee. A thin, dark-haired man in a black pinstriped suit was with her.

Mrs. Compson smiled warmly when she spotted them in the doorway. "Ah. There they are. Matthew and Sarah, come meet Mr. Gregory Krolich from University Realty."

Matt and Sarah exchanged a quick look as the man stood to greet them.

"How do you do," he said, smiling. His ring bit into Sarah's hand when he shook it. "Mrs. Compson has been telling me how much you two have been helping her lately."

"Oh, yes indeed. We'll have this place looking wonderful in no time," Mrs. Compson said. "They're both such good workers."

"I'm sure they are. I've heard a lot of good things about Exterior Architects." He smiled ruefully at Matt. "I guess I can't enlist your help, then."

Matt looked puzzled. "My help for what?"

"I'm trying to convince Mrs. Compson that the restoration isn't necessary."

"And I find his argument contrary to everything I've ever heard about selling a home," Mrs. Compson said.

Matt smiled. "Sorry, Mr. Krolich. I'm afraid I have to side with Mrs. Compson on this one. I'm not about to bite the hand that feeds me."

"Please, call me Greg," Krolich urged. "Just my luck. It's three against one. Unless . . . ?" He turned to Sarah. "You're an accountant, right? Help me explain the economics of the situation to your friend here."

His tone wasn't patronizing, not exactly, but it irritated her just the same. "Economics? Well, I'm not in real estate, but I guess you could offer Mrs. Compson less if the manor isn't yet fully restored, right?"

Mrs. Compson turned to Krolich. "Is that what's behind all this?"

He chuckled and held up his palms in defense. "Mrs. Compson, I assure you, I know how much Elm Creek Manor is worth. I'd be a fool to insult you by offering anything less than a fair price. I just hate to see you invest money in restoration when you're planning to sell the place. Save your money for your new home."

"Hmph." Mrs. Compson eyed him. "I think that's my decision, to dispose of my money how I see fit."

"You're right, you're right." He smiled agreeably. "I shouldn't butt in. Especially when you have such ardent defenders." He turned his smile on Sarah. "You have to admire someone who wants the best for her friends. That's the kind of business instinct you'll need in Waterford. You don't get far in a small town like this by making enemies."

"Thank you," Sarah replied. Then she

thought about his words and wondered if he really had complimented her.

"What are your career plans for after the manor sells?" Krolich asked Sarah.

"Now, don't you get any ideas," Mrs. Compson warned. "You'll have to be patient. I plan to keep Sarah very busy for the next few months."

"I'll wait my turn." Krolich chuckled. He reached into his breast pocket and retrieved a business card, which he handed to Sarah. "Give me a call when you're available, will you?"

Sarah fingered the card without looking at it. "I don't know anything about real estate."

"I wasn't thinking of my department. We'll try to find something for you in accounting."

"Okay. Thank you." Then she thought of something. "Could you tell me more about your company? University Realty manages student rental properties, right?"

He blinked, but his smile never wavered. "Why, yes. We do run many student properties."

"All of your properties are student rentals, right?"

"Currently, they are." His voice took on a slight edge.

Mrs. Compson looked from Krolich to Sarah and back. "What does this mean? Are you planning to turn Elm Creek Manor into some kind of frat house?"

"Certainly not. Nothing of the sort. We screen all our potential student renters very carefully. We get references, parents' addresses, all that."

Mrs. Compson drew in a sharp breath and shook her head. "I realize the number of bedrooms and baths might seem to lend itself towards that sort of thing, but you see, I couldn't bear to think of drunken undergraduates swinging from the chandeliers or performing hazing rituals in the gardens —"

"I assure you, that will never happen."

"How can you guarantee that?" Sarah asked. "Are you planning to move in and baby-sit?"

Krolich focused two steely eyes on her. "You're not long out of college yourself, are you? Would you have been swinging from the chandeliers if you'd been able to live in a place like this?"

"Of course not, but I appreciate —"

"Well, there you have it." He turned back to Mrs. Compson. "And most college students are as pleasant as your friend Sarah here. It's not fair to stereotype." He glanced at Sarah over his shoulder. "We mustn't alarm people unnecessarily."

"No one's getting alarmed as far as I can see," Matt said. "We're just asking a few questions. Mrs. Compson doesn't have to sell to you if she doesn't think you'll take care of the place."

Krolich looked wounded. "I don't know where all of this is coming from. I assure you, University Realty has an outstanding reputation in this community."

Mrs. Compson waved her hand impatiently. "Yes, yes, of course you do. No one is questioning your character or your company's willingness to properly care for a historic building."

I am, Sarah thought as she studied him.

His eyes told her he had noted her gaze, but his expression remained amiable. "Thank you for the coffee, Mrs. Compson, but I must be going. Please look over those papers, and we'll discuss them soon. No, no, I'll show myself out," he hastened to add as Mrs. Compson began to rise from her seat. He shook her hand and picked up his attaché case. He gave Sarah one last smile as he left the room. "Think about that job, will you?"

When he had gone, Mrs. Compson sighed and leaned back in her chair. A troubled frown lingered on her face, and her eyes were tired. "It's not that I want to see Elm Creek Manor become student apartments," she told them. "That certainly wasn't what I had in mind. I thought — well, a nice family, perhaps, with children . . ."

"You don't have to decide right now," Sarah said after Mrs. Compson's voice trailed off.

"I have to decide soon." Mrs. Compson stood and briskly smoothed her skirt. "They've made a reasonable offer, one I'd be foolish to simply disregard."

"What should I do about the outdoor restoration?" Matt asked.

Mrs. Compson thought for a moment. "Continue. He may use the unfinished work as an excuse to reduce his offer later, regardless of what he says now."

So Mrs. Compson didn't trust Krolich either, at least not completely. Sarah picked up the two coffee cups and carried them into the kitchen, then joined Mrs. Compson in the front foyer. Matt kissed Sarah good-bye and left for the north gardens.

As they worked upstairs, Sarah and Mrs. Compson made only a few halfhearted attempts at conversation. Sometimes, out of the corner of her eye, Sarah would see Mrs. Compson's hands drop from her work as she stared unseeing at some corner of the room.

Sarah watched and wished she could think of the right words to convince Mrs. Compson not to sell her home.

At noon Matt joined them for lunch. Sarah longed to take him aside and get his opinion about Krolich when Mrs. Compson couldn't overhear, but she didn't get an opportunity. During the meal no one mentioned the real estate agent or the manor's impending sale, and to Sarah it seemed as if the others were ignoring the morning's events. She couldn't decide if that made her disappointed or relieved.

After Matt left, Sarah remembered Gwen's notes. Mrs. Compson spread them out on the kitchen table and looked them over, nodding. "Everything seems to be arranged," she remarked. "On Gwen's end, at least. I still need to work on my own presentation if I am to be ready by the ninth. That's a Tuesday, I think."

"I didn't know it was going to be so soon."

"Soon? We have more than a week. We'll be ready. Don't worry." Mrs. Compson smiled reassuringly. "Perhaps that's what we should work on today. That may shake off our gloom."

Sarah nodded. Gregory Krolich sure knew how to ruin a perfectly good summer day. Knowing Elm Creek Manor was going to be sold was bad, and knowing it was going to be turned into student apartments was worse. But there was something else, something Krolich wasn't telling them. Or maybe it was all in Sarah's mind. Maybe she was just looking for reasons to dislike him.

"So. You don't care for our Mr. Krolich," Mrs. Compson suddenly said.

Sarah looked up, surprised.

"Oh, don't worry, dear. You haven't said anything, and I appreciate that, but your feelings are as clear as could be."

"I don't fully trust him," Sarah admitted. "But I don't know if I could like anyone who took Elm Creek Manor away from you."

"Away from you, you mean."

"That's silly. Elm Creek Manor isn't mine to begin with."

"Of course it is." Mrs. Compson reached across the table and patted Sarah's arm. "You've worked here, quilted here, heard the stories of its former occupants — though not all of its former occupants, and not all of its stories. That makes Elm Creek Manor partly yours, too."

"If Elm Creek Manor is partly mine, then I'm not selling my part."

Mrs. Compson chuckled. "I know how you feel. I don't want to sell my part, either."

"Then why are you talking to a real estate agent? If you don't want to sell, don't."

"It's not that simple." Mrs. Compson clasped her hands, fingers interlaced, and rested them on the table. "At first, I thought I wanted to sell. I admit that much. But since I've spent more time here, with you and Matthew, I've found that this is indeed my home and that I've missed it very much."

Sarah jumped to her feet. "Then let's get this settled," she exclaimed. "Matt has a car phone. I'll run out to the orchard and call this Krolich guy and tell him to forget it. I'm so glad you decided to stay, I —"

Mrs. Compson was shaking her head.

"What? What is it?"

Mrs. Compson motioned for Sarah to sit down. "It's not that I want to sell Elm Creek Manor; I have to sell it."

"Have to? Why? Is it —"

"No, it's not the money, and let's leave it at that."

"I can't leave it at that. You know how much I want you to stay. Can't you at least explain why you won't?"

"Not won't, can't," Mrs. Compson said. "You're a very demanding young woman, aren't you?"

"When I have to be."

"Oh, very well. Though I doubt if my explanation will satisfy you, here it is. Elm Creek Manor was great once. The Bergstroms made it great. But now —" She sighed and looked around the room. "Well, you see what it is now. Emptiness. Disrepair. And I am responsible for its decline."

"How can you blame yourself?" Sarah asked. "Claudia's the one who let things go. You weren't even here."

"Precisely. I should have been here. Bergstrom Thoroughbreds was my responsibility and I abandoned it. Oh, I didn't see it that way at the time, and I didn't know Claudia would fare so poorly. But that's no excuse. Elm Creek Manor will never be what it once was, and I can't bear to live here, reminded every day of what has been lost."

Sarah reached across the table and took Mrs. Compson's hand. "That's not true. You, me, and Matt — together we're going to make this place as beautiful as ever. You'll see."

"Hmph." Mrs. Compson gave her a fond, wistful look. "We can restore its beauty but not its greatness. Perhaps you're too young to understand the difference."

She squeezed Sarah's hand, then let go. "The only right action is for me to pass the estate to another family who will make the place live again. I have no direct descendants, only second and third cousins scattered who knows where around the country. I'm the only Bergstrom left, and I can't bring Elm Creek Manor back to life by myself. I'm not strong enough, and I don't have enough time left to reverse the effects of years."

Mrs. Compson paused. "Perhaps it would be best to let Krolich hand it over to the students. A bunch of young people certainly would liven up the place, and that's what I said I wanted, didn't I? What do you suppose old Great-Grandfather Hans would think of that?" She laughed quietly.

Sarah couldn't join in. "If Elm Creek Manor does comes back to life, don't you want to be here for it?"

Mrs. Compson said nothing.

"I think you're being too hard on yourself."

"I could never be too hard on myself in

this matter." Her voice was crisp. "That's enough of this. Let's go to the library and take care of my lecture materials. I have several boxes of slides to sort through. When we're finished, we can have a quilt lesson. I believe you said you're ready to start a new block?"

Sarah saw that the confidences were over, for now. "I finished the LeMoyne Star last night."

"Good. Good." Mrs. Compson rose and left the kitchen.

Sarah followed her upstairs, thoughts racing and worries growing.

Chapter 18

The several boxes of slides turned out to be four large cartons of slides, photographs, and newspaper clippings. Mrs. Compson explained that for over thirty years she had photographed every quilt she had made.

"Gwen's lucky you brought all this with you from Sewickley," Sarah said.

"Luck has nothing to do with it. I still have some of these quilts, but most of them have been sold or given away. I'd no sooner leave this record of my life's work unattended than I'd sleep outside in a snowstorm."

As Mrs. Compson opened the first box of slides, Sarah unfolded one of the newspaper clippings. The headline announced WATERFORD QUILTING GUILD TO RAFFLE 'VICTORY QUILT.' Beneath it was a photo of several women holding up a quilt pieced from small hexagons.

"Are you in this picture?" Sarah asked.

"What do you have there?" Mrs. Compson took the clipping. "Oh, goodness. Wasn't that a long time ago." She pointed to one of the women. "That's me, holding on to the corner."

Sarah looked closely at the slender young woman in the photo. She was holding her chin up and looking straight into the camera, a determined expression on her face. "What's a Victory Quilt?"

"It's not a particular block pattern, if that's what you mean. That's a Grandmother's Flower Garden quilt."

"It looks like a honeycomb."

Mrs. Compson laughed. "I suppose it does. The small pieces were well suited to using up scraps, though, and with the war on, not even the Bergstroms could afford to waste a single thread. We ladies made this quilt and raffled it off to raise money for the war effort. You can't see it in this picture, but each of the light-colored hexagons was embroidered with the name of a local boy in the service. We stitched a gold star near his name if he had given up his life for his country." She sighed and handed back the clipping. "We embroidered so many gold stars that summer."

Sarah studied the picture a little while longer before returning it to the box.

"Let's see, now," Mrs. Compson said as she took a slide and held it up to the light. "Yes, this is a good one. Sarah, take that slide projector wheel out of that box and dust it off, would you? This slide should be the first."

Two hours passed as Mrs. Compson examined slides, considered them, and either rejected them or told Sarah where to place them in the slide projector wheel. Mrs. Compson explained that she planned to discuss the history of quilting. The slides would show Gwen's students how quilting had changed over time and how it had stayed the same.

"Are you going to tell them the Wandering Foot story?"

"Yes, and perhaps a few others like it, if there's time." Then Mrs. Compson sighed and pushed the last carton away. "That's all the slides I'll need. I'll prepare my lecture notes another day, but now it's time for another quilt lesson."

They put away the cartons and returned to the sewing room, where Sarah got out her template-making supplies.

"This time I'll show you how to make the Bachelor's Puzzle block," Mrs. Compson said, a smile flickering in the corners of her mouth.

"What's so funny?" Sarah asked, wondering if there was a superstition attached to this block, too. Next thing she knew, Mrs. Compson would be telling her that a quilt with a Bachelor's Puzzle block in it would doom the maker to eternal unemployment.

Mrs. Compson's smile broadened. "It's nothing, really. An inside joke between Claudia and me. Not a very nice joke, I'm ashamed to say."

"Don't keep me in suspense. What's the joke?"

"I did say you didn't know all of the manor's stories or all of its occupants," Mrs. Compson murmured as if thinking aloud. "And she was a very important person here once." She sighed and focused on Sarah again, her cheeks slightly pink, her expression almost embarrassed. "Very well, I'll explain while we work on this new block. But I'll warn you, this story puts me in a rather bad light. I admit I was not always kind when I was younger."

"Gee, that's hard to believe," Sarah replied in a dry tone rivaling Mrs. Compson's own.

★ ★ ★

As I told you before, Richard was not fond of school. If Father had not repeatedly told him that he must have a proper education if he wished to run Bergstrom Thoroughbreds someday, he probably wouldn't have gone at all. Our semester at the Pennsylvania State College had not satisfied his thirst for travel and adventure, either. Richard often complained to me that Waterford High School was stifling him, the teachers were horrendous, the town was dull, et cetera, et cetera. When Richard turned sixteen, he and Father reached a compromise: if Richard kept his marks up, he would be allowed to attend school in Philadelphia.

"If you blame this on that baby quilt," my sister told me when we heard the news, "I'll never forgive you."

"Why, Claudia, I haven't said a word," I replied, all innocence. My amusement lasted only a moment, however. The thought of Richard's absence left me feeling hollow inside. I tried my best to feel happy for him, but I could never be so, not entirely.

So Richard went to Philadelphia to continue his education. Father had friends in the city who agreed to take him in while he was in school, so my worrying about him was really quite unwarranted. He wrote to me often, and when I read his letters aloud to Claudia and the rest of the family, it eased our hearts but made us miss him all the more.

Fortunately, James was there to brighten my spirits. He and Father were two of a kind — kindhearted, virtuous, determined men. With James's help, Bergstrom Thoroughbreds was better than it had ever been. James handled many of the more dangerous tasks that were now becoming more difficult for Father.

We had been married three years, each day happier than the last. What carefree times we had then. But of course you know what I mean, being newly married yourself, and to such a fine young man as Matthew. We were eager for children, and even after three years we weren't worried. James would always stroke my head and tell me that we had all the time in the world, that we had forever. Young brides still like to hear that sort of thing, I suppose.

So, as much as Richard's departure made my heart ache, I knew he would return when his education was complete. Maybe he would even be an uncle by then, I would think to myself, hiding a smile so that Claudia wouldn't pester me to share my thoughts. Remember, too, that it was the autumn of 1943. With so many families losing brothers and sons every day, I had no right to complain when my brother was merely away at school.

After what seemed like the longest time, the Christmas holidays finally approached. You can imagine the bustle and excitement around here then. Christmas at Elm Creek Manor was always such a lovely time, but now we had the added joy of Richard's homecoming. We had to be more creative than ever with our celebrations, due to rationing and shortages and all that, but we pushed troubling thoughts from our minds for a while. Richard was coming home at last.

On the day of his arrival, the family's impatience and expectation seemed to fill the house. All day I paced around, taking care of last-minute preparations and moving from window to window, looking out through the falling snow for him. Suddenly one of the cousins ran downstairs from the nursery shouting that a car was coming up the drive.

It seemed as if everyone was in the front entry at once, laughing and arguing over who would get to open the door for him,

271

who would get to take his coat, who would get to sit next to him at dinner. Father reached the door first, with me at his elbow. Father swung open the door, and there he was.

"Richard," I cried, leaping forward to embrace him. And then I froze.

A small figure peeked out from behind him. The biggest blue eyes I had ever seen peered up at me from beneath a white fur hood, the rest of the small face hidden behind a thick woolen muffler.

"Well, sis? Are you going to let us in or keep us standing out here in the snow?" Richard demanded, grinning at me as I stood there gaping. He took the bundled-up figure by the elbow and guided her into the house, giving me a quick peck on the cheek as he passed.

I followed them inside, still dumb-founded. Everyone tried to hug Richard at once, and their welcomes created quite a din. The bundled figure stood apart, looking anxiously from one strange face to the next.

Then Richard broke free from the crowd and turned to his companion. "Still bun-dled up, are you?" he teased gently, and the eyes seemed to smile over the muffler. Mittened hands fumbled clumsily with the hood and the coat buttons. Richard shrugged off his own coat and began to help.

The family fell silent. Even the little cousins watched them expectantly. Richard turned to face us, draping their wraps over his arm. "Everyone, I'd like you to meet my — I'd like you to meet Agnes Chevalier." He said her name just like that — Ahn-YES instead of the normal way, AGnes.

"Hello," Agnes said, her smile trembling a little. I already told you she had the biggest blue eyes I had ever seen. She also had the longest, darkest hair I had ever seen, longer than mine, even. Her skin was so fair, except where the cold had brought roses to her cheeks, and she was so small that the top of her head barely reached my shoulder. I remember thinking she looked just like a little porcelain doll.

"Welcome to Elm Creek Manor, Agnes," Claudia said, stepping forward to take their things. She handed them to a cousin with instructions that they were to be hung someplace where they would dry. Then she turned to Richard and Agnes, placing an arm around the tiny girl's shoulders. "Let's get you two by a nice warm fire, shall we?" As she guided Agnes down the hallway toward the parlor, two cousins seized Richard's hands and pulled him after them.

Father and I trailed along behind the crowd. We exchanged a quick glance, enough to confirm that the other had not known about Richard's traveling companion either.

As they warmed themselves with hot tea and warm quilts, Richard told us that Agnes was the sister of a classmate, and they had met when he went to his friend's home for dinner two months before. Her father was a successful attorney and her mother was from an enormously wealthy and prominent political family — although Richard put it more politely than I have done. They had been distressed to learn that they would not be spending the holidays with their only daughter, but they sent the Bergstroms their warmest holiday wishes.

"Maybe Agnes should be put back on the next train to Philadelphia to spend Christmas with her own family," I whispered to Claudia. I said the girl's name AG-nes, without the affected French pronunciation.

Claudia sighed. "We'll get to the bottom of this soon enough, but in the meantime, you mustn't be rude." She turned away from me and smiled brightly across the room at our unexpected guest.

It wasn't until the next afternoon that I was able to pull Richard aside for a private chat. "Isn't she just wonderful, Sylvia?" he exclaimed, his eyes dazzled. "She's just the best girl I ever met. I couldn't wait for you to meet her."

"Why didn't you say anything in any of your letters?"

Richard looked abashed. "I knew you'd tell Claudia and Father, and I didn't want them to think I was neglecting my studies. I haven't been," he hastily added, probably seeing my eyebrows rise in inquiry. "My marks are good, and I'm learning a lot, I think." He hesitated. "She's only fifteen. I know she's just a kid, but she's really special, and —"

"And you're just sixteen yourself, too young to be serious about a girl. What were her parents thinking, letting her travel across the state unchaperoned like that?"

Richard scowled. "You know me better than that. I'd never take advantage of a girl."

"Hmph. Maybe she'd take advantage of you." He bristled, and I held up a hand in apology. "Sorry. That was uncalled for. But goodness, Richard, couldn't you have given us some kind of warning?"

He grinned, and looked over his shoulder as footsteps approached. "I know you'll love her, too, once you get to know her," he whispered, giving my hand a squeeze before sauntering down the hall.

You can imagine how I felt about that. "You'll love her, too," he'd said, which meant that he loved her, or at least he thought he did. I squared my shoulders and returned to the rest of the family, hoping for the best.

Before long, I determined that just as surely as Agnes was the prettiest girl I had ever seen, she was also the silliest, most spoiled, and most childish creature ever to step foot into Elm Creek Manor.

She pouted if her tea was too cold, then batted her eyelashes at Richard until he leaped up to fetch her a fresh cup, only to send him racing back to the kitchen again because he had added too much sugar. We gave her the finest guest room, only to hear that it was "unbearably cold, not like in Philadelphia." She picked at her food, remarking that one could not expect to find Philadelphia's fine cookery so far out here in the country. She would try to participate in dinner conversation, prefacing each inane chirping remark with "Papa says . . ."

And the way Richard treated her, as if she were made of priceless, delicate china, giving her the best seat nearest the fire, carrying everything for her, taking her arm as she went upstairs, hanging on to her every word as if it fell from the lips of Shakespeare himself — my, it was tiresome.

I was not the only one who found her insufferable. We adults would exchange amazed looks at each new piece of foolishness, and even the children screwed up their faces in bewilderment as they looked from their favorite cousin to this strange creature from the apparently heavenly land of Philadelphia. We all pondered the same question: yes, she's lovely to look at, but what on earth does our dear Richard see in her?

James warned me that I had better get used to her, just in case Agnes became a permanent addition to the family. Oh, I tried to like her, and I vowed to keep my feelings hidden for Richard's sake. Surely, I told myself, once we knew Agnes better, we would come to see her as Richard did.

One afternoon Claudia and I invited her to join us as we quilted. "How charming," she exclaimed, fingering the edge of my latest quilt. Do you remember the pictures of the Baltimore Album style quilts I showed you? Well, that's what I was working on then. I much prefer piecing to the intricate appliqué required for that style, but one of my closest school friends was planning to be married in the spring. This style was not quite as fashionable as others then, but it was my friend's favorite. The quilt was going to be a surprise, you see. Her husband-to-be was fighting in Europe, and they were to be wed as soon as he came home.

But as I was saying, Agnes fingered the edge of my quilt and exclaimed, "How charming." Then she added, "In Philadelphia we can buy our own blankets, but I don't suppose you can do that out here in the country, can you?"

I removed the edge of the quilt from her tiny, grasping hand. "Quite right. There isn't a single store within a hundred miles of here. I hope you remembered to pack everything."

"Sylvia." Claudia's voice held a note of warning.

"Really?" Agnes's mouth fell open in a way that made her look quite foolish. "Not a single store?"

"Not a one," I replied. "In fact, I had never even heard of a store until Richard described them to me in one of his letters. At first I thought he was just making them up, but Father told me he was telling the truth. To me it sounded like the stuff of fairy tales, but then, I've never been to Philadelphia." I picked up my needle and continued sewing.

Out of the corner of my eye I could see Agnes staring at me in confusion, her cheeks growing pink. Then she turned on her heel and flounced out of the room.

"Sylvia, that wasn't very nice."

"After that remark, she's lucky I didn't say worse. Why make a quilt when you can just buy a blanket? Honestly."

"I agree she could be more tactful, but even so —"

"What does Richard see in her?"

"I don't know. It's a puzzle."

"She's the puzzle," I retorted, and that's how it started. From that time on, whenever Claudia or I referred to Agnes, we called her Bachelor's Puzzle. Sometimes we called her BP, or the Puzzle, as in "I wonder if Richard will bring the Puzzle home for spring break?" or "Richard writes that he and BP are going to the Winter Ball." Or "Dear me, I hope Bachelor's Puzzle can remember her own name today, indeed I do."

We never said it to her, or when anyone else other than Claudia and I could hear. But we said it all the same, and it wasn't very nice, and I'll never forgive myself for giving her that dreadful nickname.

"Sounds to me like she deserved it," Sarah said, laughing.

"Oh, no, not you, too," Mrs. Compson protested, joining in. "It isn't nice to laugh at other people, even if they are silly, foolish creatures. Especially not then." She wiped tears from the corners of her eyes.

"What did Richard say when Agnes told him about it?"

Mrs. Compson stopped laughing. "He never said anything, so I assume she didn't tell him." She fixed Sarah with a studious gaze. "And now, young lady, it's your turn."

"My turn for what?"

"I'm tired of doing all the talking around here. Now it's your turn to answer some questions."

Sarah shifted in her seat. "What kind of questions?"

"Let's start with your family. What about your parents? Any brothers or sisters?"

"No, I'm an only child. So's Matt. My father died years ago." Sarah paused.

"Your stories are much more interesting than anything I could tell. I don't see why you'd be interested —"

"Indulge me. Did your mother ever re-marry?"

"No, but she's probably set a world record for the number of boyfriends held in a single lifetime. Does that count?"

"Ah. I see I've struck a nerve." Mrs. Compson leaned forward. "Why does that bother you?"

"It doesn't bother me. She can date whomever she likes as far as I'm concerned. It doesn't affect me or my life."

"Quite right. Of course not." Mrs. Compson cocked her head to one side and smiled knowingly.

Sarah tried not to fidget. "You know, Matt and I were talking —"

"About why you're angry with your mother?"

"No. I mean, of course not. I'm not angry with her. What makes you say that?"

"Tell me about her."

"Well . . . she's a nurse, and she kind of looks like me except she has shorter hair, and she and my dad met at a bowling alley, and now she likes to take expensive trips that her boyfriends pay for. Really, there's not much to say."

"Sarah?"

"What?"

"Your storytelling abilities leave much to be desired."

"Thanks."

"Perhaps you might as well tell me what you and Matthew were discussing instead."

Sarah paused for a moment, wondering if Mrs. Compson really did intend to let her off the hook that easily. "Matt and I were wondering if you'd like to celebrate the Fourth of July with us. Bonnie Markham says there's going to be a parade downtown, an outdoor concert on the square, and a quilt show on campus. We'd like to go, and we thought you'd like to join us, maybe?"

"I think I'd like that very much." Mrs. Compson looked pleased. "And since I entered a quilt in that show myself, I suppose I ought to see how it fared."

Chapter 19

Early the next week Sarah finished cleaning two more suites in the south wing and started a new block, Posies Round the Square. Mrs. Compson warned her that this block would be the most difficult by far since it required two new piecing techniques: sewing curved seams and appliqué.

Forewarned though she was, Sarah still found herself becoming frustrated. As she gritted her teeth and attempted for the third time to join the same convex blue piece to the same concave background piece without stretching the bias edges out of place, Sarah decided that sewing a straight seam was to sewing a curved seam as brushing her teeth was to having emergency root canal. Her skills improved by the time she finished the block, however, so she admitted that curved seams were pretty, and they did create many new design possibilities. Still, she didn't want to sew any more curved seams anytime soon.

She found appliqué easier. Mrs. Compson instructed her to cut the leaf-shaped piece from the darkest fabric, but to add a seam allowance of only an eighth of an inch this time. Sarah basted the appliqué in place on the background fabric, and after securing the thread with a knot, she used the tip of her needle to tuck the raw edge of the appliqué under as she sewed it down. Sarah was pleased to see that her stitches were virtually invisible from the front of the block, and that the curves of the leaf were smooth and the two points were sharp. Before long she added a second leaf and two concentric circles resembling a flower to the design.

Sarah finished the Posies Round the Square and started a new appliqué block called Lancaster Rose on Wednesday, the same day she planned to meet the Tangled Web Quilters after work to help set up for the Waterford Summer Quilt Festival.

After sharing a quick supper with Matt, Sarah drove to the Waterford College campus, hoping she'd be able to find a parking space on the main street near the front gates, where she planned to meet Summer. To her dismay she found most of the streets adjacent to campus blocked off by blaze-orange sawhorses as city workers assembled refreshment stands and bleachers along the parade route. Finally she found an empty spot designed for a compact car and somehow managed to maneuver the pickup into it. By the time she locked the truck and ran to the meeting place, Summer was already there.

"Hi, Sarah," Summer called when she came into view, jumping up from the bench where she had been waiting. Her long auburn hair swung lightly around her shoulders.

"I'm really sorry I'm late," Sarah said, catching her breath. "Will the quilting guild still let us in?"

Summer laughed. "You're only a few minutes late. Don't worry so much. They wouldn't make us sit outside when there's so much work to do. The rest of the Tangled Webbers are already there."

The two young women hurried up the hill to the library. Sarah had never been there, but Summer claimed to have spent the equivalent of one third of her life within its walls. A security guard waved them through the turnstile when Summer flashed her student ID and explained their errand.

Once inside, Summer led Sarah around a corner and through a set of glass double doors into a long, spacious gallery. Four skylights down the center of the high ceiling left squares of light on the gleaming parquet floor. On the long wall to their left hung several portraits of library benefactors, while the opposite wall was covered almost entirely by rectangular, mirrored-glass windows separated by thin steel frames. Sarah could see the grassy hill crisscrossed by sidewalks sloping toward the main street, but the students outside would see only their own reflections. The dark tint would allow enough sunlight in to brighten the room without fading the colors of the quilts that would soon be displayed there.

Fifty or more women of all ages had gathered in several scattered groups throughout the gallery, their conversations creating a sonorous hum occasionally punctuated by bursts of laughter. At the far end of the room several women were setting up folding tables and covering them with colorful print fabric. In the middle of the room, armchairs and loveseats had been pushed aside to make room for what looked like stacks of lumber. In a group of helpers near one of the piles, Sarah and

Summer easily spotted Gwen's red hair standing out among the blonds, browns, blacks, and grays of the Tangled Web Quilters surrounding her.

They joined their friends. Summer greeted her mother with a hug and a kiss on the cheek. As Gwen laughed and brushed her daughter's hair out of her eyes, Sarah felt a pang of envy. She wondered what it would be like to have a mother who was also a friend. Summer and Gwen were always doing things together, but Sarah couldn't spend more than fifteen minutes with her mother without feeling exhausted and strained, as if every detail of her life had been dissected and denounced.

She realized she was grinding her back molars just thinking about it, and made herself relax.

The others were poking through the nearest stack of boards and chatting, and Sarah pretended she had been listening all along. She noticed that the boards were cut to specific lengths, and some of the pieces had notches carved into their ends.

"The first thing you need to do is take one of these long poles," Bonnie was saying as she pulled a long piece of wood from the pile. "Attach four of these feet so that the pole will stand up."

"I'll sort out the pile while you younger girls take care of the lifting," Mrs. Emberly said.

"Then you assemble another pole and put the crossbar across the top," Bonnie continued. "It should fit into the notches."

"Will we drape the quilts over the crossbars?" Sarah asked.

"Each quilt will have a hanging sleeve, a tube of fabric sewn on the back," Judy said. "We'll take down the crossbar, slide it into the hanging sleeve, and then put the bar back up."

"It's kind of like hanging curtains with a curtain rod, only heavier," Summer added.

The Tangled Web Quilters got to work. When they had finished three quilt stands, a tall woman wearing her dark brown hair in a pageboy cut waved to them from across the room.

"Get ready for inspection," Gwen said as the woman approached.

"Just ignore her and maybe she'll go away," Diane hissed.

"Be nice," Bonnie said. "It isn't easy to run a quilt show."

Sarah didn't have time to ask who the woman was before she reached them. "We're so glad you could make it," she exclaimed. She squinted at their quilt stands. "How are things going over here?"

"Just fine, Mary Beth," Bonnie said.

Mary Beth grasped the nearest pole and shook it. "Seems sturdy enough. Maybe a little wobbly."

Diane frowned. "No one will be grabbing the poles like that during the show, so we're probably safe."

"Oh, you'd be surprised. You wouldn't believe some of the things we've seen at these shows. Someone could trip and fall, bump into a pole and knock it on someone's head, and then it's lawsuit city."

"We'll be sure they're safe before you put the quilts on them," Judy said.

"That's all we ask," Mary Beth said. "When you're done, we'll double-check them just to be sure." She smiled and hurried across the room to inspect another group.

"Must she refer to herself as 'we'?" Diane grumbled.

Gwen grinned. "You're just annoyed because she's been guild president six years in a row." She turned to Sarah. "After her first two years, Diane offered to take over —"

"I thought she might want a break from it, that's all. It's a lot of work."

"— but Mary Beth took it the wrong way."

"She acted like Diane was plotting a military overthrow," Judy said.

"That's because it looked like I was going to win."

Mrs. Emberly sighed. "It was quite unpleasant. At the meeting before the election, Mary Beth stood up in the front of the room and asked us if we'd feel comfortable putting the guild and the Waterford Summer Quilt Festival in the hands of someone who had never won a ribbon."

"How mean," Sarah exclaimed. "What did you do?"

"You won't believe this," Gwen said. "Diane just laughed it off."

"Until after the meeting, that is," Summer said. "Then she totally blew up. I'd tell you what she said, but Mom covered up my ears for most of it."

"I did not."

"Soon after that, and not coincidentally, our bee seceded from the Waterford Quilting Guild," Judy explained. "We still enter our quilts in the shows and help out with various projects, but for weekly meetings, we prefer our own little group."

"Most guilds aren't so political," Bonnie

said. "And not everyone in the Waterford Quilting Guild is like Mary Beth. You'll find that out when you get to know them."

That evening, though, Sarah was too busy to meet anyone new. Several hours passed as she and the other Tangled Web Quilters assembled the large wooden stands and moved them into rows. The wooden pieces were heavy, and after a while Sarah began to grow weary.

When the last stands were in place, Mary Beth went to the front of the room and waved her arms in the air to get everyone's attention. "Thanks again for all your help," she called out. "We'll see you tomorrow at the quilt show. Now we have to ask everyone who isn't on the Festival Committee to leave, please. Thanks again."

The helpers began to move toward the doors.

Even though it was almost midnight, Sarah was dismayed. "But I wanted to see the quilts," she protested as the Tangled Web Quilters went outside. They headed down the hill to the main street where Sarah and Gwen had parked their cars; the others lived close enough to campus to walk home.

"Only members of the Festival Committee are allowed to see the quilts before the show opens tomorrow," Summer explained. "They'll hang the quilts and get them ready for the judges."

"How will they decide who gets a ribbon?"

"There are six categories according to style and size, with ribbons for first, second, and third place in each category. Then there's Best of Show, which means exactly that: the best quilt out of all categories. Each of the four judges also gets to pick a Judge's Choice, and then there's Viewers' Choice. If you get to the show early enough you get to vote for your favorite quilt."

"How early?" Sarah asked, thinking about Mrs. Compson's entry.

"Before ten. My mom won one of those a few years ago, and she said it was the highest honor any one of her quilts had ever received."

"That's because judges' methods are utterly inscrutable," Gwen said. "You might make an absolutely stunning quilt, but a judge might disregard it if you quilted it by machine rather than by hand, or for some other reason whose grounds are wholly personal."

Bonnie sighed. "Now Gwen, be fair."

"Who's not being fair? I didn't mean to suggest that judges make arbitrary choices, just that matters of personal taste strongly influence how we evaluate art. That being the case, I'd prefer the appreciation of a broad range of people, quilters and nonquilters alike, rather than the stamp of approval from a few select so-called experts."

"Mom's had some conflict with judges in the past," Summer explained to Sarah in an undertone.

"I never would've guessed."

"Then again," Gwen mused, "the Viewers' Choice ribbon poses problems of its own. Does one pander to the opinions of the general public or does one pursue one's own artistic vision? What if those two paths cannot coincide? And then there's that whole problem of pitting artists against each other. Talk about stifling artistic cooperation. What should one do then?"

"Stop entering your stuff in quilt shows, I suppose," Diane said. "I could do without your competition, especially if you're going to fret about it so much."

Everyone laughed.

"Fine," Gwen said, pretending to be wounded. "I'll just continue to wrestle with these important moral issues myself, thank you very much."

They reached Sarah's truck. "I'll see you all tomorrow at the celebration," she called, unlocking the truck and climbing inside. They waved good-bye, and she drove home.

Chapter 20

When Matt and Sarah pulled up behind the manor the next morning, Mrs. Compson was waiting on the back steps wearing a red-and-white-striped dress, white tennis shoes, and a wide-brimmed blue hat decorated with red and white flowers. Sarah opened the passenger door and slid over to the middle of the seat.

"Good morning, you two. Are you ready for some fun?" Mrs. Compson said.

"We're always ready," Matt assured her.

Since the parade route had been closed to traffic, they parked in a municipal lot near the edge of campus and joined the hundreds of people already milling through the streets. Dixieland music floated through the warm and hazy air. "What should we do first?" Sarah asked. "Do you want to go to the quilt show?"

"Let's see what there is to see downtown first," Mrs. Compson replied, smiling as a juggler in clown makeup passed unsteadily on a unicycle, an impromptu parade of delighted children close behind.

The next few hours passed quickly as they strolled around the downtown enjoying the street performers. Musicians entertained the crowds from small stages in the intersections. A magician's bewildering display of sleight-of-hand sparked a hot debate between Mrs. Compson and Matt regarding who was and who wasn't watching carefully enough to figure out how the tricks worked. Children seemed to be everywhere, shouting and laughing, darting in and out of the crowd, balloons tethered to their wrists. Parents gathered in friendly groups wherever a storefront window or a tree offered shade, laughing and chatting as they kept one eye on their friends and the other on their rambunctious offspring. The delicious fragrance of popcorn and broiling chicken and spicy beef drifted through the streets.

Matt must have noticed it, too, for he glanced at his watch. "It's almost noon."

"Already? I can't believe it," Mrs. Compson exclaimed. "Is anyone else ready for lunch?"

They all were, so they approached the closest food vendor and ordered three

Cajun-style blackened chicken sandwiches with curly fries and lemonade. Mrs. Compson insisted on treating them. Matt carried Mrs. Compson's lunch for her as they made their way through the ever-increasing crowd to the square, where a ten-piece band was belting out dance tunes from the forties. They managed to find a seat on a tree-shaded bench for Mrs. Compson, and Sarah and Matt sprawled out on the grass nearby. Mrs. Compson tapped her foot in time with the music as they ate and talked.

Sarah noticed that people were starting to gather along the sidewalks, some sitting in folding chairs facing the street. "The parade must be about to start," she guessed, just as the band wrapped up its final set.

"I'll grab us a spot," Matt called over his shoulder as he dashed into the crowd, his curly head bobbing above those surrounding him. Sarah and Mrs. Compson disposed of their trash and followed more slowly, joining him in a clear space right next to the street, the perfect spot to view the parade as it approached the judges.

Several parade officials wearing red, white, and blue sashes passed, motioning the last stragglers off the street and onto the curbs. A cheerful woman in colonial dress handed them each a small flag. In the distance they heard a marching band and cheers from spectators lining earlier stages of the parade route. Soon the first float came into view, and the crowd responded with appreciative cheers and flag-waving. Sarah told the others what Summer had told her the night before, that each Waterford College fraternity and sorority entered a float into the competition. Between the floats came marching bands from each of the local junior and senior high schools. The mayor, the police chief, and the Dairy Princess, all clad in eighteenth-century costume, were driven by in an old Model T. Behind them marched Betsy Ross, George Washington, and Ben Franklin, waving and throwing candy to the audience.

Betsy Ross passed within a yard of their spot. "Hi, Sarah," she called, beaming.

Sarah stared at her. "Diane?" But by then she was gone.

Then a murmuring chorus of adoring parents signaled the highlight of the event: the Children's Bike Parade. First came cautious five-year-olds on tricycles, followed by older children on two-wheelers with training wheels, and lastly by sixth graders on fifteen-speeds and off-road bikes. Each bike was festooned with red, white, and blue crepe paper streamers and balloons. There would be prizes, Sarah overheard, for the best decorated bike in each age group.

As the last child passed and the next float drove slowly by, Sarah turned to Mrs. Compson with a grin. "What do you think?"

"Oh, it's delightful. The children are so charming."

A group of sequin-clad teenage girls whirled by, batons flashing in the sunlight. After the next float the crowd suddenly quieted, and then there began a sprinkling of applause that grew louder each moment. Sarah heard a lone snare drum beating out a measured march. Mrs. Compson placed a hand over her heart and gave Matt a quick elbow in the ribs. He hastily snatched off his baseball cap.

A color guard marched slowly past, holding the flag high. Behind them in two open convertibles sat seven elderly men, their lined faces stern and proud. "World War One," Matt said, nodding to their uniforms. Behind them twenty other men clad in uniforms from the Second World War stiffly marched in four rows. Some wore medals; some also wore empty jacket sleeves rolled up and pinned at the shoulder. Other veterans, men and women who had fought in later wars, followed, some smiling and waving to the crowd, others staring straight ahead, faces grim. One long-haired man in his forties held his flag clenched in his teeth because his hands were occupied with propelling his wheelchair along.

Mrs. Compson sighed. "I think I'd like to sit down now."

Sarah nodded and took her elbow. Matt cleared a path for them through the crowd, and they made their way back to the square and the shady bench. The lawn was now empty except for discarded sandwich wrappers and cups. Mrs. Compson eased herself onto the seat. They heard the Waterford College marching band approaching, playing a stirring Sousa march that soon had the spectators clapping along.

"Quite a patriotic town you have here," Matt remarked, stretching out on his back on the grass and resting his head in his hands.

"Patriotic? Hmph. I suppose they would call it that."

Matt's brow furrowed slightly. "Wouldn't you?"

Mrs. Compson shrugged and looked away. "This might sound petty, but it's hard for me to see their frenetic flag-waving in an entirely positive light."

"Frenetic?" Sarah laughed. "Don't you think that's a little harsh?"

"I'm entitled to my point of view. This town wasn't very friendly to the Bergstroms when I was a young woman because of their so-called patriotism."

"I don't understand. Your family immigrated to America a long time ago, right? I thought you said they've been here since your great-grandfather's time."

"I did."

Matt and Sarah exchanged bewildered looks.

Mrs. Compson noted them, and gave a wry smile. "I'll tell you what happened. Maybe then you'll see why I have mixed feelings about this town."

Matthew, I assume that Sarah has told you most of what I have already said about my family and Elm Creek Manor, but if you get lost, stop me and I'll explain.

It was March of 1944, and I was twenty-four years old. Father's declining health had put me and James all but entirely in charge of Bergstrom Thoroughbreds by this time, and Richard was still away at school in Philadelphia. Our family business, which had grown so much since my great-grandfather's time and had survived the Depression and the Great War, was now struggling. It seemed selfish then to worry about our own fortunes when so many were suffering, so we did what we could to maintain the business until the war ended and we could properly invest in it again.

In Waterford, everyone's thoughts were on the war effort. Claudia's young man, Harold, was the assistant air raid warden for our area. Although James assured me we were safe, the whole town picked up the habit of nervously scanning the skies for German bombers who might mistake us for Pittsburgh or Ambridge, to the west. It was a difficult time, but we made the best of it.

Richard's letters did little to put me at ease. He wrote about his friends who were going off to war and how he envied them the grand adventures they would have. Oh, and remember his childhood friend Andrew, from the playhouse? Richard had looked him up in Philadelphia and they were two peas in a pod again. When Richard wrote and reminded me that both he and Andrew were seventeen and men now, I felt my heart quake, but I tried to put it out of my mind.

For Claudia and me, our weekly quilting guild meeting was our escape. Every member saved scraps of fabric to make raffle quilts to raise money for the war effort, like that Grandmother's Flower Garden quilt in the picture you saw, Sarah. That was our first Victory Quilt. We'd made it the previous summer, when I was guild president, when I thought the war couldn't possibly last much longer.

But the following March it seemed that we had always been at war, and hanging blackout curtains, and rationing everything. We worked on new Victory Quilts and talked in hushed tones about husbands, brothers, and sons overseas. When one of us experienced the worst sort of loss, the others would do what we could to comfort and console her.

One evening our meeting was held in the high school cafeteria, and I was sitting at a quilt frame with Claudia and four other women as the other quilters worked in smaller groups on other projects. I mentioned that in two weeks Richard would be coming home for spring break.

"The rich little German schoolboy's

coming home. Not like my boy," a voice muttered behind me.

I spun around. "And what exactly is that supposed to mean?" I demanded, only to be met by stony silence.

I looked around the quilt frame. Only Claudia's eyes, wide with shock, met mine.

"Better not to have those Krauts fighting with our boys, anyway," a different voice hissed.

"Not unless you want to wake up with a knife in your back," said a third.

"Must be nice to have enough money to buy your way out of the service."

Claudia flushed, and her eyes brimmed with tears. She opened her mouth as if to speak, then scrambled to her feet, snatched her sewing basket, and fled.

"If any one of you has anything to say to me or my family, say it now." Inside I felt as if I were trembling to pieces, but my voice sounded like stone.

No one said a word.

"Very well, then," I said, turning an icy gaze on each of them in turn. "You can apologize to my sister next week." I spun on my heel, grabbed my sewing basket, and marched out the same door Claudia had taken.

Even though it was early March, it was

still bitter cold. I found Claudia walking toward home, her shoulders shaking. I ran to catch up with her. "Claudia?"

She was crying into her handkerchief. "For months it's been like this, at the grocery store, the library, everywhere, but this is too much. How could they? How could my own friends be so hateful?"

I put my arm around her. "Don't mind them, Claudia. They're just upset. Everyone is. It's the war, that's all. They don't mean it. Everything will be fine next week."

"I have to wonder." She sniffled. We walked the rest of the way home in silence.

Claudia had always been so popular with the local girls, and so their comments wounded her much more than they did me. Their behavior confused her. There were so many German families in Waterford, and some who taunted us were of even more recent German origin than we. Remember, too, that our name and a significant portion of our heritage were Swedish. We were hardly just off the boat from Berlin. Why had we been singled out?

I understood well enough.

Although Father and our uncles had fought in the Great War, we were one of the few families in town who did not have someone currently in the military. James was already twenty-six, though there were plenty of men even older who had enlisted. Richard was still too young, and the only cousins of suitable age were girls. What's more, our wealth had always made us the target of envious remarks. They weren't shunning us because we were German but because we were fortunate.

I tried to explain this to Claudia, but I don't think she ever really understood. You'd think that of all people Claudia would recognize jealousy when she saw it, but in this matter that wasn't so.

The next week's guild meeting was even worse. I could feel their accusing glares boring into the back of my head, their hateful whispers burning in my ears. Claudia and I sat close together and looked at no one, trying to pretend we didn't notice.

At the end of the evening, the guild president, Gloria Schaeffer, drew us aside. She didn't even apologize as she politely suggested that we leave the guild for the duration. Can you imagine? For the duration. Honestly. And from Gloria *Schaeffer*, of all people.

I clamped my mouth shut before I let loose with exactly what I thought of her and her petty little friends. I gathered up our things, took Claudia by the elbow, and steered her out of there before she could burst into tears. If we had to leave, best to leave with as much dignity as we could muster.

Sarah, you've wondered why I won't join the Waterford guild, and now you know. Yes, I realize most of the people there that night aren't around anymore, but it's the principle of the thing. They didn't want us then, fine. I don't want them now.

We tried to forget the guild and how our so-called friends had treated us by throwing ourselves into preparing for Richard's homecoming. How wonderful it would be to see him again.

His first dinner home, he talked endlessly about Andrew, his friends away in Europe, and of course, the Puzzle. Father beamed at him adoringly. I suppose we all did, though I could have done without all that talk about the war.

"No one at school is cruel to you because of your ancestry, are they, Richard?" Claudia asked suddenly.

James gave her a sharp look, and I kicked her, none too gently, under the table. She let out a squeak and glared at me.

Richard set down his fork. "No, of

course not. Everyone who knows me knows how I feel about Hitler. Why do you ask?" Claudia swallowed and glanced at me. I gave her a warning stare, which Richard immediately recognized. "Come on, Claud, don't let Sylvia shut you up. What's going on?"

Hesitantly, Claudia told him how the residents of Waterford had been treating us lately. As she continued, Richard's jaw clenched ever tighter and his eyes narrowed into icy blue slits.

Father looked around the table in bewilderment. "Sylvia, James? You've been keeping all this from me? Why?" His voice was troubled and hurt, and we couldn't bear to meet his gaze. "I cannot understand their behavior, when we Bergstroms have done so much for this town. No one has ever questioned our family's patriotism. I fought in the Great War and lost two brothers to it. What further proof do they require?"

Grimly, Richard resumed eating, his white-knuckled fists trembling with rage. His expression filled me with fear.

When everyone else had gone to bed, Richard drew me and James aside. "Whatever happens, I want you to promise me you'll look after Agnes."

My eyes widened. "What do you mean, whatever happens?"

"You explain it to her," Richard said to James over my head.

"I'm standing right here. Talk to me." My voice broke, and I clutched at Richard's sleeve. My baby brother was now taller than I by several inches, but he was still only a boy of seventeen. "What are you planning? You need to finish school, and then you're needed here."

James placed an arm around me and pulled me away. "We'll talk about it in the morning. In the morning, Richard," he emphasized. "I'll expect you to be here."

Richard nodded. He watched us climb the stairs and disappear around the corner.

Somehow I managed to sleep that night, but I woke the next morning with an uneasy knot in the pit of my stomach. I shook James awake. "Something's wrong," I whispered, my voice an anxious hiss between my teeth.

We hurried into our clothes and downstairs, where Claudia was bustling about the kitchen, humming cheerfully as she helped Cook prepare breakfast. Richard was an early riser, and by all rights he should have been there before us, charming Cook out of a scarce pastry made with carefully conserved sugar rations. Claudia's bright smile faded when she saw our faces.

A quick search of the manor and the grounds established that Richard and his suitcase were gone. He wouldn't have left without saying good-bye, I was certain, or at least without leaving a note. The house was in an uproar, with James at the center trying to calm the storm. My thoughts were in a whirl, when suddenly I remembered the playhouse.

I ran as fast as I could to the dilapidated old structure near the stables. The door had long since fallen from its hinges, and I ducked past it, my eyes searching the musty room.

Then I spotted it — a folded edge of paper sticking out from beneath a rusted coffee tin in the middle of the floor, where Richard had known I would find it right away. I unfolded the paper with shaking hands.

"Dear Sylvia," he had written. "I'm sorry to go off like this, but I know you'll forgive me. I figured you'd find this note soon, but not soon enough to stop me. Andrew and I have been thinking, and what Claudia said tonight clinches it. We're going to enlist, and whip those Germans until they know they're licked. No one is going to say Bergstroms are chicken, or question our loyalties, not as long as I can do something to prove otherwise. Remember what I asked you to promise me. Don't worry. I'll be fine."

I fled back to the manor clutching the note to my heart. The others had not even noticed my absence, and they broke off their argument when I rushed in. I held out the paper and sank into a chair. James hurried over and held my hand as he read the note, grim-faced.

He crumpled it in a fist. "I'll get Harold and we'll catch the next train to Philadelphia."

"How do you even know he's heading for Philadelphia? He could enlist here just as easily."

"That's where Andrew is, and from the sound of Richard's note, they're signing up together." His voice was calm for everyone else's benefit, but his eyes told me the truth. He didn't know if Richard had returned to Philadelphia, but it seemed a reasonable conclusion. For all our sakes, it had to be the correct one.

"James, if anything happens to him —"

James gripped my shoulders with both hands. "Don't worry. I'll take care of it."

He kissed me, quickly, then hurried off to pack his bag.

He and Harold wired us two days later with dreadful news.

They had found Richard at school, packing his things. He and Andrew had already enlisted in the army and were to report in less than two weeks. With the Chevaliers' reluctant blessing, Richard and Agnes had married. They would be bringing her back to Elm Creek Manor on the next train.

When they finally returned, James and Harold looked resigned, the Puzzle was tearful, and Richard could barely contain his excitement. I hugged him so hard he had to gasp for breath. "What have you done?" I cried, not expecting or receiving an answer.

That night, when James and I were alone, he took me in his arms. His face wore the strangest expression — regret, love, concern, I don't know. I assumed he thought I was angry, or thought he had failed.

"James, I know you did the best you could," I said, trying to comfort him. "I know you tried to stop him. It's in God's hands now."

"Sylvia, I'm going, too."

I stared at him. "What?"

"It was the only way. Sylvia, it was the only way. He had already joined up, and if I signed up right away, we would be placed in the same unit. Harold signed up, too, although I'm not sure why. It was clear he didn't want to."

"My God." I pressed a hand to my lips and sank down upon the bed. The room spun about me.

"I'll look after him. I promise you that. I promise we'll all come home safe to you. Sylvia, you have my word. I'll always come home to you."

What could I say to him then? What more could he say to me?

The next morning we learned that Harold had asked Claudia to marry him and that she had accepted. I tried to be happy for her sake.

After the shortest week of my life, James, Richard, and Harold left us. Around the same time I realized I was pregnant, they were sent to the Pacific to fight the Japanese.

The parade had ended, and revelers filled the square as a jazz quartet began to play in the concert shell. Mrs. Compson, Sarah, and Matt listened without speaking for a time.

Then Mrs. Compson rose. "I think I'd like to see that quilt show now, wouldn't you?" Her smile was forced. "Perhaps I've taken a ribbon or two."

Sarah nodded, and Matt attempted a smile. They walked along the parade route toward the campus.

Chapter 21

Two women at the library entrance took their admission fees and offered them programs. Sarah was disappointed to learn they had arrived too late to vote for the Viewers' Choice award.

"Come on, you two," Mrs. Compson urged them. "You'll miss everything if you poke around like that all day."

The library concourse was full of enthusiastic quilt lovers of all ages, and the stands Sarah had helped assemble were now displaying the quilters' handiwork. They viewed each quilt in turn, reading the program for the artists' names and thoughts on their work. Guild members wearing white gloves mingled through the crowd, ready to turn over an edge so a quilt's backing could be examined.

Mrs. Compson knew so much about block patterns, design elements, and construction techniques that Sarah and Matt felt as if they were enjoying a museum tour with an expert guide. Often Sarah noticed that other spectators were listening in on Mrs. Compson's analyses of the pieces, nodding occasionally in agreement.

Sarah was pleased to find that even with a beginner's eye she could study an unfamiliar block and figure out how the quilt had been constructed. She was able to see how subtle variations in color and contrast made a traditional quilt sparkle, and how other quilts used the traditional as a starting point for devising something truly innovative. Soon the show became a dizzying and enthralling display of color and pattern, inspiring in that she saw so many possibilities, and humbling in that her own handful of simple pieced blocks couldn't begin to compare.

"I'll never be able to make a quilt like this," she said, gazing at a particularly stunning Dresden Plate variation whose wheel-shaped blocks had pieced "spokes" intensifying in hue as they radiated outward. A pieced border resembling a twisted ribbon spiraled along the outside edges. The quilting stitches were too tiny to be believed.

"You shouldn't make a quilt like this. You should make your own quilt," Mrs. Compson chided.

"What I meant was I'll never make a quilt as good as this one."

"Not with that attitude you won't," Matt said, grinning.

"My thoughts exactly." Mrs. Compson gave Sarah a pointed look. "This particular quilter has been working on her skills since before you left high school. If you've already decided you'll never make a quilt so fine, then you never will, and my lessons will be wasted on you. If, however, you're willing to stick to it and keep in mind that few if any first quilts are as lovely as this one, well, then, perhaps there's still hope for you." She turned and moved on to the next quilt.

"See? Just like I've been telling you all along: think positive," Matt said over his shoulder as he followed her.

Sarah sighed and went after them.

The Tangled Web Quilters had done well. Bonnie's blue-and-gold Celtic knotwork quilt had taken first place in the appliqué/large bed quilt division, and Judy's log cabin variation had also won a blue ribbon in the pieced/small bed quilt category. Together Gwen and Summer had claimed a second place in the innovative division for a family tree quilt that blended piecing, appliqué, and photo transfer techniques. When Sarah came across Diane's floral appliqué wall hanging, she was delighted to see a third-place ribbon hanging by its side. Sarah admired Diane's first ribbon and promised herself that next year she would enter a quilt, too.

Matt, eager to see how Mrs. Compson's entry had fared, went on ahead to find it.

"Mrs. Compson, do you think I'll be able to finish my quilt in time for my anniversary?" Sarah asked as soon as he was out of earshot.

"Well, that depends. When is it?"

"August fifth. I'd like to have my quilt done by then so I can give it to Matt for a present. It'll be our first anniversary spent in Waterford, so I want to give him something special. What could be more special than my first quilt? I'd like to use a garden maze setting, too, and maybe a pieced border."

Mrs. Compson held up her hands, chuckling. "Slow down. You still have a few blocks to go. August fifth, hmm? Even if I help you with the quilting, that might be pushing things a bit." She thought for a moment. "Perhaps it's time to teach you how to machine piece. I suppose I could let you use my sewing machine."

"Really?"

"If you promise to be careful."

"Of course I'll be careful." They rounded the corner and found Matt standing in front of Mrs. Compson's quilt, grinning from ear to ear. "But don't say anything to Matt. I want the quilt to be a surprise."

Mrs. Compson nodded and wove her way through the onlookers to see her quilt, with Sarah following close behind. She recognized the blue, purple, green, and ivory eight-pointed star quilt immediately. It was the same one she had seen on the sofa the first time she'd visited Elm Creek Manor.

Beside the quilt hung a blue ribbon for first place in the pieced/large bed quilt category, a purple Judge's Choice ribbon, another purple ribbon for Best Hand Quilting, and a gold ribbon for Best of Show.

"You won more ribbons than anyone else here," Sarah exclaimed.

Mrs. Compson bent forward to examine the ribbons herself. "Hmph. No Viewers' Choice?" Her voice sounded amused, but Sarah detected how pleased she was.

"Congratulations, Mrs. Compson." Matt tipped his baseball cap in her direction.

"Why thank you, Matthew." Other viewers who had overheard offered their congratulations, which she graciously accepted.

"Sarah?" someone called out.

Sarah spun around and caught a glimpse of red hair in the throng of people behind them. "Oh, hi, you guys. I was hoping I'd run into you. There's someone I'd like you to meet." She beckoned to Mrs. Compson, and they made their way back through the crowd. "Gwen, Bonnie, and Summer, I'd like you to meet Mrs. Compson. Mrs. Compson, this is Gwen, Bonnie, and Summer, a few of the Tangled Web Quilters."

"We've met," Bonnie said.

Mrs. Compson nodded pleasantly to the others, then turned to Gwen. "Professor, it's a pleasure to meet you. I'm looking forward to meeting your students next week."

"And they're looking forward to meeting you, too. They'll be impressed when they hear about this." Gwen indicated Mrs. Compson's awards.

"Ooh, how did you do?" Summer asked, stepping through the crowd for a closer look. Mrs. Compson went with her, responding to Summer's stream of eager questions as rapidly as they came.

Gwen caught Bonnie by the elbow before she could follow. "Where's Mrs.

Emberly?" she whispered, looking around anxiously.

"She left earlier, with Judy and Emily." Bonnie turned to Sarah. "Judy raised a stink when they told her she couldn't bring Emily's stroller in here. Diane would've been proud."

Gwen released Bonnie's arm. "Thank goodness. That was a narrow miss."

Sarah's brow furrowed. "What do you mean? What's wrong?"

Gwen and Bonnie exchanged a look. "Mrs. Compson and Mrs. Emberly don't exactly —" Bonnie hesitated. "Well, you know Mrs. Emberly said they had a falling out, but it's worse than that. It would be very awkward if they happened to run into each other here."

"Rumor has it they've been feuding for more than fifty years," Gwen added. "They could just ignore each other while they weren't living in the same town, but it's been more difficult ever since Mrs. Compson returned to Waterford."

Sarah thought back. "Was Mrs. Emberly one of the people who kicked Mrs. Compson out of the Waterford Quilting Guild?"

Gwen's eyes widened and she exchanged a surprised look with Bonnie. "She got kicked out? That's news to me. We never even knew she had been a member."

"That's not it, though," Bonnie said. "It's a family quarrel. Mrs. Emberly and Mrs. Compson are sisters-in-law."

Sisters-in-law? "Oh, my God. Mrs. Emberly is the Puzzle."

"The what?"

"Nothing — I mean, her first name is Agnes, right? She married Mrs. Compson's brother Richard?"

Gwen nodded. "That's right."

"Those two." Bonnie shook her head in exasperation. "It's such a shame, what with most of the family gone. Honestly — to have to dodge your own sister-in-law at a quilt show, rather than speak to her."

"Maybe we should stop running interference for them," Gwen mused. "Maybe if they're forced to speak to each other they'll achieve some sort of reconciliation."

Bonnie looked dubious. "I don't know. From what I've seen, Sylvia Compson's temper is as flammable as her quilts."

"I think you mean volatile," Gwen said. "But I know what you mean. What do you think, Sarah? You know Mrs. Compson pretty well."

"Apparently there's still a lot I don't know." Sarah's thoughts were in a whirl. If

Mrs. Emberly was the Puzzle, then shouldn't her name be Agnes Chevalier instead of Agnes Emberly? But no, that wasn't right, either; her name should be Agnes Bergstrom.

Just as Sarah was about to press Bonnie and Gwen for more details, Mrs. Compson and Summer returned. "Are you ready to go on and see the rest of the show?" Mrs. Compson asked.

Sarah nodded. The Tangled Web Quilters joined them as they viewed the remaining quilts. Mrs. Compson chatted pleasantly with the group, especially with Summer, but Sarah barely listened to the conversation. She should have guessed from Mrs. Emberly's remarks that there was more to her relationship with Elm Creek Manor than she had mentioned.

After the show, Sarah, Matt, and Mrs. Compson had dinner at an outdoor restaurant, then went to the Waterford College stadium for the fireworks display. As Matt and Mrs. Compson gazed at the brilliant spectacle overhead and let out murmurs of awe and cheers of delight, Sarah watched in silence. When Mrs. Compson eyed her and remarked that she was being rather quiet, Sarah made an effort to seem cheerful and relaxed. Mrs. Compson seemed to accept that, but inside Sarah was troubled. The quiet, pleasant woman she had come to know through the Tangled Web Quilters seemed nothing like the foolish, exasperating girl from Mrs. Compson's stories. Mrs. Compson was more of a puzzle than Agnes Chevalier had ever been.

Chapter 22

Mrs. Compson began Monday afternoon's quilt lesson by arranging Sarah's blocks on the table. She checked over the list of remaining blocks and worked out some problems on a calculator, then jotted down some notes on a pad. "Since you finished the Lancaster Rose block over the weekend, that makes eight. I'm surprised you were able to finish it so fast."

"I like appliqué. What are you doing?" Sarah gestured toward the calculator. "I'm good with math. Can I help?"

"Thank you, dear, but I'm finished. I'm calculating the necessary measurements for your Garden Maze setting." She frowned. "If I'm going to teach you how to machine piece today, I think we had better select the easiest of your remaining blocks. Let's go ahead and work on the Sister's Choice."

"Will it make any difference in the finished quilt that some of the blocks are machine pieced and some are hand sewn?"

"Not enough to matter." Mrs. Compson produced Sarah's template-making tools and spread them out on the table.

When Sarah had finished making her templates and cutting out the block pieces, Mrs. Compson showed her how to use the sewing machine. With the older woman hovering close by, Sarah practiced sewing on a few scraps of cloth before risking her quilt block pieces. It had been a long time since she had used a sewing machine in her junior high Home Ec class, but soon Sarah felt fairly comfortable with the tiny black machine. She pressed a seam open with her fingernail and inspected the neat, even stitches with a smile. This was definitely faster than hand piecing.

"Where can I get a sewing machine like this?" Sarah asked.

"Hmph. Depends. How much are you willing to spend?"

"That bad, huh?"

"I bought mine new many years ago, but if you can find one, and if the owner can bear to part with it, you might pay three hundred, five hundred dollars, depending upon its condition. Of course, I've heard of some people with incredible luck who have managed to snatch them up at garage sales for only a fraction of that." Mrs. Compson tilted her head to one side. "Of course, there's always —" She broke off suddenly and smiled, her eyes glinting in merriment.

"What? There's always what?"

"Nothing." But a faint smile played around the corners of her mouth. Sarah suspected she was up to something, but when she said so, Mrs. Compson merely smiled.

The next morning Sarah awoke with nervousness gnawing in her stomach. As she went to the bathroom to shower, she ordered herself to stop being so ridiculous. Mrs. Compson was the one who had to stand in front of Gwen's class and talk, not Sarah. All she had to worry about was running the slide projector.

She put on her interview suit and carefully arranged her long hair instead of merely pulling it back into a ponytail as she usually did for work. When Sarah and Matt arrived at Elm Creek Manor, Mrs. Compson was waiting in the back foyer with a box of slides and lecture notes. She wore an attractive lightweight pink suit and pearls.

Matt wished them good luck and strode

off for the north gardens as Sarah helped Mrs. Compson into the truck. As they drove to Waterford College, Mrs. Compson gave Sarah some last-minute instructions. Sarah listened and nodded when appropriate, but her stomach was in knots.

The security guard at the west entrance to the campus gave them a short-term parking permit and a map. Gwen was waiting behind the classroom building when they pulled up.

"I'm glad you're here early," she said, taking the box of slides from Mrs. Compson. "When word got out about your talk, some of the other professors asked if their classes might join us. I said it was okay. Was it?"

Mrs. Compson shrugged. "Certainly. The more the merrier."

"I'm glad you feel that way. We had to move into the auditorium."

"The auditorium?" Sarah's voice quavered.

Mrs. Compson looked surprised. "Classroom, auditorium — what's the difference? Why are you so pale?"

Gwen peered at her. "Are you okay, Sarah?"

"Sure. Why wouldn't I be?" She hoped she sounded more confident than she felt.

She did feel better when she learned that she would be working at the top of the auditorium in the projection booth where no one would see her. Gwen showed her where the various light switches and controls were, then left to take Mrs. Compson backstage while Sarah set up the equipment. Almost all of the seats were full, and Sarah could hear the students buzzing noisily below. Before long a crackle of static came over an intercom to her left. "Sarah, are you there?"

She fumbled for the white button next to the speaker. "Yes, Gwen. I'm here and I'm all set."

"We're ready, too. House lights down, stage lights up."

Sarah glanced at the control panel and found the switches. "Okay, I've got them. Uh . . . over and out."

The students quieted as the lights went down and Gwen came out to introduce Mrs. Compson. Sarah clutched her hands in her lap, glad to see that Mrs. Compson was greeted with a smattering of applause as she came onstage and approached the podium. She tilted her head in Sarah's direction and smiled, though Sarah was sure Mrs. Compson couldn't see her. Mrs. Compson greeted the audience, and at that

Sarah took a deep breath and turned on the slide projector.

At first Sarah sensed skepticism from the students, but to her relief, Mrs. Compson's wry humor quickly won them over. After discussing quilting's origins in ancient times through its use as padding for knights' armor in the Middle Ages, Mrs. Compson moved on to a discussion of quilting in colonial America and in the days of westward expansion. She concluded by describing contemporary quilting from the upsurge in interest sparked by the Bicentennial to present-day quilt artists who incorporate everything from traditional patterns to computer-aided design in their craft. Sarah found the discussion so fascinating that she almost missed a few cues, but she didn't think anyone noticed.

When it was over, the students gave Mrs. Compson an enthusiastic round of applause, and she inclined her head and smiled graciously. As class ended and Sarah switched on the house lights, a few listeners approached the stage with questions as the others left the auditorium. Sarah glanced at the stage, and finding Mrs. Compson surrounded by students, decided to use the time to pack up the slides. When she finished she left the projection booth and carried the box of slides to the stage, where Mrs. Compson and Gwen were saying good-bye to one lingering student.

"That was really interesting, Mrs. Compson," Sarah said. "You did a great job."

"Who would've thought that young people would find quilt jokes so amusing?" Mrs. Compson shook her head as if amazed, but she looked pleased.

Gwen looked pleased as well. "I can't thank you enough, Mrs. Compson. I think my students got a lot out of your lecture."

Mrs. Compson patted her on the arm. "Any time you want me to come back, I'd be delighted to. I thoroughly enjoyed myself."

Sarah noted the remark and tried to keep her features smooth and nonchalant. Inside she felt like shouting with triumph. She couldn't wait to tell Matt.

"I'm going to take you up on that," Gwen said. She walked them to the truck, and as they were about to drive away, she approached the passenger side window and peeked in. She gave Sarah a knowing glance and turned to Mrs. Compson. "Maybe Sarah can talk you into joining the

Tangled Web Quilters at our meeting this week?"

"I've tried, believe me," Sarah said.

Mrs. Compson pursed her lips. "It's not the Waterford Quilting Guild?"

"No. We defected a long time ago."

"Very well, then. Perhaps I'll consider it."

Gwen grinned. "Hope to see you there." She backed away from the window and waved before returning inside.

Sarah drove them home to Elm Creek Manor.

"I think that went quite well, don't you?" Mrs. Compson asked.

"Oh, definitely. You had them in the palm of your hand."

"Well, I was an art teacher once, you know."

"No, I didn't, although I remember you mentioned studying to be one. But I thought you left college."

"I did, but I returned to school later and earned my degree. Not at Waterford College, though."

Sarah nodded. Mrs. Emberly had mentioned something like that at one of their quilting bees, but she didn't think she should tell Mrs. Compson that. Not yet.

Inspired by Mrs. Compson's successful

presentation, they decided to ignore the work waiting upstairs and spent the rest of the afternoon quilting. As Sarah and Matt drove home that evening, she told him about the presentation and, most importantly, the promise Mrs. Compson had given Gwen. "She said any time Gwen wants her to deliver another lecture, she will. That must mean that she's thinking about staying, right? I mean, how could she give another presentation if she leaves Waterford?"

Matt nodded, considering. "It could be a good sign, I guess."

"You guess? If she feels needed, that's one more reason to stay, right?"

"Don't get your hopes up too high, honey. I don't want you to be hurt if things don't work out."

Sarah rolled her eyes. "Well, if that doesn't impress you maybe this will. She's also thinking about joining the Tangled Web Quilters."

"Does she know Mrs. Emberly is a member?"

Sarah paused. "I don't know. I don't think so."

"How are you going to work that?"

"I don't know." Sarah frowned and sank back into her seat, deflated.

They pulled into their parking lot. Matt draped an arm around Sarah's shoulders as she unlocked the door and went inside. "Sarah, something about this University Realty deal bothers me."

"Everything about it bothers me."

Matt took off his baseball cap and ran his hand through his hair. "I've been thinking about how much it would cost to remodel the interior of the manor so that it could be used for apartments, and frankly, I don't see how University Realty can hope to make any kind of profit. They'd have to charge incredible rents just to break even, and what college student has that kind of money to throw around? And most students want a place with all the modern amenities and aren't willing to sacrifice them just to say they lived in a historic mansion. Especially one that isn't within walking distance of campus."

"It never sounded very logical to me, either."

"The remodeling costs are only part of it. Tony's currently working on a similar project but on a much smaller scale, a three-story home near downtown that the owners want to convert into three apartments. You wouldn't believe all the laws and ordinances he has to follow and all the fees the owner has to pay just to get the place up to local code for rental units." He shook his head. "I don't know. It just seems to me that it would be more logical for University Realty to buy some land and start from scratch rather than try to make Elm Creek Manor into something it isn't."

Sarah's pulse quickened. "Maybe that's what they're doing."

"What do you mean?"

"Maybe they're only interested in the grounds, not in the manor itself."

Matt's eyes widened. "You mean tear down Elm Creek Manor —"

"And start from scratch, just like you said." Sarah's thoughts raced as she pictured how many modern efficiency apartments could be squeezed onto the grounds, each one pouring a generous rent into Gregory Krolich's pocket every month. "That has to be what they have planned."

"But that's crazy. Converting Elm Creek Manor is one thing, but tearing it down is another. Mrs. Compson would never sell knowing Elm Creek Manor would be demolished."

"I don't think she does know. We don't even know for sure. But think about how carefully Krolich chooses his words. Remember when Mrs. Compson said she was worried that students would trash the place, and he said it would never happen? I bet he meant it will never happen because there won't be any Elm Creek Manor left for them to trash."

"We have to tell her."

"Not until we know for sure. I don't want to upset her."

"I can talk to Tony. He's been in this town a long time and knows everybody in the business." Matt reached out and stroked Sarah's head. "Don't worry. We'll find out what's going on and tell Mrs. Compson before she signs anything. It's her home, and we have to respect her decision even if we don't like it, but she deserves to know the truth."

Sarah nodded. How could she not worry? Only a few moments before, she'd thought she would have Mrs. Compson and Elm Creek Manor all summer, at least. Now she felt as if they were already slipping away.

Chapter 23

The next morning Sarah's mood did not reflect the bright and pleasant weather outdoors as she trudged from the truck to the back steps of the manor carrying her best blue interview suit on a hanger.

Mrs. Compson greeted her at the back door with a smile and a glint in her eye. "Let's go right upstairs and get started, shall we?"

Sarah had slept poorly, too worried about Elm Creek Manor to rest. To make matters worse, she felt ill prepared for her job interview later that day. She hooked the hanger over the doorknob and returned Mrs. Compson's cheery greeting halfheartedly. "I wanted to remind you that I have another job interview this afternoon," she added as she climbed the stairs behind the older woman.

Mrs. Compson gave a start. "Oh, of

course. That's fine. I'm sure you'll do well." She continued down the hall, past the suite they had begun two days before but had not yet finished.

Sarah hesitated at the door. "Mrs. Compson?"

"Hmm?" Mrs. Compson turned. "Oh, yes, that. Don't bother with that room right now. I want you to work somewhere else today." She resumed her pace, motioning for Sarah to accompany her.

Sarah trailed after her, wondering what had gotten into Mrs. Compson that morning.

Mrs. Compson stopped in front of a door near the end of the hall. "This was my sister's room," she said, placing her hand on the doorknob. "I admit I've put off this suite as long as possible, but yesterday I thought of — well, never mind. You'll see for yourself." She pushed open the door and waved Sarah in ahead of her.

This room had been used more recently than the others. A pink-and-white quilt was spread across the queen-size bed, and a white lamp with a frilly pink shade sat on a bedside table. White eyelet lace curtains stirred in the breeze from the open west-facing window. A small, square quilt of pink, yellow, and white triangles arranged in the shape of a basket hung opposite the bed.

Mrs. Compson motioned for Sarah to follow her into the suite's adjoining room. Most likely it had been Claudia's sewing room, Sarah guessed, noting the sewing machine nearby. It resembled Mrs. Compson's other machine, except the interlocking pattern painted in gold on the shiny black metal was slightly different, and it was set into a wooden table with a single drawer.

Mrs. Compson pulled back the chair and gestured for Sarah to take a seat. "What do you think? Like it?"

Sarah ran a hand over the smooth, polished surface of the table. "It's gorgeous."

"It's yours."

"Mine?"

"Consider it an employee-of-the-month bonus. Now, it's not the same model as mine, but in my opinion it sews just as well. It just isn't portable because of the table. The light's on the back of the machine rather than above the needle, but a good lamp at your left will illuminate the area sufficiently."

"Mrs. Compson, I can't accept this. It's too —"

"What? Don't you like it?"

"Are you kidding? Of course I like it. I love it."

"Then take it and be grateful." Sarah started to speak, but Mrs. Compson silenced her with a raised palm. "Make an old lady happy by accepting her gift in the spirit in which it has been given. Surely you don't want to insult me?"

Sarah grinned. "Definitely not. Anything but that."

After Sarah dashed downstairs to fetch her Sister's Choice block pieces, Mrs. Compson showed her how to operate the machine. It had all kinds of attachments whose uses Sarah couldn't discern, and she soon realized that she could operate the machine better in her stocking feet than with her shoes on, since the foot pedal was actually no more than a single button she could depress with her right big toe.

Matt surprised them by arriving early for lunch.

"Look at my new toy, honey," Sarah greeted him, making Mrs. Compson laugh.

Matt gave them a tight-lipped smile. "That's great, Sarah. Mrs. Compson, I hope you don't mind if I take Sarah to her job interview early? I have a meeting with my boss in town and I can't be late."

"Oh, and we were having so much fun."

"I'll come back after the interview," Sarah promised. "After all, we should get some work done today, shouldn't we?"

With an anxious Mrs. Compson barking out directions and warnings as they went, Sarah and Matt carried the sewing machine downstairs and set it up in the west sitting room opposite the sofa. Sarah changed into her suit and joined Matt in the truck.

"I don't really have a meeting, Sarah," he said as soon as she shut the door. "I had something to tell you, and I don't think you're going to like it."

"What is it?"

Matt started the truck. "Tony checked with a friend in the city licensing department. University Realty has applied for a demolition permit."

"For Elm Creek Manor?"

Matt nodded, eyes fixed on the dirt trail as they drove past the barn into the forest.

"But they haven't even bought it yet," she exclaimed. "How can they apply for permits already?"

"Tony says the Waterford Zoning Commission can take as long as six months to grant approval to raze historic buildings. Apparently Krolich wants to be able to tear down the place as soon as his check clears."

"I can't believe he'd buy Elm Creek Manor without telling Mrs. Compson what he plans to do with it. We have to do something."

"I know."

Sarah thought for a moment. "Let's go see him right now."

Matt glanced at her, then quickly returned his gaze to the narrow road. "What about your interview?"

"We have time."

Soon Matt was parking the truck in front of the three-story Victorian building that housed University Realty's downtown office. Sarah raced up the front stairs as Matt fed coins into the meter. He joined her inside at the receptionist's desk, where Sarah was asking to see Mr. Krolich.

"Who may I say wishes to see him?" the receptionist asked as she reached for the phone.

"Just tell him it's important." Sarah craned her neck, trying to see the work space beyond the desk. Men and women in solemn business attire strode through the hallway, but Krolich was not among them.

"I'll need your names."

"Sarah and Matt McClure. He knows us."

The receptionist phoned Mr. Krolich's office, exchanged a few words, then replaced the receiver. "I'm sorry, but he's due in a meeting. If you'd like to schedule an appointment he'd be happy to see you sometime next month —"

Then Sarah spotted a familiar figure. She grabbed Matt's sleeve. "There he is." She marched down the hallway with Matt close behind, ignoring the receptionist's protests. Krolich's back disappeared around the corner into an office. By the time Sarah and Matt burst in, he had reached his desk.

He paused only slightly before settling down into the high-backed leather chair. "Hello again, Sarah, Matt." He gestured toward two chairs facing his desk. "Please, take a seat."

"We'll stand," Sarah said.

Krolich shrugged. "Suit yourself. So, to what do I owe the pleasure of this unexpected visit? Are you interested in that job after all, Sarah?"

"We want the truth about your plans for Elm Creek Manor."

Krolich frowned. "You must realize I can't discuss confidential business matters with anyone other than my clients and other involved parties. As much as I'd like to help you, well, you can understand the spot I'm in."

"Sarah is Mrs. Compson's personal assistant," Matt said. "And both of us are her friends. That makes us involved parties."

"So you might as well tell us your plans for tearing down Elm Creek Manor," Sarah said.

Krolich's eyes widened almost imperceptibly. "Oh, so you've heard about that." He picked up a gilded letter opener and fingered it. "Tell me, have you mentioned this to Mrs. Compson?"

"Not yet, but we plan to."

"I see." He returned the letter opener and folded his hands, resting his elbows on the desk. "I was planning to tell her myself, you know."

"Yeah, right," Matt said. "When? Before or after she signed the place away?"

"If Mrs. Compson wants to sell Elm Creek Manor, that's her business. Who are you to interfere?"

Sarah tried to keep her voice steady. "We're her friends, and we care about her, which is more than you can say."

"It's not that I don't care."

"Then why hide your plans from her?"

Krolich sighed. "Are you sure you won't sit down?" When Sarah and Matt didn't move, he nodded in acceptance. "Okay. I guess you're determined to see me as the villain here. But hear me out. I do care about Mrs. Compson. I'm trying to do right by her."

Matt snorted. "You have a funny idea of what's right."

Krolich's expression became earnest. "Hasn't it occurred to you that she already knows we plan to raze Elm Creek Manor?"

Sarah shook her head. "No way. She would've told me."

"Think about it, Sarah. My offer is the only one she's had, the only one she's likely to get. If she accepts it, she's agreeing to have her family home torn down. Do you think she'd admit to knowing that, even to herself?"

"So you're saying she's known all along, and she's lied to me?"

"Not exactly. I'm saying she doesn't want to know."

"That's ridiculous," Sarah shot back, but doubt trickled into her mind. She shoved it away. "You deliberately glossed over your plans for Elm Creek Manor because you knew she wouldn't sell it to you otherwise."

"I knew nothing of the sort."

"You had to suspect it, at least, or you would've told her."

"You're letting sentiment cloud your

judgment. Not a good practice for an aspiring businesswoman." He shook his head as if regretful. "This discussion is getting us nowhere. I'm afraid I'm going to have to ask you both to leave."

Sarah opened her mouth to retort, but Matt caught her arm. "Let's go, Sarah. It's not worth it." He gave Krolich a hard look. "Anyway, we got the answers we came for."

Krolich frowned but said nothing.

Sarah and Matt hurried down the hallway, ignoring the stares of Krolich's employees. "We have to tell her right away," Sarah said as they climbed into the truck.

Matt shook his head and pulled into traffic. "Your interview, remember?"

"That's right." Her heart sank. "But what if he gets her to sign something before I'm done?"

"You go to your interview, and I'll go talk to Mrs. Compson."

"I think I should be the one to tell her," she argued. Then she sighed. "But we can't risk waiting. You're right. You tell her."

They pulled into the accounting firm's parking lot and exchanged a quick kiss before Matt drove away and Sarah hurried inside. She glanced at her watch, relieved to see she was still two minutes early.

A clerk took her name and guided her to a waiting room, where she took a few deep breaths to compose herself. An image of Matt breaking the bad news and Mrs. Compson's grief-stricken face flashed through her mind. She tried to shake it off.

Not five minutes later the clerk returned and led her to another office. "You'll be meeting with our new assistant director of operations, Thomas Wilson," he said.

Sarah started. She knew that name. The clerk opened the door for her and she entered the room.

From behind his desk Thomas Wilson looked up in surprise. "So you're Sarah McClure." He rose and shook her hand. "How funny. All those times I've seen you and I never got your name. Please, have a seat."

Sarah sank into the opposite chair, smiling uncertainly. Usually her interviews began with introductions between strangers, and the change was disconcerting. "Congratulations on your new job," she said, then wondered if she should have.

He smiled. "Thanks. Sure beats constant interviewing. Well, let's get started, shall we?"

He began with the few perfunctory questions she had heard so often before, and she provided her familiar responses. At first she felt hopeful, thinking that he was sure to be a sympathetic listener since until recently he had been on the other side of the interviewer's desk himself. Before long, however, her confidence began to erode. She noticed that he never once looked her in the eye or wrote down any remarks. The more Sarah tried to sound positive and confident, the more she began to wonder if this man really was the same person who had been so talkative only a few weeks ago.

When she was in the middle of responding to his question about why she left her former employer, he suddenly pushed her résumé aside. "Sarah, I'm a busy man. Let's save ourselves a lot of time and trouble and call it quits, okay?"

"What do you mean?"

"We both know you don't want this job."

"But I do. I wouldn't be here if —"

He raised his voice to drown out her protests. "Did you think I had forgotten our conversation — oh, what was it, two, three weeks ago? You made it clear that you really aren't interested in accounting work. I'm afraid I can't in good conscience hire you knowing you won't be satisfied with us."

"I will be satisfied. You know I can do the work and —"

"Being able to do the work isn't enough. If the desire isn't there, productivity won't be, either."

Sarah's cheeks grew warm. "I've always done the very best I could at every job I've ever held. I'd do the same here, I promise you."

"Thanks for stopping by. We'll let you know." He turned back to his papers as if Sarah had vanished.

Sarah knew she should leave, but his abrupt dismissal angered her. "Are you even going to consider me?"

He didn't look up. "We'll hire the most qualified candidate, and that's more than you need to know."

She stood and stared at him for a moment. Then she turned on her heel and left without another word, her eyes burning.

Matt was waiting in the truck, grim-faced. "I told her," he said as soon as she sat down. He sped out of the parking lot. "I don't think she's taking it very well."

"How did you expect her to take it?" Her voice was sharper than she had intended. Krolich, Wilson, that stupid guy with his stupid grocery store question — she should have realized that they were all alike. If business these days was some kind of game, then the players broke all the rules. No, that wasn't quite it. They followed rules, all right, but not any kind of rules Sarah could live with.

They drove the rest of the way in silence.

When they reached the manor Matt took her hand and squeezed it. "Everything will work out."

She tried to smile. "I know." She kissed him and hurried inside.

She found Mrs. Compson in the sewing room, sitting in a chair with her hands clasped in her lap, staring straight ahead at nothing. She looked up when Sarah entered. "Hello, dear. How did it go?"

"Fine. It went —" And then Sarah broke down, the words tumbling out and falling over each other, angry sobs choking her throat. Murmuring sympathetically, Mrs. Compson took her hand and pulled her over until Sarah's head rested in her lap. She stroked Sarah's long hair and listened while Sarah told her what had happened.

Sarah's tears subsided. She took a deep breath and closed her eyes, comforted by Mrs. Compson's motherly touch. It had been a long time since her own mother had so much as hugged her. "I'm just going to have to face it," Sarah said. "I'm never going to find a job."

Mrs. Compson's hand paused for a moment. "You already have a job, I thought."

"Sure, but how long is it going to last, what with you ready to pack up and leave as soon as you get the chance?"

"True enough." Mrs. Compson sighed and resumed stroking Sarah's hair. "I might as well tell you. I've decided not to sell to Mr. Krolich."

Sarah sat up and wiped her eyes. "Really?"

"Of course. What else could I do? I could hardly sell knowing his intentions. I'm grateful to you and Matthew for discovering the truth before it was too late. Elm Creek Manor will stand for a long time yet."

"So what happens now?"

Mrs. Compson shrugged. "I wait for a better offer." She eyed Sarah intently. "Can you make me a better offer?"

Sarah barked out a laugh. "Not unless you're planning to give me a huge raise. You know Matt and I could never buy this place."

"Must you be so literal? I don't mean for you to submit a bid, silly girl. I'm telling you to give me a reason to stay. You're a smart young woman. Use your imagination. This place —" Her voice faltered, and she looked around as if seeing through the walls and taking in the entire building. "This place was so full of life once. I'm just one old woman, but I don't want to sell my family home. There's time enough for Elm Creek Manor to be out of Bergstrom hands after I die."

"Don't talk like that."

"Don't interrupt your elders when they're making a point. And here's mine: I'm giving you the chance to convince me to keep Elm Creek Manor. Show me how to bring Elm Creek Manor back to life and I'll never sell it. I promise."

"I don't think — I'm not sure how."

"Well, don't panic, dear. I didn't expect you to have an answer already. Give it some time. But not too much time." She smiled and patted Sarah's shoulder. "Everything will come out all right in the end."

"Matt said something almost exactly like that when he dropped me off."

"A wise man indeed," Mrs. Compson said, her voice solemn. Then she smiled.

Sarah's mind raced. A better offer. How could they make Elm Creek Manor live again? She shook her head. She should approach this problem as a businesswoman would, collecting and analyzing the evidence before submitting a proposal to the client.

"Mrs. Compson, there's more I need to know."

"What's that, dear?"

"I need to know why you left, and why you didn't come back for so many years, and why you don't speak to your sister-in-law when as far as I can tell she might be your only living relative." Mrs. Compson's smile faded, but Sarah plowed on ahead. "Before I can help you figure out how to bring Elm Creek Manor back to life, I need to understand how it died in the first place."

Mrs. Compson took a deep breath. "I suppose. Perhaps if you know the whole story you'll understand. Or perhaps you'll just think I'm a foolish old woman who deserves to be unhappy."

Maybe that's what Mrs. Compson thought of herself, but Sarah didn't care what Mrs. Compson had or had not done. She would never agree that Mrs. Compson deserved such remorse.

She waited, and Mrs. Compson explained.

Chapter 24

I suppose if James and Richard and Harold had never gone off to war I might have lived at Elm Creek Manor all my days and would have had a very different life. But they did go, and at the time my only consolation was that they would be together. I prayed that they would stay alive long enough to outlast the war.

As for the Elm Creek Manor homefront — well, I had the baby to think about, and Claudia and I both had our hands full trying to comfort Agnes. She seemed perpetually on the verge of tears, and usually did begin to sob uncontrollably if no one rushed to her side with a hug and some consoling words. I admit I became quite impatient with her. I too wanted someone to convince me that everything would be all right in the end, but when no one could, you didn't see me collapsing into hysteria.

I don't know. Perhaps I was also angry at myself for wishing that someone would comfort me as we all tried to comfort Agnes. A grown woman shouldn't need that. A grown woman in charge of an entire household should definitely not need that. When you're the strong one of the family you must be the strong one all the time, not just when it's convenient.

Spring turned into summer. Letters from the men were infrequent and often censored so thoroughly that we were hard-pressed to find a single comprehensible sentence. Still, we were relieved and thankful to learn that they were alive, together, and unharmed.

To help pass the time and distract our thoughts, Claudia and I would quilt and talk about more pleasant things. Sometimes my starry-eyed sister would launch into a fanciful description of her upcoming wedding. You would think we were royalty, her plans were so elaborate. As we worked, Agnes would linger around, sulking and pretending she wasn't interested. One day while I was working on a Tumbling Blocks baby quilt, Claudia whispered to me that Agnes deserved a second chance. To keep the peace, I relented and asked my sister-in-law if she wanted to learn how to quilt.

To my astonishment, she agreed. We set about planning a sampler just as you and I did, Sarah, but she refused to follow the simplest instructions. First she fought me over making a sampler, saying they were too simple. My instinct was to retort that a sampler would be all the more appropriate in her case, but a warning look from Claudia helped me bite my tongue. I lost that fight, so I tried to salvage the project by encouraging her to at least pick a simple block, like the Sawtooth Star or a Nine Patch. But she would have no part of any of my advice. Once she spotted that Double Wedding Ring pattern she made up her mind. She was going to make a Double Wedding Ring quilt and no one was going to stand in her way.

"Agnes," I said in my most reasonable tone, "look at this pattern more carefully. See all these curved seams, all these odd-shaped pieces with bias edges? Trust me, this isn't the best choice for your first quilt. You're just going to end up frustrated."

But she tossed her head and said that she hadn't had much of a wedding and no engagement whatsoever and she hadn't seen her husband in five months, and no one was going to tell her she couldn't have a quilt named Double Wedding Ring if she wanted it. I gave in very reluctantly, I assure you.

That quilt was doomed to failure from the first. We made our templates differently back then, but not as differently as the Puzzle did. She drew her shapes haphazardly, glaring at me when I warned her that even small errors could result in pieces that wouldn't match up. It had been enough trouble to convince her to use scraps, even when I reminded her there was a war on, but then she decided to make the entire quilt — yes, including the background pieces — out of red fabric. This quilt would have no contrast at all.

So many problems and she had not even begun sewing yet, which meant, of course, that the worst was yet to come. She handled the pieces so awkwardly that the bias edges stretched hopelessly out of shape, then she would mutter to herself as she jabbed pins into them to try to get them to behave. She jabbed herself more than once, too, and made sure everyone in the house heard it. Her stitches were large and crooked, but eventually I gave up telling her to take them out and do them over.

On one especially hot, muggy day a week later, Agnes, her forehead beaded with perspiration, triumphantly waved a ring in my face. "You didn't think I could do it, but here it is. So there."

I chose to ignore her childish behavior. "Very good, Agnes," I replied, taking it from her and placing it on a table for inspection. I tried to keep my face expressionless. An entire week's labor had gone into this? The ring buckled in the middle rather than lying flat, pieces didn't meet properly, stitches were so loosely sewn that the thread could be seen from the front of the block, and all that red blended together so that the pattern was unrecognizable. The forlorn assemblage of fabric begged for a mercifully swift delivery into the final resting place of the scrap bag.

"What do you think?" Agnes demanded when I had been silent for a while.

"Well," I said carefully, "it's fine for a beginner, but you need to remember that small trouble spots multiply into big problems when you have a big quilt. Even if you're only off by an eighth of an inch, if you have eight of those mistakes, that's an inch worth of inaccuracy."

She scowled. "So how do I fix it?"

"You'll have to rip out some of these seams and do them over."

"Rip them out? It took me forever to put them in!"

"It's nothing to get angry about, Agnes. I've had to rip out plenty of seams. Every quilter does."

"Well, I guess I'm not a quilter, then." She snatched up her work and stormed out of the room.

Claudia had overhead everything. "You'd better go after her," she said, sighing.

I nodded and followed Agnes down the hall toward the front entry. I was relieved to see that Claudia had decided to accompany me.

"Where do you think she's going?" I asked as we crossed the marble floor. I didn't have to wonder long, as I spotted her yellow dress through the open door.

Agnes stood frozen in place on the veranda, her back to us. As we joined her, the unfinished quilt fell from her hand and dropped silently to the floor. Her face was no longer angry, but she stared straight ahead as if she had not heard us approach.

"Agnes, what —" Claudia's voice broke off as she followed Agnes's line of sight and spotted the car driving slowly up to the manor.

Icy fingers clutched at my heart.

Two men in formal military dress climbed out of the car and walked toward us. One was older, with brown curly hair graying at the temples and a grim expression. The younger man's face was pale behind a sprinkling of freckles. He swallowed repeatedly and avoided meeting our eyes as they climbed the right-hand set of curved stairs. Each man carried a yellow slip of paper.

I thought they'd never reach the top of those stairs. Claudia slowly reached out and clasped my hand.

Then they were standing at the top of the stairs and removing their hats. "Mrs. Compson?" the older man asked.

I nodded.

The man came up to me and glanced down at the paper in his hand. "Mrs. Compson, ma'am, I regret that it is my duty to inform you that . . ."

A distant roaring filled my ears, blocking out his words. I watched his lips working silently.

James was dead.

Through the fog I became aware that the younger man was fingering his paper uncertainly. He looked from Claudia to Agnes and back again. "Mrs. Bergstrom?"

Mrs. He said Mrs., not Miss. That means —

Agnes's eyes welled up with tears. The younger man's voice trembled as he repeated the older man's message.

Not Richard, too. This can't be happening.

Agnes began to wail. She sank to her knees, clutching the paper to her chest.

Claudia buried her face in her hands and murmured the same phrase over and over, her shoulders shaking. Then she looked up, tears glistening on her cheeks. "Thank God," she sobbed. "Thank God."

The roaring in my ears seemed to explode white hot. I slapped Claudia across the face, so hard my palm stung. She cried out. I grabbed the older man by his lapels. "How?" I screamed in his face. "How did this happen? He promised! He promised me!" The younger man leaped forward to pull me away. I felt fabric tear in my fists. "You're wrong! You're lying!" I kicked at them both.

Searing pain stabbed across my abdomen. *They shot me,* I thought, watching the dark red blood pool around my feet.

Agnes shrieked. Then I sank into cold, silent blackness.

I remember little about the next few weeks. I suppose that's a good thing. I do remember lying in a hospital bed holding my daughter's still little body and sobbing. She actually lived for almost three days, can you believe that? What a little fighter. If only —

But it doesn't matter now. She's with her daddy. That's enough.

Soon her grandpa joined them. Father collapsed from a stroke when he heard the news. They buried him before I was released from the hospital. I think I begged the doctors to let me go to the funeral, but they wouldn't let me. I think that's what happened. I don't remember it clearly. Can you imagine, missing my own father's funeral?

For weeks after returning home I felt as if I were shrouded in a thick woolen batting. Sounds were less distinct. Colors were duller. Everything seemed to move more slowly.

Gradually, though, the numbness began to recede, replaced by the most unbearable pain. My beloved James was gone, and I still didn't know exactly how. My daughter was gone. I would never hold her again. My darling little brother was gone. My father was gone. The litany repeated itself relentlessly in my mind until I thought I would go mad.

A few hesitant visitors from the quilting guild would come by, but I refused to see them. Eventually they stopped trying.

Then the Japanese surrendered, and Harold came home, thinner, more anxious, his hairline even farther back than when he had left. When he first returned to Elm Creek Manor I thought his receding hairline was the funniest thing I had ever seen. I laughed until my stomach hurt and the others stared at me. You'd think they would have been glad to see me laugh for a change.

Claudia lost little time planning her wedding. She asked me to help, and I agreed, but my mind wandered and I had trouble remembering to take care of all the little details. She exploded at me more than once, but it didn't bother me as much as it used to. Instead she turned to Agnes, who for some reason had decided to remain at Elm Creek Manor rather than return to her own family. Perhaps she felt Richard's presence here. I know I did.

Then one evening we had a visitor. Andrew stopped over for the night on his way from Philadelphia to a new job in Detroit. I was glad to see him. He walked with a limp now and sat stiffly in his chair as if still in the service. He was pleasant enough to everyone, but he had barely a cold word for Harold, who seemed to go out of his way to avoid our visitor. I found this strange, since I had always heard that veterans shared a bond almost like that of brothers. But I decided that perhaps seeing each other reminded them of the war, which everyone in Elm Creek Manor would rather forget.

After dinner Andrew found me alone where I was working in the library. He took my hand and pulled me over to the sofa, his face nervous and angry.

"If you want to know, Sylvia," he said, his voice strained, "I can tell you how it happened. I was there. I can tell you if you want to know, but I don't think it will comfort you."

"Nothing can comfort me." I knew that as certainly as I had ever known anything. "But I need to know how they died."

This is what he told me.

He, James, Richard, and Harold were in an armored division on an island in the South Pacific. Richard and another soldier in one tank and James and Harold in a second were completing a routine patrol of the beach. On a high bluff some distance away, Andrew and some others were preparing to relieve them.

Andrew heard the planes before spotting them in the night sky. He and his companions breathed sighs of relief upon realizing they were our boys.

"They're coming in awfully low," one of the other fellows said.

"You don't suppose they're going to try to land, do you?"

Andrew felt a cold prickling on the back of his neck. "If I didn't know better I'd think they were about to —" And then the beach exploded in flames.

Andrew flung himself onto the sandy ground. "Get down," someone screamed.

Another grabbed a radio. "Call it off. Call it off. It's us, damn it!"

Andrew scrambled to his feet, choking and wiping the grit from his eyes. One of the tanks was engulfed in flames.

He ran straight down the steep bluff to the beach, knowing he would never make it in time.

He saw the hatch to the second tank lift. James climbed out and jumped for the ground. He ran to the flaming tank, shouting over his shoulder. Harold's head poked through the opening just as James reached the other tank. He climbed to the top and tried to open the hatch. Andrew was closer now, and through the flames he could see the tendons in James's neck straining as he struggled to open the hatch.

James shouted something to Harold and stopped wrestling with the hatch long enough to gesture frantically for him to help. Harold stared at him, licking his lips nervously, seemingly frozen in place.

The breeze picked up, fanning the flames and carrying some of James's words to Andrew's ears. "Goddammit, Harold, help me. With two of us —"

"Hang on," Andrew yelled as he raced by Harold's tank. "I'm coming! I'm —"

He heard the second plane droning overhead and saw Harold duck back into the tank. Then the explosion knocked the ground out from beneath his feet. Heat seared his eyes and wet soil rained down all around him.

Andrew was sobbing. "I'm so sorry, Sylvia," he wept, his voice breaking. "He saved me when we were just kids, but I couldn't save him. I'm so sorry."

I rocked him back and forth and tried to comfort him as best I could, but I had no words for him. All I knew was that James had died trying to protect my little brother as he had promised me, and Harold had let them both die rather than risk his own neck.

The next day Andrew left, and I never saw him again. I waved good-bye to him as his cab drove off, and turning back inside, I vowed not to tell Claudia and Agnes what I had learned. But still I felt uncertain. Should Claudia, at least, be told?

Wouldn't she want to know this about her husband-to-be? Then I thought about her words on the veranda that terrible day. "Thank God!" she had said. "Thank God! Thank God!" Angry tears sprang into my eyes at the memory. No, Claudia would prefer her blissful ignorance. And Agnes was too fragile for the truth.

I found them in Claudia's sewing room, giggling like schoolgirls. Agnes stood on a stool in the middle of the room as Claudia fitted her for a dress.

Their conversation broke off when I entered. "Do you — do you like it, Sylvia?" Agnes asked, holding out her skirts and smiling nervously. "It's my matron of honor dress for Claudia's wedding."

Claudia nudged her and flushed.

I started. "But I thought — but you already asked me to —"

Claudia tossed her head. "I changed my mind. After all, you've hardly been very helpful with my wedding plans. You're always too busy. You don't care about my wedding at all. Agnes does."

Agnes jumped down from the chair. "Stop it. Please. I won't listen to any fighting." She fled from the room.

Claudia threw down her tape measure and glared at me. "Now look what you've done.

You just can't leave her alone, can you?"

"What on earth do you mean?" I gasped. "You're the one who asked me to be your matron of honor and then dropped me behind my back. Claudia, I'm your sister."

"She's our sister, too, now," Claudia snapped. "Can't you be unselfish for once in your life? My God, Sylvia, she lost her husband."

My anger swelled. "Have you forgotten? I lost my husband, too. And my brother, and my daughter, and Father. And you know who's to blame?" And then the truth I had vowed not to reveal burst from my lips. "That cowardly fiancé of yours! He let James and Richard die!"

"How can you blame him for that? It isn't Harold's fault he couldn't get the hatch open."

"What? He never even tried. Whatever he told you — Claudia, he never left his tank. Andrew was there. He told me everything."

"You're just jealous because my man came home and yours didn't. You've always been jealous of me, always —"

"He does not belong in this family!" I screamed. "You will not marry him. I am the head of the Bergstrom family now, and I forbid it!"

"You forbid." Claudia's voice was cold, her face pale with rage. "You can forbid nothing. Harold risked his life to protect Richard. How dare you — how dare you speak of him this way. He is as fit as any man to join the Bergstrom family."

"The Bergstrom family is dead," I choked out. "Dead!"

"If you can say that, then perhaps you're the one who doesn't belong here."

"Perhaps you're right." I turned my back on her then. I couldn't bear it anymore. I stormed to my room and threw my things into my suitcases. No one tried to stop me.

I left Elm Creek Manor that day and never returned until this spring. I never again spoke to my sister, or to Agnes, or to Harold.

The sitting room was silent for a long time. Sarah could hear birds chirping outside, and farther away, the sound of Matt's lawn mower.

"Where did you go?" she finally asked.

Mrs. Compson shrugged and wiped at her eyes with an embroidered handkerchief. "I stayed with James's family in Maryland for a while. They were happy to have me. Then I returned to college. I studied art education at Carnegie Mellon, where they taught things I had already learned from my mother and great-aunt, though my mother and great-aunt didn't use words like 'color theory' and 'composition.' After I received my degree, I taught art in the Pittsburgh area until my retirement. Since then I've had my quilting to keep me busy. I think I've done all right, but it wasn't the life I had hoped for."

"What happened to the others — to Claudia and Agnes?"

"Claudia and Harold married, but they had no children. Several years later Agnes married a professor from the college and moved out of Elm Creek Manor. Claudia and Harold took over Bergstrom Thoroughbreds, and you've seen the results of their keen business sense already. But I have no one to blame but myself for the business's failure. If I had remained here to manage things . . ." She sighed and placed her hand on Sarah's. "Well? Did my long-winded reminiscing solve any riddles?" Her voice was slightly mocking, but not unkind. "Will that help you think of a way to bring Elm Creek Manor back?"

"I'm not sure. I'm going to try."

"Well, you do that. I'm counting on your help." She patted Sarah's hand and sighed.

Chapter 25

The next day Sarah interrupted her cleaning to ask Mrs. Compson if she would like to join the Tangled Web Quilters for their meeting that evening. Mrs. Compson thought about it for a moment, then shook her head. Although Sarah persisted, the older woman would neither change her mind nor explain her refusal.

So Sarah drove to Mrs. Emberly's home alone.

The red-brick colonial house was only a few streets away from Diane's, in an older part of the Waterford College faculty neighborhood. Sarah was the first to arrive, and Mrs. Emberly took her into the kitchen.

"Help yourself," Mrs. Emberly said, indicating the counter covered with snacks.

Sarah pushed a bowl of pretzels aside to make room for her plate of cupcakes.

"Thanks. Maybe later, when the others get here."

Mrs. Emberly glanced back toward the front door. "So, you came alone?"

Sarah nodded.

"I thought Sylvia might come with you this time, since she was so friendly with everyone at the quilt festival."

"You heard about that?"

"Bonnie told Diane, and Diane told me." Mrs. Emberly sighed. "I suppose she would've come if not for me."

"It's not that. I don't think she knows you're a member."

"Really?" Mrs. Emberly brightened for a moment, then looked puzzled. "You didn't tell her?"

"No." Sarah gave her a wry smile. "Just like you never told me you're Mrs. Compson's sister-in-law."

Mrs. Emberly's cheeks went pink. "I assumed that you would've heard it from one of the others long ago, or from Sylvia herself. I suppose she never mentioned me, then?"

"She did, but she called you Agnes, and I didn't know you were Agnes. The Tangled Web Quilters always call you Mrs. Emberly."

"Diane started that. I used to baby-sit

her when she was a little girl. She's always known me as Mrs. Emberly, and I suppose the habit was too strong. The others picked it up from her."

"I wish I would've known."

"I didn't mean to deceive you, but I was afraid you'd feel caught in the middle if you knew." Mrs. Emberly took a seat at the kitchen table. "Though I suppose there isn't anything for you to be in the middle of."

"What do you mean?"

"Sylvia and I have no relationship now. Oh, Claudia and I kept tabs on her as best we could through the years, but we had only secondhand information from mutual friends. That's not enough to hold a family together."

Sarah took the seat beside her. "I think Mrs. Compson would be glad to see you again."

"Really?"

"She's very lonely. She feels like she's the last Bergstrom."

"Perhaps she is." Mrs. Emberly twisted her hands together in her lap. "Claudia was a true sister to me, even after I re-married, but Sylvia —"

"Would you be willing to see her again?"

Mrs. Emberly hesitated. "Yes — that is,

if you think she'd welcome me."

"I know she would."

"I'm not so certain. Sylvia holds on to a grudge with both hands."

Sarah couldn't argue with that. "What if we —"

Just then Summer burst into the room. "Hey, I'm the second one here. That must be like a new record for me or something."

Mrs. Emberly laughed and pushed her chair away from the table. "Then come on over here and celebrate with one of Sarah's cupcakes." She avoided Sarah's eyes.

The moment was over, and as the rest of the group arrived Sarah knew she wouldn't get another chance that evening to talk to Mrs. Emberly alone.

As the others quilted, Sarah made templates for her latest block, Hands All Around. Her conversation with Mrs. Emberly and Mrs. Compson's stories played over and over in her mind. Somewhere in their stories there had to be a solution.

Diane's voice broke in on her thoughts. "Isn't that a Hands All Around, Sarah? You're smart to hand stitch all those curved seams and set-in pieces."

Sarah hid a smile. "Actually, I've been machine piecing for several days now."

"Please tell me you're joking."

"Welcome to the twentieth century, Sarah," Gwen said.

The others laughed, but Diane glared at them. "You guys are a bad influence." That just made them laugh harder, and even Diane had to smile.

Sarah looked around the circle of friends. This was what Mrs. Compson needed. This was what Elm Creek Manor used to have and had lost.

Maybe Gwen was right, and Mrs. Compson and Mrs. Emberly should be forced into seeing each other again. They were both lonely, especially Mrs. Compson; they both needed to forgive each other. And if Mrs. Compson felt that she had family in Waterford, she might be willing to stay at Elm Creek Manor.

Or the first sight of each other might rekindle all of those smoldering resentments until any hope of reconciliation burned to ashes.

Sarah wished she could figure out what to do. If only she had more time.

By the middle of the next week, Sarah had finished the Hands All Around block and another block, the Ohio Star. Then she had only one block left to piece.

The next day, Mrs. Compson held the

book open to the page so that Sarah could see the picture. "Here it is," the older woman said. "It's not the most difficult block, but it's a good one for using up scraps, so I saved it for last."

Sarah carried the book to the table and studied the diagram. The block resembled the Log Cabin pattern, but instead of only one center square, there were seven arranged in a diagonal row across the block. The strips of fabric on one side of the row were dark, and the strips on the other side were light. She looked to the title for the block's name. "Chimneys and Cornerstones," she read aloud, and smiled. "It's a Log Cabin variation, and its name also alludes to houses. That's appropriate, don't you think?"

Mrs. Compson was fingering her glasses and staring into space.

"Mrs. Compson?"

"Hmm? Oh, yes, the name is quite fitting."

"What's wrong?"

"Nothing's wrong. I just remembered something I hadn't thought about in a long time." Mrs. Compson sighed and eased herself onto the sofa. "My great-aunt made a Chimneys and Cornerstones quilt for my cousin when she left Elm Creek Manor as a young bride. She and her husband were moving to California, and we didn't know when — or if — we would see them again. It wasn't like today, when you can hop on a plane any time you like."

I was a very young child then. This happened before my mother passed away, before Richard was born, even before my first quilt lesson.

I admired my cousin Elizabeth very much. She was the eldest of the cousins, and I wanted to be just like her when I grew up. How confused and sad I was when she told me that she would be going away. I didn't understand why anyone would want to live anywhere but Elm Creek Manor.

"Why do you want to go away when home is right here?" I asked her.

"You'll understand someday, little Sylvia," she told me. She smiled and hugged me, but there were tears in her eyes. "Someday you'll fall in love, and you'll know that home is wherever he is."

That didn't make any sense to me. I pictured Elm Creek Manor sprouting wings and flying along after my cousin and her husband, settling back down to earth wherever they stopped. "Home is here," I insisted. "It will always be here."

She laughed then and hugged me harder. "Yes, Sylvia, you're right."

I was happy to see her laugh, and thought that meant she wouldn't be leaving. But the wedding preparations continued, and I knew my dear cousin was going away.

Claudia helped the grown-ups as best she could, but I resented anyone who did anything to hasten my cousin's departure. I hid my aunt's scissors so that she couldn't work on the wedding gown; I took the keys to Elizabeth's trunk and flung them into Elm Creek so that she couldn't pack her things. I earned myself a spanking when I told her fiancé that I hated him and that he should go away.

"If you aren't going to help, then just keep out of the way and stay out of trouble," my father warned me.

I pouted and sulked, but no one paid me any attention. Eventually I pouted and sulked my way into the west parlor, where my great-aunt sat quilting. She was my grandfather's sister, the daughter of Hans and Anneke, and the oldest member of the family.

I stood in the doorway watching as she worked, my lower lip thrust out, my eyes full of angry tears.

My great-aunt looked up and hid a smile. "So, there's the little troublemaker herself."

I looked at the floor and said nothing.

"Come here, Sylvia."

In those days, when a grown-up called you, you went. She pulled me up onto her lap and spread the quilt over us. We sat there, not speaking, as she sewed. I watched as she took a long strip of fabric and sewed it to the edge of the quilt. The softness of her lap and the way she hummed as she worked comforted me.

Finally my curiosity got the better of me. "What are you doing?" I asked.

"I'm sewing the binding onto your cousin's quilt. See here? This long strip of fabric will cover the raw edges so the batting doesn't fall out."

Raw edges? I thought. I didn't know quilts had to be cooked. Not wanting to reveal my ignorance, I asked a different question. "Is this her wedding quilt?"

"No. This is an extra quilt, one to remember her old great-aunt by. A young wife can never have too many quilts, even in California." She pushed her needle into her pincushion for safekeeping, then spread the quilt wide so that I could see the pattern.

"Pretty," I said, tracing the strips with my finger.

"It's called Chimneys and Cornerstones," she told me. "Whenever she looks at it, she'll remember our home and all the people in it. We Bergstroms have been blessed to have a home filled with love, filled with love from the chimneys to the cornerstone. This quilt will help her take a little of that love with her."

I nodded to show her I understood.

"Each of these red squares is a fire burning in the fireplace to warm her after a weary journey home."

I took in all the red squares on the quilt. "There's too many. We don't have so many fireplaces."

She laughed. "I know. It's just a fancy. Elizabeth will understand."

I nodded. Elizabeth was older than I and understood a great many things.

"There's more to the story. Do you see how one half of the block is dark fabric, and the other is light? The dark half represents the sorrows in a life, and the light colors represent the joys."

I thought about that. "Then why don't you give her a quilt with all light fabric?"

"Well, I could, but then she wouldn't be able to see the pattern. The design only appears if you have both dark and light fabric."

"But I don't want Elizabeth to have any sorrows."

"I don't either, love, but sorrows come to us all. But don't worry. Remember these?" She touched several red squares in a row and smiled. "As long as these home fires keep burning, Elizabeth will always have more joys than sorrows."

I studied the pattern. "The red squares are keeping the sorrow part away from the light part."

"That's exactly right," my great-aunt exclaimed. "What a bright little girl you are."

Pleased, I snuggled up to her. "I still don't like the sorrow part."

"None of us do. Let's hope that Elizabeth finds all the joy she deserves, and only enough sorrow to nurture an empathetic heart."

"What's emp— empa—"

"Empathetic. You'll understand when you're older."

"When I'm old like Claudia?"

She laughed and hugged me. "Yes. Perhaps as soon as that."

Mrs. Compson fell silent, and her gaze traveled around the room. "That's how I feel about Elm Creek Manor," she said. "I love every inch of it, from the chimneys to the cornerstone. I always have. How could I have stayed away so long? Why did I let my pride keep me away from everyone and everything I loved? When I think of how much time I've wasted, it breaks my heart."

Sarah took Mrs. Compson's hand. "Don't give up hope."

"Hope? Hmph. If I had any hope left, it died with Claudia."

"Don't say that. You know that isn't true. If you had no hope, you wouldn't have asked me to find a way to bring Elm Creek Manor back to life."

"I think I know when I'm feeling hopeful and when I'm not, young lady." But the pain in her eyes eased.

Sarah squeezed her hand. "I'm glad this block is in my quilt."

"I'm glad, too."

By the end of the week Sarah finished the Chimneys and Cornerstones block, and then all twelve blocks were finished.

On Monday Sarah prepared the blocks for assembly into the quilt top.

"Don't slide the iron around like that. Just press," Mrs. Compson cautioned as Sarah ironed the seams flat. "If you distort the blocks they won't fit together."

As Sarah handed her the neatly pressed blocks, Mrs. Compson measured them with a clear acrylic ruler exactly twelve and a half inches square. Each of Sarah's twelve blocks was within a sixteenth of an inch of the intended size.

"Fine accuracy, especially considering this is your first quilt," Mrs. Compson praised her. "You'll be a master quilter yet."

Sarah smiled. "I have a good teacher."

"You flatterer," Mrs. Compson scoffed. But she smiled, too.

To Sarah's surprise, Mrs. Compson announced that their next step was to clean the ballroom floor. "Or at least part of it," she added. She took a battered vacuum cleaner from the hall closet and gave it to Sarah, while she carried the twelve sampler blocks.

Mrs. Compson had mentioned once before that the ballroom took up almost the entire first floor of the south wing, but Sarah still took in a breath as she looked around the room. A carpeted border roughly twenty feet wide encircled the broad parquet dance floor, which still seemed smooth and glossy beneath a thin coating of dust. Above, three chandeliers hung beneath a ceiling covered with a swirling vinelike pattern made from molded plaster. At the far end of the room was a raised dais where musicians or honored guests could be seated. In the far corner, a large object — a table, maybe, with chairs on all sides — rested beneath a dusty sheet. Rectangular windows topped by semicircular curves, narrow in proportion to their height, lined the south, east, and west walls.

Mrs. Compson moved from window to window pulling back curtains, but the drizzle outside permitted little light to enter. She went to a panel in the far corner, flicked a switch, and gave the chandeliers a challenging look. The lights came on, wavered, and then shone steadily, casting shadows and sparkling reflections to the floor below.

After Sarah vacuumed a small portion of the carpet, she and Mrs. Compson arranged the blocks on the floor in three rows of four, then stood back and studied them.

"I think I want the Schoolhouse block in the middle instead," Sarah said, bending over to switch two of the blocks. "And the Lancaster Rose next to it. Since it's more complicated I want to show it off."

Mrs. Compson chuckled. "Spoken like a true quilter. Then you can place the two blocks with curved piecing opposite each other, here and here. And since you have three star blocks, and another that resembles a star, you can put them in the corners like this . . ."

They spent half an hour arranging and rearranging the blocks until Sarah was satisfied with their appearance. In the upper-left-hand corner she placed the Ohio Star block, with the Bachelor's Puzzle, Double Nine Patch, and LeMoyne Star blocks completing the row. The middle row held the Posies Round the Square, Little Red Schoolhouse, Lancaster Rose, and Hands All Around blocks. The Sawtooth Star, Chimneys and Cornerstones, Contrary Wife, and Sister's Choice blocks made up the bottom row.

"I don't think this is going to be big enough for a queen-size bed," Sarah said.

"Don't worry. We're a long way from binding it yet."

"If I make any more blocks, I'll never finish the quilt in time."

"Oh, we'll contrive something."

"Like what? You mean the setting? That should make it bigger, but not by much."

"Not the setting. You just let me worry

about that," Mrs. Compson said, and Sarah couldn't persuade her to say anything more.

They left the blocks in place and returned to the west sitting room, where Mrs. Compson showed Sarah how to make a Garden Maze setting. They began by making three templates: a small square, an even smaller triangle, and a narrow rectangle that tapered off to a point on both ends. To save time, Mrs. Compson traced the pieces — the tapered strips from the cream fabric and the other two shapes from the darkest blue — while Sarah cut them out. Sarah simply used her ruler rather than making a template for the narrow, dark blue pieces Mrs. Compson called block border strips.

Sarah sewed the hypotenuse of each small triangle to a tapered edge of the longer strips; when four triangles were attached, pieced sashing strips fourteen inches in length were formed. Meanwhile, Mrs. Compson sewed the dark block border strips around the edges of each block. They worked for the rest of the afternoon, and when it was time for Sarah to leave, Mrs. Compson told her to go ahead and leave everything where it was.

Sarah took in the fabric scraps, snipped

threads, and quilting tools of all kinds scattered wildly around the room and had to laugh. "If you can live with this mess, I guess I can," she said as she left.

At home, Matt went to check the mailbox while Sarah went inside to study the cupboard shelves and try to figure out what to make for supper. When he returned he tossed her a thick beige envelope. "Something came for you." He leaned against the counter and watched her.

The return address announced "Hopkins and Steele" in bold blue lettering. Sarah tore open the envelope and scanned the letter.

"Well? What do they say?"

"They're offering me the job."

Matt let out a whoop and swung Sarah up in his arms. Then he noticed he was the only one celebrating. "Isn't this good news? Don't you want the job?" he asked as he set her down.

"I don't know. I guess so. I mean, I thought I did, but — I don't know."

"You want to stay with Mrs. Compson."

"Would that be so bad? You were the one who got me started working there in the first place, remember?"

Matt grinned and held up his palms in

defense. "If you want to keep working at Elm Creek Manor, that's fine by me."

"It's fine by me, too, unless Mrs. Compson decides she doesn't need me anymore after we finish cleaning the place. I'm surprised I still have a job now, since the whole point of it was to help prepare the manor for sale."

"Maybe she likes having you around."

"She doesn't have to pay me for that." Sarah went into the adjoining room and slouched into a chair, spreading the letter flat on the table.

Matt took the opposite chair. He turned the letter around and read it. "They want you to respond within two weeks."

"That's two weeks from the date of the letter, not from today."

"Either way, you don't have to decide this minute. Take some time to think about it. Talk it over with Mrs. Compson, maybe."

"Maybe." Sarah sighed. Every day seemed to bring a new and more pressing deadline.

Chapter 26

That week Mrs. Compson and Sarah spent their mornings finishing up the south wing's bedrooms and used their afternoons to finish piecing Sarah's quilt top. They sewed blocks and sashing strips together to make the three rows, then they fashioned four long sashing rows by alternating sashing strips with the two-inch squares. When the block rows were joined to the long sashing rows and then to each other, the sampler's garden maze setting was complete.

Thursday came and went, and once again Sarah went to the Tangled Web Quilters' meeting alone.

On Friday, Mrs. Compson instructed Sarah to cut long, wide strips from her background fabric and attach these borders to the outside edges of her quilt. Sarah's shoulders and neck ached from hanging curtains all morning, and sitting at the sewing machine didn't help. Their anniversary was quickly approaching and she hadn't even started the quilting yet.

Behind her she heard the cedar chest opening and the rustle of tissue paper. "Sarah?" Mrs. Compson asked.

"Just a sec. I'm almost finished with the last border." Sarah backstitched to secure the seam and clipped the threads. "There." She removed the quilt top from the machine and brushed off a few loose threads. "I still don't think it will be big enough. Almost, but not quite."

"Maybe this will help."

Sarah turned in her chair. Mrs. Compson was spreading four long strips of pieced fabric on the sofa.

"What are those?"

"Oh, just a little something I've been working on in the evenings after you leave. Did you think I just sat around all night waiting for you to return in the morning?"

Sarah rose for a closer look. "This looks like my fabric."

"That's because it is your fabric."

Sarah held up one of the pretty quilt tops, if that's what they were. Maybe they were table runners. There were two long and two shorter pieces, all with the same pattern of parallelograms and squares on background fabric.

Then Sarah remembered. "These look like the twisted ribbon borders we saw at the quilt show."

"You seemed to admire the pattern, and I thought it would suit your sampler." Mrs. Compson hesitated for a moment before hurrying on. "But only if you want them. I took the liberty of making them for you so that you could have the large quilt you wanted, but you don't have to use them."

"These are for my quilt? Really?" Sarah snatched up her quilt top and held it against the border, trying to see how the finished product would look. "Thank you so much."

"You don't have to use them, mind. Maybe you wanted the whole quilt top to be made by your own hands. I can understand that. Don't think you have to sew them on so you won't hurt my feelings."

"Are you kidding? I'm sewing them on right now and you just try to stop me."

Mrs. Compson smiled in response. Soon Sarah finished attaching the twisted ribbon outer borders, and she held up the finished quilt top for inspection. "What do you think?"

Mrs. Compson picked up the other edge of the quilt. "It's lovely. You've done well."

Sarah studied the quilt top. "I can't believe I made this — except for the border, I mean."

"Believe it. But it's a long way from finished."

"What's next?"

"Now we need to mark the quilting designs." Mrs. Compson rummaged around in her tackle box and produced a pencil.

Sarah clutched the quilt top to her chest. "You want to draw on my quilt? I don't think that's such a good idea."

Mrs. Compson rolled her eyes heavenward. "She makes one quilt top and now she's the expert." She reached out for the quilt top. "Will you relax, if you please? I've done this before."

Sarah handed it over. "Okay, but . . . be careful."

They spread the quilt top on the table and pulled up two chairs. Mrs. Compson handed Sarah the pencil and told her to give it a closer look. As she did, Mrs. Compson explained in a very patient voice that this was a fabric pencil, not a typical Number 2, and if the marks were made lightly they would wash out later. She then explained how to mark the quilting designs on the quilt, either by using a stencil or by slipping a printed pattern from a book or a magazine beneath the fabric and tracing it. They used dressmaker's chalk instead of pencil on the dark fabrics.

Sometimes the quilting designs were simple, like the straight lines a quarter inch away from the seams called outline quilting. Others were more complex, especially where they had open space to decorate, but to Sarah's relief none were as complicated as those she had seen on Mrs. Compson's quilts. She wasn't sure that she was ready for anything so difficult.

At the end of the day Sarah decided to take the quilt top home and finish tracing the designs over the weekend.

"That's fine," Mrs. Compson said. "But don't you think Matthew will notice?"

Sarah frowned. She wanted the quilt to be a surprise, but she was running out of time.

Mrs. Compson patted her on the shoulder. "I'll work on it. I don't know if I'll have it finished by Monday, but I'll do my best."

"I don't want you to go to so much trouble."

"Trouble?" Mrs. Compson laughed. "I haven't had so much fun in I don't know how long. It's nice to feel a part of things again." She ushered Sarah outside to wait for Matt so that he wouldn't walk in on them and see the quilt spread out on the table.

All weekend long Sarah's thoughts kept returning to Elm Creek Manor. She couldn't shake the feeling that her time for finding a way to bring Elm Creek Manor back to life was rapidly running out.

Unfortunately, Matt meant well but was little help when it came to finding a solution. He couldn't understand why anyone would never speak to her family again just because she didn't get to be matron of honor at some old wedding. And even if Mrs. Compson was still holding a grudge, her sister was gone, so why stay angry? "You don't see guys acting like that," he concluded, shaking his head in bafflement.

"You're missing the point," Sarah told him. "Think of everything she'd been through. She was angry at Claudia and Agnes for shutting her out, but she was even angrier at herself for needing them. She left instead of facing up to all the pain. I can understand why she left, but she sees it as abandoning her responsibilities." Then suddenly she understood. "That matron of honor business — that didn't mean anything. They fought about that because they couldn't fight about what was really hurting them — their loss, their rivalry. It was too painful to face."

Matt studied her. "Sort of the way you and your mother fight about her boy-friends."

Sarah stiffened. "It's not the same thing."

"Well, sure it is, if you look —"

"It's *not*."

"Okay, okay." Matt backed down. "You know your mother better than I do."

"We're talking about Mrs. Compson, not about me."

"If that's the way you want it."

Sarah's thoughts churned. She didn't want to think about her mother, couldn't afford to spend a moment there when her time for saving Elm Creek Manor was dwindling so rapidly.

Then, suddenly, an image flashed into her mind, an image of herself as an old woman cleaning up her childhood home, sorting through her dead mother's things, still wrestling with anger and resentment and pain, forever denied reconciliation.

One day Sarah would be as angry and alone as Mrs. Compson.

Suddenly fearful, she flung the image from her mind.

By Monday morning she felt no closer to

a solution. Worsening matters was the Hopkins and Steele letter, a persistent reminder that other deadlines were closing in. As Sarah and Matt drove to work, Sarah found herself looking forward to her quilting lesson later that day. Not just looking forward to it, she suddenly realized, but needing it. Tangled, anxious thoughts relaxed when she felt the fabric beneath her fingers and remembered that she was creating something beautiful enough to delight the eyes as well as the heart, something strong enough to defeat the cold of a Pennsylvania winter night. She could do these things. She, Sarah, had the power to do these things.

Sarah knew Mrs. Compson recognized the power of quilting, too. Quilting certainly seemed to bring Mrs. Compson's joy to life; maybe it could do the same for Elm Creek Manor. If Mrs. Emberly was one piece of the puzzle, maybe quilting was the second.

A vague shadow of an idea began to form in Sarah's mind as the truck pulled up behind Elm Creek Manor.

Mrs. Compson had finished marking all but a small portion of the quilt top, and she was completing that section when Sarah walked in.

"Did you remember to buy the batting and backing fabric like I told you?" Mrs. Compson asked, pausing long enough to peer at Sarah over the rims of her glasses.

Sarah nodded and showed her the Grandma's Attic bag. "And the fabric's washed and pressed, as ordered."

"Good girl." Mrs. Compson set down the pencil and removed her glasses. "Now it's time to prepare the quilt layers."

"I've done that part before, and I was thinking —"

"You've done this before?"

"Yes, with the Tangled Web Quilters. And that's who I wanted to talk to you about. I was thinking —"

"You never told me you've used a quilt frame before. This is indeed a surprise."

Sarah opened her mouth to speak, but then Mrs. Compson's words registered and she forgot what she was going to say. "Quilt frame?"

"Yes, of course." She folded the quilt top and draped it over her arm.

"Oh." Sarah frowned. "I thought you were talking about basting the quilt sandwich."

"With this quilt frame you don't need to baste, thank goodness. Life's too short to baste a quilt if you don't have to. Bring the bag." She turned and beckoned Sarah to follow.

Sarah hurried to catch up as Mrs. Compson walked to the ballroom. "Basting goes fast if you have lots of people to help. And that's what I wanted to talk to you about."

"What did you wish to say?"

"I was thinking that maybe this weekend we could invite the Tangled Web Quilters over for a quilting party. You know, like you used to have here? They could come over Friday after work and we could quilt and get a pizza or two, and they could spend the night, and then we could finish up on Saturday."

Mrs. Compson looked doubtful.

"Don't say no, Mrs. Compson. It would be a lot of fun. And I only have a little more than a week to finish the quilt in time for our anniversary."

Mrs. Compson stopped with her hand on the ballroom door and eyed Sarah suspiciously. Then her face relaxed. "A quilting party, you say?"

Sarah nodded.

"Sounds more like a slumber party to me. Aren't you a little old for slumber parties?"

Sarah shrugged and gave her a pleading look.

"What will Matthew say?"

"He can survive without me for one night, I think."

"Hmph. You may be surprised." Mrs. Compson paused. "As you say, it might be fun."

"You won't have to do any of the work. I'll take care of all the food and getting the rooms ready and everything."

"Hmph. No, you won't; I wouldn't let you do all that alone." She sighed. "How many people are we talking about?"

"Six. Seven including me."

"Eight including me. That's plenty of help for finishing the quilt."

"Most of them you've met already, at the quilt show, I mean, and you already know Bonnie and Gwen pretty well, and —"

Mrs. Compson held up a palm. "You can stop babbling now, Sarah. I agree. We may have your quilting party."

"Oh, thanks, Mrs. Compson." Impulsively, Sarah hugged her. "This will be great. You'll see."

"I believe I may regret this. You have something up your sleeve, my dear, and don't think I don't know it."

Sarah assumed her best wide-eyed-innocence expression. "Who, me? You're the one with all the surprises."

"Hmph. We'll see." Mrs. Compson passed the quilt top to Sarah, pushed open the door, and led Sarah to the large object in the corner of the ballroom. She grasped the edge of the sheet covering it. "This is the quilting frame I told you about, the one Claudia and I used before I left home. Let's see if it still works."

She pulled off the sheet, and a cloud of dust rose. Coughing and sneezing, Sarah peered through the cloud to find a rectangular wooden frame roughly four feet across and six feet long perched on four legs that raised it to table height. At the corners were strange assemblies of knobs and gears with slender rods running the length of the frame between them. On either side of the tablelike surface was a small wooden chair. And draped across the middle —

"Why, there's a quilt still on the frame," Mrs. Compson said when the dust had settled. "What on earth?" She bent over the faded cloth and studied the pieces.

Sarah could tell that it was a scrap quilt, and many if not most of the pieces were not typical cotton quilting fabrics. She guessed it was decades old, maybe as much as fifty years. Pieced blocks alternated with solid fabric squares of the same size. The block pattern resembled a star, but not quite. Eight narrow triangles with their smallest angles pointing toward the center formed an octagon in the middle of the block. There were eight squares, one joined to each edge of the octagon, and between the squares were eight diamonds, each with a tip touching a corner of the octagon. Four triangles and four parallelograms finished the design. The quilt sagged in the middle, as if the mechanism holding it taut and secure had weakened over time.

"Look over here," Sarah said. "The points of these diamonds are chopped off. Didn't you say that's a sign of Claudia's piecing?"

"Castle Wall," Mrs. Compson murmured. "Well, if that doesn't just fit. Castle Wall."

"Mrs. Compson?"

"Safety and security and comfort behind the Castle Wall. Except you have to come back home before home can be your safe castle, your refuge. Of all the choices."

"Mrs. Compson?" Sarah gripped her by the shoulders and gave her a small shake. Startled, Mrs. Compson gasped and tore her eyes away from the quilt. "Are you all right?" Sarah asked.

Mrs. Compson pulled away. "Yes. Yes, I'm fine. This was just . . . a bit unexpected."

"Is this Claudia's work?"

Mrs. Compson nodded and turned back to the quilt. "And the Puz— and Agnes's, too." With a trembling finger she traced one of the quilt pieces, a blue pinstriped diamond. Then she reached out and stroked a central octagon made from tiny red flannel triangles. "See this?" She indicated the blue diamond. "That was from the suit James wore on our wedding day. And this red flannel — why, I spent a good part of my married life threatening to burn this wretched work shirt." She touched a soft blue-and-yellow square. "This —" With an effort she steadied her voice, but Sarah saw tears spring to her eyes. "This was from my daughter's receiving blanket. My lucky colors, you know, blue and yellow —" She choked up and pressed a hand to her lips. "They were making this for me. They were making me a memorial quilt."

Sarah nodded. A memorial quilt, a quilt made from pieces of a deceased loved one's clothing, made as much to comfort the living as to pay tribute to the dead.

"They must have started it after I left, but — but why? After the way I left them? They must have thought I'd come back one day, but when I didn't — yes, that must be why they didn't finish it."

Sarah touched her on the shoulder. "Mrs. Compson?"

She jumped. "Yes? Oh, don't look so alarmed, poor girl. I'm perfectly all right." She took a lace-edged handkerchief from her pocket and wiped her eyes. "Don't worry. I was just caught off guard, like I said. I never thought — well, never mind. It can't be helped, not now." She forced her lips to curve into a smile. "There, see? All better."

"I'm not fooled."

"No? Well, I didn't think you would be."

Mrs. Compson stared at the quilt for a long while. Then, with Sarah's assistance, she removed it from the frame and folded the unfinished layers. She placed the bundle on the raised dais at the south end of the room and stood there stroking the fabric, her eyes full of pain.

Chapter 27

They worked no more on Sarah's quilt that day. Mrs. Compson isolated herself in the library, and Sarah worked alone in a west wing suite.

The next morning, though, Mrs. Compson met Sarah on the back steps. "I've been going over a list of things we'll need for the party," she said after greeting her. "Perhaps you and Matthew can pick them up sometime this week."

Sarah agreed and stuffed the list into the back pocket of her denim shorts. She'd been half afraid Mrs. Compson would cancel the quilting party after the unexpected surprise the previous day. Sarah was relieved that she wouldn't have to devise some other scheme. It had been difficult enough to come up with this one.

They went to the ballroom, where Sarah noticed that the quilt frame had been dusted and pulled away from the corner.

Sunlight streamed in through the open windows, and a gentle cross breeze cooled the room. The memorial quilt was nowhere to be seen.

Mrs. Compson guided Sarah through the steps of placing the backing, the batting, and finally the quilt top around the rollers along the long sides of the quilt frame. By adjusting the gears, the three layers could be held firmly and smoothly without being stretched to the point of distortion. The middle of the quilt top was visible now, but when they finished that section they could bring the other parts into view by adjusting the rollers.

"James built me this frame," Mrs. Compson remarked as she directed Sarah to one of the chairs. "Before then, we would lay our quilts on the floor and crawl around on our hands and knees thread basting. Not too gentle on the knees or the back, I assure you." She dug through her tackle box. "I think we'll start you off with a nine between, if I have any. I usually use twelves — ah, here we are."

"A nine between what?"

"Hmm? Oh, that's what quilting needles are called. Betweens. They're thicker and sturdier than regular needles, which are called sharps. The number indicates the size. The higher the number, the smaller the size."

"Then I'll take the lowest number you have."

"A nine will be just right. Don't worry about making your stitches small at first; just concentrate on making them of equal length, both on the top and on the bottom. The more you quilt, the smaller your stitches will become. You'll see."

Mrs. Compson threaded two needles and handed one to Sarah. She showed Sarah how to tie a small knot at the end, to pull the needle from the back through to the front on one of the drawn quilting lines, then to give the thread a careful tug to pop the knot through the back and into the batting. It took Sarah a few tries before she could get the knot to stay in the middle of the quilt instead of popping right on through the top.

"Are you right-handed? Then put your thimble on your right hand and put your left hand underneath the quilt," Mrs. Compson ordered, and she proceed to demonstrate how to sew through all three layers. First, using the finger protected by the thimble, she pushed the needle through the top of the quilt. When the tip of the needle touched her left forefinger on the other side, she pushed the tip of the needle back through the layers to the top. By rocking her right hand back and forth in this manner, she gathered a few stitches on her needle. Then she pulled the needle and the length of thread all the way through to the top, leaving behind four small running stitches in a straight row along the penciled quilting design.

Sarah tried it, awkwardly gathering three stitches on her needle before bringing the needle and thread completely through the layers. She paused to inspect her work. "They're even and straight, but they're huge."

Mrs. Compson bent over for a look. "Those are toenail catchers for sure, but fine for your first try. Go ahead and see how it looks from the back."

Sarah ducked her head beneath the quilt frame. "They look the same to me. Huge, but equally huge."

"Good. That's what you want: nice even stitches the same length on the bottom as on the top."

They continued for a while, Sarah on one side of the quilt frame and Mrs. Compson on the other. At first Sarah tried to match the other woman's brisk pace, but soon gave up and proceeded more slowly, trying to make her stitches even and small. The quilt came alive beneath their needles as the quilting stitches added dimension to the pieced pattern. Before an hour had passed, Sarah's shoulders and neck ached and her left forefinger stung from so many needle pricks. She withdrew her hand from beneath the quilt and stuck her sore finger in her mouth, stroking the quilt with her other hand.

Mrs. Compson looked up. "You'll develop a callus there eventually, and it won't hurt as much. But perhaps that's enough quilting for now."

Sarah popped her finger out of her mouth. "No, let's go on just a little while longer, okay?"

Mrs. Compson laughed and shook her head. She tied a knot in her thread, popped it into the batting, and trimmed the trailing end. "No, it's important to rest every once in a while. Besides, you want to save something for your friends to do this weekend, don't you?"

"Even if we worked eight hours a day between now and then, there would still be plenty left," Sarah said, but she set her needle and thimble aside.

They spent the rest of the day working in the west wing. That evening Sarah phoned the Tangled Web Quilters and invited them to the party. She called Mrs. Emberly last and spoke with her for almost an hour.

On Wednesday, Sarah and Mrs. Compson bustled about arranging six bedrooms with fresh linens and pretty quilts for their guests. Twice they interrupted their work to spend some time quilting. They stitched and discussed the upcoming party with growing excitement. Mrs. Compson was cheerful and animated, and Sarah was about to burst with anticipation and nervousness. So many things could go wrong, but she tried not to think about that.

Finally she had to say something. "Matt's finished the north gardens," she said, trying to sound nonchalant. "How about if we take a look at them on Friday before our guests arrive?"

Mrs. Compson set down her rag and brushed the dust from her hands. "I'm ready for a rest. Why don't we go now?"

"No," Sarah exclaimed, and Mrs. Compson jumped. "I mean, I'd rather go Friday, Friday afternoon around four. I want to make sure we get this cleaning done. How about this — visiting the gardens can be our reward when we finish getting everything ready for the party, okay?"

Mrs. Compson studied her, bemused. "Very well, then. Friday it is." She walked off, shaking her head.

Idiot, Sarah berated herself. She had almost ruined everything.

Thursday passed quickly, with little time for quilting. At the Tangled Web Quilters' meeting that evening, Sarah explained her plan to everyone and made sure Mrs. Emberly understood her part. Mrs. Emberly's eyes were wide with worry, but she nodded. Sarah was sure she looked just as anxious herself.

At home that night, Sarah packed an overnight bag while Matt sat on the bed and watched her. "Mrs. Compson's important to me, too, and I'd like to help. Are you sure I can't come?" he asked.

"If you come you'll spoil my surprise for you." She kissed him on the cheek. "But you already have an important role. I couldn't pull this off without you."

"All I get to do is play chauffeur," he complained, but he cheered up a little.

Friday morning came. Matt dropped Sarah off with a kiss, an encouraging grin, and a promise to be at the appointed place on time. As he started to drive away, Sarah waved him to a stop and jogged over to his window. She took an envelope from her bag, held on to it for a moment, then passed it to him. "Do you think you'll have time to mail this for me today?"

"Honey, for you I'll make the time," he said, grinning. Then he noticed the address. "What's this? Your response to Hopkins and Steele?"

Sarah nodded.

"You're refusing their offer, right?"

"That's right." Sarah shifted her weight from one leg to the other.

"Have you thought this through? Shouldn't you wait and see if your plan works first?"

"If Mrs. Compson doesn't like this idea, I'll keep trying until I find one she does like. But if I take a new job, that will be the end of my days at Elm Creek Manor. If I'm not here, I think it will be much more difficult to come up with a new plan."

"I guess I can't argue with that." He leaned his head out of the window for another kiss. "I hope you know what you're doing."

"So do I," Sarah replied as he drove away.

She went inside and found Mrs. Compson in the kitchen humming and mixing something in a large bowl. "I thought I'd make us some sweet treats for tonight," she explained with a smile. "I know how much quilters like to nibble."

"You're going to fit in just fine with this crowd," Sarah said, laughing.

They hurried to finish all the last-minute preparations. Mrs. Compson had gathered wildflowers from around the barn and placed them in each quilter's room. Sarah made sure the kitchen was well stocked with snacks and beverages while Mrs. Compson checked for extra quilting supplies. As the day passed, Sarah's anxiety grew. Maybe her plan was a bad idea. Maybe she would make things worse.

But Mrs. Compson didn't have a phone, so Sarah had no way to call things off. She tried to force the negative thoughts from her mind. She had no choice but to go ahead with her plan, so there was no point to worrying about it.

At four o'clock she met Mrs. Compson in the front foyer. "Everything's ready, I believe," Mrs. Compson announced. She looked excited and happy.

Sarah hoped she wasn't about to change all that. "We still have an hour before everyone's due to arrive. Why don't we go see the gardens now?"

Mrs. Compson agreed and returned to the kitchen for her hat. They left by the cornerstone patio exit and strolled along the gray stone path toward the gardens.

"I hope Matt worked some miracles out here," Mrs. Compson said. "There was so much work —" Her voice broke off at the sight of the gardens.

Large bushes encircled the oval clearing where only weeds had grown before; although they would not bloom now, so late in the summer, in the spring the garden would be fragrant with the scent of lilacs. In the four planters, rosebushes and white bachelor's buttons were surrounded by lush ivy and other green foliage. The weeds and grass had been removed from between the gray stones beneath their feet, and the fountain of the mare and two foals had been cleaned and polished. The gazebo's fresh coat of white paint was dazzling in the sunlight. The terraces behind the gazebo had been rebuilt, and now displayed blossoms of every color and variety.

A breeze carried refreshing mist from the fountain and the scent of roses to them as they stood at the edge of the garden, taking in the beautiful sight.

"I can't believe it. I never would have thought it possible," Mrs. Compson gasped. "It's as lovely now as it ever was. Even lovelier."

Just then a small figure stepped out from behind the gazebo.

Mrs. Compson stared.

Sarah's heart thumped heavily in her chest. She clenched her hands together and swallowed. "Mrs. Compson, this is —"

"Agnes," Mrs. Compson breathed.

Hesitantly, Mrs. Emberly approached them. "Hello, Sylvia."

"Mrs. Emberly is one of the Tangled Web Quilters," Sarah said. "I thought — I thought maybe you two would like to see each other before the rest of the group shows up."

"It's been a long time, Sylvia." Mrs. Emberly stopped a few paces in front of them. She gave Mrs. Compson a slow, sad smile, and clutched her purse like a shield. "We have a lot of catching up to do."

Mrs. Compson stared at her, her lips pursing then separating slightly as if she struggled to speak.

Sarah willed Mrs. Compson to speak, to say hello, to say something, anything.

Agnes's lower lip trembled. "I've — I've missed you. We all did, when you went away."

"I found the quilt."

Mrs. Emberly blinked. "The —"

"The memorial quilt. The one you and

Claudia were working on for me."

Mrs. Emberly's mouth formed an O. "Of course. The Castle Wall quilt."

"You did well. Both of you. Fine workmanship."

"Thank you." She looked grateful, and then her eyes filled with tears. "Oh, Sylvia, is there any chance we could ever be friends? I know I wasn't the sister-in-law you hoped for, but now that everyone else is gone —"

Mrs. Compson strode forward and gripped Mrs. Emberly's shoulders. "Now, you stop that. We'll have no crying here today. My behavior all that time ago had nothing to do with you. I was selfish and wanted Richard all to myself. I was wrong to treat you so badly, and I was a fool to leave home." She took Mrs. Emberly's hands in her own. "Richard loved you, and if I were any kind of decent sister I would have respected that."

"You were a decent sister," Mrs. Emberly insisted. "I was a spoiled, flighty little child concerned for no one but myself. You cared about your family and your home, and I should have been more understanding."

"You may have been foolish, but that's not as bad as being deliberately mean."

"Well, perhaps you were overbearing and bossy and always thought you knew better than everyone else, but at least you didn't blunder in unwanted only to divide a family and place enmity between sisters."

"Nonsense. Claudia and I always squabbled, as far back as I can remember. You had nothing to do with that."

Sarah looked from one tear-stained face to the other. "Mrs. Compson, Mrs. Emberly —"

Mrs. Compson didn't even turn around. "Remember, Sarah, never interrupt your elders when they're in the middle of making a point. Will you excuse us for a while? Agnes and I have some matters to discuss. It's time for me to stop being a self-righteous old bag of wind and make amends while the sun shines." She gave Mrs. Emberly a small, hesitant smile, which the other woman returned. Then Mrs. Compson gave Sarah a look over her shoulder that said as clearly as if she had spoken, *As for you, young lady, I'll deal with you later.*

Sarah nodded, then turned and hurried back to the house, leaving Mrs. Compson and Mrs. Emberly alone in the garden.

Chapter 28

Sarah waited outside on the back stairs for the other guests to arrive. A few minutes before five o'clock, Bonnie and Diane pulled up in Diane's car.

"How did it go?" Bonnie asked in a stage whisper as they walked toward the manor.

"I don't know yet. They're still out in the garden."

Diane sat down on the steps beside her. "Well, at least they didn't kill each other. That's something, anyway." She nudged Sarah and grinned.

"I think it's wonderful that you're trying to bring those two together, Sarah," Bonnie said. "It couldn't have been easy, considering how long they've been estranged."

"Bonnie's right. If you can pull it off, it'll be a nice thing you've done for them."

Sarah reddened. "It's no big deal. I'm just trying to save my job, that's all."

Diane rolled her eyes. "Do you expect us to believe —"

"Look, Judy's here," Sarah interrupted, relieved to be able to change the subject. She stood and waved to Judy as she pulled up in her minivan. Close behind came Gwen and Summer.

As always, everyone had brought a dessert; Sarah guided them to the kitchen, where they set their trays and boxes next to the pile of goodies already awaiting them. Then she led them through the manor and out the front entry to the veranda. The others' reactions made her smile. She had gawked even more her first days here, and that was a layer of dust or two ago. They still had more to do, Sarah reminded herself. Matt's work and her own had done much to restore Elm Creek Manor, but they weren't finished yet.

They waited on the veranda in adirondack chairs she and Matt had arranged there. Their conversation broke off when Mrs. Compson and Mrs. Emberly came around the north side of the building walking arm in arm. They hesitated at the foot of the stairs as the others watched them.

"Well?" Mrs. Compson finally barked, glaring up at them. "What are you all looking at?"

After the barest pause, Mrs. Emberly burst into laughter, and the others joined in.

Mrs. Compson smiled sheepishly. "Not much of a welcome, was it? Please accept my apologies. It's not every day hell freezes over." She clapped a hand over her mouth. "And now I'm cursing. Goodness, what has gotten into me?"

They went inside to the ballroom, where everyone oohed and ahhed appropriately as Sarah showed them her quilt. Then they decided they were hungry, so Judy used her car phone to order pizza. By the time the delivery car pulled up behind the manor, all the women — including Mrs. Compson — were chatting and laughing like old friends.

After a casual supper on the veranda, they got to work. Four people sat quilting on one side of the quilt frame and three on the other while the eighth person threaded needles, fetched quilting tools, or ran for snacks. Every so often the runner would trade places with one of the quilters so that everyone had a chance to rest their fingers. As they worked they talked about themselves, their quilts, their families, and their jobs, and often the ballroom would echo with laughter.

Occasionally everyone would take a break from quilting, and they would hurry to the kitchen for snacks and conversation, giggling like kids at recess, until their fingers felt ready to pick up their needles again. Sarah was delighted to see how quickly eight pairs of hands virtually flew over the fabric. Beside the more experienced hands, Sarah thought her own plodded along clumsily, but she had to admit her stitches were improving.

As the evening waned, one by one the quilters sighed and stretched and pushed their chairs away from the quilting frame — Mrs. Emberly first, then Diane, then Judy, and then the others until only Sarah and Mrs. Compson were left.

"It's nearly midnight," Mrs. Compson finally said, straightening and working out the kinks in her shoulders. "Perhaps it's best to stop for the night."

Although they were tired, no one wanted to go to bed just yet, so they went out to the veranda to watch the fireflies flickering in a silent dance on the lawn. They chatted more quietly now, and Sarah could feel the gentle sound of the rearing stallion fountain lulling her to sleep.

Her eyes were about to close for good when Mrs. Compson placed a hand on her shoulder. "Let's show our guests to their rooms, shall we?"

Sarah nodded and pulled herself up from her chair. Carrying Mrs. Emberly's overnight bag, she led the others inside and upstairs to their rooms. Sleepy though they were, the Tangled Web Quilters were pleased with their suites, with the lovely Amish furniture, the pretty quilts on the beds, and the cut flowers Mrs. Compson had so carefully arranged. Sarah showed them where the bathrooms were and wished them good-night.

She carried Mrs. Emberly's bag into her room for her and placed it in the corner. "I'll see you in the morning," she said, closing the door behind her.

"Sarah?" Mrs. Emberly called before the door was completely shut.

Sarah pushed the door open again. "Yes?"

Mrs. Emberly stood in the center of the room, hands clasped at her waist. "Thank you for today."

Sarah smiled. "It was my pleasure."

Mrs. Emberly gave her a searching look. "Tell me something, Sarah. Did you select our rooms for us or did I end up with this room by chance?"

"Well, actually —" Sarah hesitated,

glancing over her shoulder to see if Mrs. Compson was near. "Originally we picked these rooms because they're close together and already cleaned, and we were just going to have everyone pick whichever room they liked best. But when you were in the kitchen with Judy, Mrs. Compson told me to make sure you got this one. Why? Is something wrong?"

"Oh, no. Quite the contrary." She looked around the room, a thoughtful, sad smile on her lips. "This was my first husband's room when he was young." She pointed to a desk next to the door. "His initials are on that brass plate right there. We stayed here together before he went into the service."

"I see."

"And Sylvia wanted me to have this suite. What do you suppose she intended?"

"I don't know. Maybe you should ask her."

"No. That won't be necessary. I think I know."

Sarah smiled, then nodded and left.

Her own room was two doors down and across the hall. After changing into a short cotton nightgown, she padded down the hall in her slippers to the nearest bathroom. When she returned, she found Mrs. Compson sitting on the bed.

"Well, young lady, you certainly had a busy day full of surprises, didn't you?"

"You aren't angry, are you?"

"Of course not." She rose and gave Sarah a hug. "You forced me to do something I should have done on my own a long time ago. I suppose I just needed a push."

"How did it go? In the garden, I mean, talking with Mrs. Emberly."

"Better than I could have expected or hoped." Mrs. Compson sighed. "But we have a long way to go until we're as close as sisters ought to be. As you know from my stories, we were never friends, and we've both changed so much since we knew each other last. Who can say? Perhaps those changes will allow us to be friends in a way that simply wasn't possible then." She gave Sarah an affectionate smile. "As I said, we have a long way to go, but at least we've finally begun a journey we should have made fifty years ago." She turned and stepped through the open doorway. "Good night, Sarah."

"Good night."

Sarah shut the door behind her and switched off the light. She climbed into bed and inhaled the fragrance of the freshly washed, smooth cotton sheets. The room was cool and comfortable for a warm summer's night. Moonlight spilled in through the open window, and a soft wind stirred the curtains. Sarah rolled over onto her side and ran her hand along the empty space in the bed beside her. This was the first time she had slept without Matt since they were married, and it felt strange. She rolled onto her back and stared up at the ceiling wide-eyed, memories of the day crowding into her thoughts. She knew she would never fall asleep with so much to think about.

Then sunlight was dancing on the braided rug and someone was knocking on the door. Sarah leaped out of bed and fumbled on the bedside table for her watch.

"Get up, sleepyhead," Summer's voice rang out on the other side of the door.

"Come on in," Sarah called.

Summer entered, grinning. "Are you going to sleep all day while the rest of us work on your quilt?"

"Is everyone else up already?" Sarah ran a comb through her long hair and snatched up her shower bag.

Summer nodded. "Mom and I got up and went running early. She always does, rain or shine. The grounds are awesome. Mrs. Compson said to let you sleep until one of the showers was open. She said, and

I quote, 'All of that mischief Sarah's been up to lately must have taken a lot out of her.' "

"That sounds like her." Sarah laughed. She hurried off to the shower while Summer joined the others downstairs.

As quickly as she could, Sarah showered, dressed, and went down to the kitchen, where the other quilters were talking and laughing over coffee, bagels, and fruit. After breakfast they returned to the ballroom to finish the quilt.

After they had been quilting and chatting for a while, Sarah looked around the quilt frame to Diane, Judy, Mrs. Emberly, and Gwen. "So," she said, changing the subject. "Did you guys have fun at quilt camp the other week?"

"Go on, tell us," Bonnie urged. "Mrs. Compson didn't get to hear you talk about it before."

Gwen launched into a vivid description of quilt camp, with the others occasionally speaking up to add a detail or share an anecdote. Sarah noted that Mrs. Compson seemed interested in the discussion, especially when Judy and Mrs. Emberly gushed about the new techniques they had learned in the different classes they had been able to take.

"Sounds like fun, doesn't it, Mrs. Compson?" Sarah asked when they had finished. To her satisfaction, Mrs. Compson agreed.

At noon they broke for a picnic lunch in the north gardens. Matt met them there, and after pulling Sarah aside for a kiss and murmuring "I missed you last night" in her ear, he proceeded to badger the quilters with questions about this mysterious surprise for which an overnight party was necessary. He pretended to be crushed when they refused to divulge the secret, but they knew he was only teasing them. After a lunch of chicken salad sandwiches, fruit, and iced tea, Matt led them on a tour of the gardens, explaining the restorations he and his coworkers had completed so successfully.

Before long Matt left for the orchards and the quilters returned to the ballroom. While the others put the last quilting stitches in Sarah's sampler, Gwen and Summer created a long strip of binding for the raw edges of the quilt by cutting a large square of the cream fabric into two triangles, then seaming them together so that they formed an offset tube from which they cut the narrow bias strip.

Then Sarah finished quilting the last section of the last design.

Mrs. Emberly, Mrs. Compson, and Bonnie removed the quilt from the frame and spread it flat on the dance floor. While Sarah carefully trimmed the backing and batting even with the edges of the quilt top, Diane folded the long binding strip in half, wrong sides facing inward, and pressed it with a hot iron so the crease would stay. She explained to Sarah that doubling over the strip increased its durability, which was important because the edges of a quilt experienced so much wear and tear. When that task was completed, the others relaxed on the veranda while Mrs. Compson showed Sarah how to sew the binding strip around the edges of the top of the quilt with the sewing machine. Sarah had to pull out stitches and try again when it came to mitering the binding at the corners, but in the end she was pleased with the results.

Sarah and Mrs. Compson carried the nearly finished quilt outside, where the others had arranged their chairs in a rectangle on the shady veranda. After a debate over whether blind stitches or whip stitches were best — the blind stitch advocates won — they showed Sarah how to fold the binding strip over the raw edges of the quilt and sew it to the quilt back. Each quilter worked on her one-eighth of the quilt circumference until the raw edges were covered by the smooth strip of fabric.

Sarah thought the quilt was finished, but to her surprise, the others flipped the quilt over to the back and turned to Summer. The youngest quilter reached into her sewing kit and pulled out a rectangular patch trimmed in blue, which she placed in Sarah's lap.

"What's this?" Sarah asked, lifting the piece and examining it. There were words printed on the right side, and she read them aloud:

SARAH'S SAMPLER
*Pieced by Sarah Mallory McClure
and Sylvia Bergstrom Compson*

Quilted by the Tangled Web Quilters

*August 3, 1996
Elm Creek Manor, Waterford, Pennsylvania*

"It's a tag to sew on the back," Summer explained. "I ironed some fabric to freezer paper and ran it through my laser printer. That printing won't wash out."

Sarah gave her a grateful smile. "Thanks, Summer. Thanks a lot." She looked around at her friends' smiling faces. "That goes for all of you. I can't thank you enough for all your help."

"Well, sew on the tag so we can declare this quilt officially finished," Diane urged.

Using an appliqué stitch, Sarah attached the tag to the back of the quilt in the lower-left-hand corner. She tied off the thread and rose, holding two corners of the quilt in outstretched arms. Mrs. Compson and Summer each took another corner, and the three women held the quilt open between them. The others stepped forward to look.

Sarah's first quilt was finished, and it was beautiful.

Judy began to applaud and cheer, and the rest joined in.

"You just finished your first quilt, Sarah," Bonnie said. "How do you feel?"

"Tired," Sarah quipped, and the others laughed. Sarah realized she felt a little sad, too. She almost wished she hadn't finished the quilt, because now she wouldn't be able to work on it anymore.

"What are you going to do for an encore?" Diane asked.

"I don't know," Sarah said, then Mrs.

Compson caught her eye. She was standing with an arm around Mrs. Emberly, smiling proudly at her student. Then again, maybe the perfect project already awaited her. Somewhere inside Elm Creek Manor there was a memorial quilt that needed to be completed.

It was almost four o'clock when the Tangled Web Quilters finished gathering their things and loading their cars. They left thanking Mrs. Compson for the wonderful party and hoping they could do it again sometime. Mrs. Compson and Sarah stood on the back steps and waved to their departing guests as they drove away.

Then they returned inside and started cleaning up the mess.

As Sarah finished washing the dishes, Mrs. Compson entered the kitchen carrying the last bundle of linens. "I'll drop this off in the laundry room, but then let's go sit outside on the veranda for a while. I'll worry about the rest of this tomorrow."

Sarah drained the sink, dried her hands, and followed her outside. Mrs. Compson eased herself into one of the adirondack chairs with a sigh. Sarah sat beside her on the floor and leaned back against the chair. Not speaking, they enjoyed the peaceful stillness of the sun-splashed front lawn and the distant forest, broken only by the soothing waterfall sound of the fountain and the music of songbirds.

Then Sarah decided that she wasn't likely to find a better time to speak. She turned and looked up at Mrs. Compson.

"About that better offer I'm supposed to think up," she said. "I can put on one of my interview suits and give you a formal proposal with visual aids and the works, or I can just tell you what I have in mind right now, as is. Which method would you prefer?"

Chapter 29

"This will do," Mrs. Compson said, folding her hands in her lap.

Sarah rose and took the seat beside her. "You're an art teacher, correct?"

"If thirty years in the Allegheny County School District count for anything, yes."

"And you enjoyed giving that lecture for Gwen's class, the party this weekend, and teaching me how to quilt, right?"

Mrs. Compson nodded. "Especially your lessons."

"So I can conclude that you find fulfillment in many ways, three of the most significant being quilting, teaching, and being with people you care about, am I right?"

"You demonstrate wisdom beyond your humble years."

"Thank you. I try. I also noticed that you paid particular attention to the Tangled Web Quilters' conversation about the quilt camp they recently attended."

"Certainly. It sounded as if they had a marvelous time, and what an opportunity to interact with other quilters and perfect one's craft. Sensible critiques of one's work are a crucial part of any artist's development. Perhaps next year you and I could —" She inclined her head to one side, eyes narrowing. "Hmm. Are you about to propose what I think you're about to propose?"

Quickly, before Mrs. Compson could voice any doubts, Sarah launched into a description of her plan to turn Elm Creek Manor into a year-round quilters' retreat where artists and amateurs alike could share their knowledge and their love for quilting.

Nationally known quilters could be brought in to teach special programs and seminars, while Mrs. Compson and other members of the permanent staff would provide most of the instruction. Sarah would handle all of the accounting and marketing matters just as she had done at her previous job. She presented the financial details and legal requirements she had investigated, showing, she hoped, that they had the resources and the abilities to make the project work. Getting the project under way would be neither easy nor quick, but before long Elm Creek Manor could become a haven for the quilter who longed for a place in which to create — if only for a week, a month, or a summer at a time. Mrs. Compson would be involved in the activities she loved most, and best of all, Elm Creek Manor would be alive again.

When she finished her proposal, Sarah studied Mrs. Compson's face for some sign of her inclinations, but Mrs. Compson merely gazed off at the distant trees.

Finally she spoke. "It sounds like a lovely dream, Sarah, but you've never even been to quilt camp. How do you even know you'd care for it?"

How could anyone not care for it? "Okay, that's true enough, but I've done a lot of research and I plan to do more. You and I could attend a few sessions together and talk to their directors and their participants. We should also talk to the quilters who don't attend and find out what's been missing. I'm willing to invest all the time and energy it takes. That's how much I believe in this."

Mrs. Compson still looked doubtful. "That's all well and good, but I fear you may be confusing running a quilters' retreat with attending one. I thought you hated accounting and all things business. I wouldn't want you to start a new business for my sake, only to find yourself unhappy in your work."

"I don't hate accounting, and I wouldn't be unhappy." That was the least of Sarah's worries. "What I disliked about my old job was the sense that I was just going through the motions, plugging in the numbers and spitting out sums, and none of it mattered. I wanted my work to have some — some relevance. I wanted it to mean something." She struggled to explain how she felt, how she had been feeling for so long. "This would matter. We would be creating something special. I would have a purpose here."

Mrs. Compson nodded, and to Sarah her expression seemed less skeptical, if only by the smallest degree. "What about teachers for these classes? I couldn't teach them all myself, and although you're a fine quilter, you're not quite ready for that yet."

"I've already spoken to the Tangled Web Quilters. Mrs. Emberly would be able to teach appliqué, Diane could teach introductory piecing classes, Bonnie could teach some of her Celtic knotwork and clothing classes here in addition to those at her shop, and you could handle the advanced piecing and quilting sections. If it turns out we need more help, we can always hire someone by advertising in quilt magazines, or better yet, we could find someone local through the Waterford Quilting Guild."

"Hmph." Mrs. Compson drummed her fingers on the arm of her chair. "I spot one fundamental flaw in your plan."

Sarah's heart sank. "What's that?" She had been sure she had covered everything. "If you don't want to risk your own capital, I'm sure we can find investors."

"That's not it. I'm certainly not about to use someone else's money for something I can well afford on my own." She sighed. "It's another matter altogether. I don't think you considered how difficult it would be for me to take care of so many overnight guests by myself. I can't be running up and down stairs at everyone's beck and call all the time."

"I guess I see your point."

"There's only one solution, of course. You'll have to move in, and you can be at everyone's beck and call instead."

"Move in here? To Elm Creek Manor?"

"I can see if the playhouse is still standing, if you'd prefer it. Naturally, I'd expect you to bring Matthew along. Yes, I see no other way around this problem except having you move in, and I'm afraid that's one condition I must insist upon, so if you don't want to live here —"

Sarah laughed and held up her hands. "You don't have to talk me into it. I'd be thrilled to live here."

"Very well, then. But you should check with Matthew before packing your things."

"I have a condition of my own."

Mrs. Compson raised her eyebrows. "So, this is to be a negotiation, is it?"

"You could call it that. My condition is that you have to have a phone line installed so our clients can contact us." Sarah rubbed her wrinkled, waterlogged hands together. "And a dishwasher."

"That's two conditions. But very well. Agreed. And now I have another requirement." She gave Sarah a searching look. "You may not like it."

"Go ahead."

"I don't know what kind of conflict stands between you and your mother, but you must promise me you'll talk to her and do your best to resolve it. Don't be a stubborn fool like me and let grudges smolder and relationships die."

"I don't think you know how difficult that will be."

"I don't pretend to know, but I can

guess. I don't expect miracles. All I ask is that you learn from my mistakes and try."

Sarah took a deep breath and slowly let it out. "All right. If that's one of your conditions, I'll try. I can't promise you that anything will come of it, but I'll try, Mrs. Compson."

"That's good enough for me. And if we're going to be partners, I must insist that you call me Sylvia. We'll have no more of this Mrs. Compson this and Mrs. Compson that. You needn't be so formal."

For a moment Sarah thought Mrs. Compson was teasing her. "But you told me to call you Mrs. Compson. Remember?"

"I said no such thing."

"Yes, you did, the first day we met."

"Did I?" Mrs. Compson frowned, thinking. "Hmph. Well, perhaps I did, but that was a long time ago, and a great deal has happened since then."

"I couldn't agree more." Sarah smiled. "Okay. Sylvia it is."

"Good." Mrs. Compson sighed and shook her head. "An artists' colony. Sounds like something right out of my college days." She sat lost in thought for what seemed to Sarah to be the longest silence she had ever had to endure.

Say yes. Just say yes. Sarah clenched her hands together in her lap. *Please please please please —*

"I suppose all that's left is for us to select a name for our fledgling company."

Sarah felt as if she would burst. "Does that mean yes?"

Mrs. Compson turned to Sarah and held out her hand. Her eyes were shining. "That means yes."

Sarah let out a whoop of delight and shook Mrs. Compson's hand. Mrs. Compson burst into laughter and hugged her.

As they sat on the veranda brainstorming, Sarah's heart sang with excitement. Mrs. Compson seemed even more delighted, if that were possible. Sarah suspected that, like her, Mrs. Compson could already envision the beautiful quilts and the strengthened spirits of their creators bringing the manor to life once more.

The first question was easily settled — the name for their quilters' haven.

Elm Creek Quilts.

About the Author

Jennifer Chiaverini lives with her husband and two sons in Madison, Wisconsin. In addition to the five volumes in the Elm Creek Quilts series, she is the author of *Elm Creek Quilts: Quilt Projects Inspired by the Elm Creek Quilts Novels* and designer of the Elm Creek Quilts fabric line from Red Rooster Fabrics.